I0564655

SILVER LININGS

CHRISTINE CHIANTI

Golden Lark Publishing

Silver Linings
Published by Golden Lark Publishing
Copyright © 2014 Christine Chianti
Cover design by Robin DeMarco
Cover art photos:
Composite Businessman © Wavebreakmedia Ltd | Dreamstime.com
Office Building © Ben Goode| Dreamstime.com
Excerpt from Misappropriated Means © 2014 Christine Chianti

This is a work of fiction. Names, characters, places and incidents
are either from the author's imagination or are used fictitiously. Any
resemblance to actual individuals, living or deceased, businesses,
establishmentsor events is entirely coincidental.

All rights reserved.
This book, or parts of this book, may not be reporduced in any
form without written permission. Information address: Golden Lark
Publishing, P.O. Box 1602, Lockport, New York 14095-1602

ISBN: 978-0615996929

Golden Lark Publishing
P.O. Box 1602
Lockport, New York 14095-1602
www.goldenlarkpublishing.com

CHAPTER 1

"Morning, Lieutenant," I said to my supervisor, Aaron Walker, as I walked into the squad room at Police Headquarters.

"Detective." He studied my face for a moment. "Monica, you know that you've got to start taking better care of yourself. It doesn't look like you slept much again."

I sighed. "I know, Lieutenant. I've been trying to get things back under control, but the situation last night just brought everything to the forefront. Again."

"It's been almost a year since Bill was killed. You need to let him go."

"I know. I'm seeing the department counselor, but when I'm on the scene where an officer has been shot, I just can't control the memory."

He placed a hand on my shoulder gingerly and gave it a soft squeeze. "Try."

I turned and looked at the room. Fourteen desks covered the shared space. Most of the occupants had brought in small knick-knacks to personalize their space. Only two desks sat void of personal clutter.

I'd cleared Bill's desk out the week after a hyped-up crack addict had gunned him down.

His death had hit me harder than anything I'd known to date. He'd been my mentor, my trainer and my friend. I'd been invited to share holidays with him and his wife, Judy, more times than I could remember. All of that was stripped away by some twenty-three year old punk who'd been too concerned about where his next hit was coming from.

I dropped my purse on the second clear desk and settled into my corner to attack the paperwork I so hated.

"Dietz!" I heard a voice yell an hour later, and turned to see Commander Willoby standing in the middle of the room.

Eric Willoby was a good boss. He'd been on the force for nearly thirty years, and the gray was starting to show in his thick black hair. He had broad shoulders and at six-eight, was commanding even when standing still. His skin was a pale white, but his eyes of piercing blue, screamed cop.

"Yes, Sir," I said timidly, wondering what I had done that would bring him down to find me.

He motioned me to follow him as he led me toward someone standing by the door. A woman of about twenty-five, dressed in a sweater and skirt and hands folded, stood there. A large leather purse was slung over her right shoulder.

"Detective, I'd like you to meet the department's newest detective, Jackie Gannon." He motioned to the woman standing there, "Detective Gannon, this is Detective Monica Dietz, your new partner. My head snapped to glare at him, "My what?" I managed to splutter out.

His eyes twinkled as the edges of his mouth curved up into something between a smile and a grin. "I knew you'd be excited. Detective Gannon was just promoted and transferred to this division, and since you need a partner, the two of you will be working together. Good day, ladies," he said as he strolled down the hall whistling a tune that sounded familiar, but I couldn't place it.

"Guess he caught you by surprise, huh?" my new partner remarked.

When my eyes focused on the woman I looked intently at her. My first reaction was that she was exactly my polar opposite. She was about six inches shorter than my height of five-ten. She had the body of a model, and a face that was sure to cause speech impediments. When this was combined with her pin straight hair, and with the way she filled out the sweater combo, I would guess she was going to be spending quite a bit of time fending the single men in our squad off. I would have given up right there, but I saw something else.

I recognized the look in her eyes. I had seen it in my bathroom mirror for the past eight years.

I huffed out a breath, "Yeah, he did. I should have expected it, but he got the drop on me with the idea of a partner. Welcome aboard, Gannon." I held out my hand.

She smiled, shook my hand, "Please, call me Jackie."

"Well, come on in and meet the rest of the team," I said as I led her back into the room.

"Who we got here, Dietz?" Matt Jenkins called out.

"The loud mouth over there with the broad shoulders and crew cut is Matt Jenkins. He's mostly harmless, and he keeps assuring everyone that he's had all his shots. When push comes to shove, he's a great one to have in your corner. Next to him is his partner, Ted Anderson. They spend most of their day working with the schools and juvenile.

"Over here," I said pointing to the other side of the room, "we have Sylvia Crowne and her partner, Bill Kenner. They tend to do quite a bit with the narcotics teams. Across the side of the room, we've got Mark Sibly, Nate Martin, Adam Westly, Todd Cunnigham, Dave Lerch, Ken Fricano and Kerri Marsbury. Keri is usually partnered up with the Lieutenant. The others tend to pair up in odd ways, but they stick to most of the everyday stuff."

"And you handle what?" Gannon asked.

"I keep seeing dead people," I deadpanned. "Actually, I'm more of a troubleshooter. I've got a knack for dealing with the minutia that tends to be overlooked. Because of that, I get the cases that require it, high profile cases like homicide and kidnapping. Thankfully, we don't usually have too many of those here in Blackberry Creek. We'll jump in and do whatever needs to be done, but if we end up with one of those cases, most likely, the captain will pull us off whatever we were working on to take the high profile one."

I led her back to our little corner, "This will be your—" the words caught in my throat.

Jackie looked at me, and I could see the sympathy in her eyes. "The Commander told me that your last partner was killed in the line. I'm very sorry."

I nodded, "I keep thinking that I'm past it, but every once in a while it comes up and sucker punches you. The case that I was working for the last four days blew up last night. It ended with the suspects having a shoot out with police. Both perps were killed, but more worrisome are the three officers they shot and the two civilians who were run over when the perps tried to flee the scene of their latest robbery." I didn't have to tell her that it brought everything that had happened with Bill back to the surface again."

"What are we working on now?" she asked.

I slid the paper work over to her, took my own seat, and proceeded to fill her in.

It was getting close to lunchtime, and the paperwork was completed. "Thanks for the help, Jackie," I said as I stood to stretch. "I'll drop this on the Lieutenant's desk, then we can—" the phone on my desk cut me off.

"Dietz," I answered.

"You and your partner are to report to my office immediately. We've got a heck of a case to break your new partner in on."

"We're on the way, Sir," I said as I hung up the phone. "Let's go, Jackie. Time to go see the boss." I checked to ensure that my badge was on my waistband and my weapon was still in the holster on my hip, and then tossed a light jacket over my shoulders. I headed over to the Lieutenant's desk to drop off the paperwork and turned and waited for my partner.

"Do I take it we're going on one of those high profile cases?" she asked with trepidation.

"If I was a gambler, I'd say that the odds are pretty good, but until we know, we don't worry about it."

We walked to the captain's office in relative silence, the only noise being the constant clack of Jackie's high heels. I wondered how she would fare if we had to chase anyone down today. All I could do was hope that we wouldn't need to test that theory.

I knocked on Commander Willoby's door, and was greeted with a terse "Come".

"You sent for us, Commander?"

He looked up from his desk, motioned to the two seats across from his desk. "We've got a bit of situation. Looks like a robbery gone bad. About fifteen minutes ago, Cathy's Collectibles was attacked. That's the best word that I can use to describe it.

"The shop owner from across the street called it in and reported that it sounded like a war zone. The nine-one-one dispatcher said she could hear what sounded like automatic weapon fire. Uniforms arrived at the scene within three minutes. They found the carnage. At the present, we've got one confirmed dead, one in the hospital and one who is still unaccounted for."

"Sir, what exactly is Cathy's Collectibles? And who is the missing person?" Jackie asked timidly.

She was going to have to toughen up, but helping her through that process was going to be my job.

The Commander looked at her briefly before he continued. "From what I've been told, the store was a high end antique and specialty shop. People paid big bucks for the merchandise. As for who the missing person is, we don't have an identification."

"How do you know that they're missing then?" Jackie asked.

The Captain looked at her for a moment. "The eyewitness, a neighbor from across the street, said she saw a woman whom she thought to be the owner go in to open the store this morning. The car that was pointed out as the owner's is still there, but there is no sign of her. Three men were seen to have gone in. There are conflicting reports about what they had when they came out. Reports say that two men carried a large bag together while the third man continued to fire into the building. The responding officers have the information on the vehicle."

"Thanks, Captain," I said. "We've got it from here. Let's roll, Gannon."

"One more thing, Detective. Keep me in the loop on this. I want reports daily."

I turned back to him, "Yes, Sir."

Cathy's Collectibles sat in the middle of a block of small shops on Main Street. The plate glass windows were now scattered with the debris from the gunfire. I pulled the departmental Dodge Challenger over behind a black-and-white that had its lights going.

"What did they teach you about investigations, Jackie?" I asked as I pulled the crime scene kit out of the trunk.

"Well up until the promotion became official three hours ago, I'd been a uniformed officer. Basically I just secured the scene."

We started walking toward shop, "Okay, lesson one. Listen to the evidence." She turned her head to look at me, and I could see the question she wanted to ask. "I know it can't say a verbal word, but it is your best resource. As long as the scene has been properly secured, the evidence will tell you the story. It won't lie or change its story. It is the one thing that we can depend on.

"Lesson two, we look at the whole thing first. Document where everything is, get as many photos as we can and identify everything that we can. This is all done before we go and talk to any of the witnesses. Questions?"

"I don't think so, Monica. I'm just really, um, you know, nervous right now."

I stopped a few feet short of the doorway. "Are you afraid that you wont be able to hold through this?" I asked sternly.

"No, it's not that. I've seen dead bodies before. It's just that I'm starting to understand how important what we're about to do is, and I'm worried about making a mistake."

"Buck up, Jackie. We all make mistakes. It's how we learn. The trick is to work together so that we can back each other up. Keep each other from making those mistakes. We'll talk about every step that we're going to take and we'll do it together."

She smiled, "Okay. Thanks."

"All right then, let's do this."

We ducked under the crime scene tape, and I flashed my badge at the officer who started over. "Detective Dietz," I said and he waved us on. "Good grief," I muttered as I rounded the edge of the doorway.

Every window in the building appeared to have been blown out and glass sparkled in the sun covering the hardwood floor. What I guessed to be the main counter was only defined by the steel framing, it's glass sides and top decimated. The wall nearest the entry way looked like a colander. "There has to be at least fifty bullet holes in this little area alone," I stated.

"What were they after with that kind of fire power?" Jackie asked.

"I don't know. But obviously there was something here that was of major importance to somebody and they weren't worried about people noticing that they were here."

I leaned in and traced one of the bullet holes with my finger. "Doesn't look too big."

"That'd be a good thing, right?" Jackie asked.

"Depends on what else we find. Either way, it should help us narrow down what kind of weapon or weapons were used here."

As we came around the main counter, I noticed that there was a small room off to the right. I could see three officers standing just inside the door. "What've we got?" I asked as I approached the door.

One of the officers turned and when he saw me, his eyes lit up. "Dietz, how you doing?"

"That you Lockhorn?" I asked with a grin of my own. "They letting you out to play a little now?"

"I'm not a rookie any more, Monica. In fact, I'm sitting for my sergeant's exam in a bit over a week."

"Good luck, Mike." I waved Jackie over. "Jackie, this is Officer Mike Lockhorn. I had the dubious pleasure of training him when he was a rookie. That was just before I upgraded to detective. Mike, this is Jackie Gannon. My new partner."

They shook hands briefly, and then Mike's smile faded. "It's bad, real bad, Monica. Coroner is coming for the guy over in the corner. Room's been disturbed by rescue personnel as they were working to save the other vic. Don't know what they were looking for, but, man, they blasted everything."

"Well, let's take a look. Did you get an ID on the deceased?"

"I fished out his wallet," Mike said as he pointed to a clear plastic evidence bag that was set on the floor a few feet from the body. "Contained a Massachusetts Drivers license in the name of Toby Williams, age fifty-two. He shows an address over on Weston Woods. Not sure if he was an employee of the shop or a customer."

Jackie peered over at the body again, "Whichever, he was in the wrong place today."

"Mike, what else do we have on the other two victims?"

"EMS took one, a young guy probably in his twenties, maybe early thirties, to the hospital. Nobody's said anything to us. I know that an officer was going in to stand guard. As far as the woman who is missing? Best guess there is that that is the proprietor, Catherine Evans, age is listed on DMV records as thirty-five. She actually lived upstairs."

"Okay. Thanks, Mike." I turned my attention to the body on the floor. "What can you tell me, Toby?" I whispered as I made my way towards the body.

I stepped over the broken pottery that lay on the floor and knelt by the body. Pulling out the small digital recorder that I habitually carried, I flicked it on. "Deceased is a male, mixed-raced identified as Toby Williams. The body is lying with the head pointing north-east and on the left side. Visual inspection shows seven bullet entrance wounds on the back, three exit wounds on the chest." I paused the recorder, "What were you trying to protect that got you shot in the back, Toby?"

"Monica?" Jackie asked softly. "How do you know that the wounds on the back are entrance wounds as opposed to exit wounds?"

"Look at the sizes. See how these on the back are relatively small and circular? This indicates that the projectile was spinning along its axis when it went in. In the front, notice how irregular the holes are shaped? That tells us that the shot hit something inside and began to flip around."

I took a cursory glance around the room. "Did anybody find a safe or an alarm button back here?" I asked the officers who were still standing guard.

Mike looked over, "Honestly, I never even looked, Monica. Do you want us to do a quick search?"

I thought about this for a brief second. "Yeah. Be careful of the evidence, but do a quick sweep. Williams took it in the back for a reason, and we need to know what that reason was."

By the time we left the shop, it was after six, and we still hadn't figured out what the perpetrators were after. "So much for lunch", I said to Jackie. I noticed that she was starting to limp a bit. "You okay there, Gannon?"

She grimaced at me, "I didn't exactly think that they were going to be throwing me out into the field right away. I thought that I'd get a day playing desk-jockey before this happened. I ended up wearing the wrong shoes."

I chuckled. "You've just figured out lesson three there, Jackie. Dress comfortably, because there is no telling what's going to happen."

"I'll be ready tomorrow," she said as we climbed back into the car. "What happens next, anyway?"

I pulled out into traffic, and aimed the car towards the police station. "Well, the F.B.I. is treating this as a kidnapping. We're playing nice with them, and they're going to let us work the homicide end of things, so we'll start by meeting with the witnesses, and going over their statements. From there, we'll check on the progress of the Medical Examiner, and see what he can tell us. At some point, we're going to need to run by the lab and get briefed on what we've found. Somewhere in this mess is the answer to what happened here."

As I watched her drive away, I turned my own car towards home, dinner and Sam, and thought about what I had told Jackie. Somewhere in this mess was the answer. But where?

CHAPTER 2

I opened my eyes and peered into the darkness, and my heart was beating as if I'd just finished running five miles at a full sprint. My recurring nightmare had struck again. For some unknown reason, I'd found myself back in that alley, watching the whole scene unfold when Bill was gunned down. It was so real, I swore that I felt his blood trickling through my fingers as I tried to stop the bleeding.

I could hear Sam's faint snores coming from the foot of the bed, and took comfort in his presence. Consciously, I tried to match my breathing with his, and gradually it slowed. Reaching over, I flicked on the reading light and repositioned myself into a sitting position. I squinted to read the numbers on the clock, two-seventeen.

It could be worse, I reminded myself.

In the days right after the shooting, I found myself having this experience at least once an hour. This was the first time I'd had it now in over five months. That's progress, I reminded myself.

I swung my feet off of the edge of the bed and fought gravity to sit up. My head throbbed.

A cold wet nose snuck under my arm, and my face was bathed in the wet kisses from my dog, Sam.

I laughed lightly, scratched his ears, "Well, Sam, I think that definitely qualifies as one of the worst nights I've had."

Sam simply responded by pushing his big body closer and increasing the frequency of kisses.

We sat there, him the 150-pound Newfoundland nestled precariously on my lap and his head on my shoulder, and me with my arms wrapped lightly around his neck.

I ran my fingers through his thick fur, "I didn't think this case would hit me so hard," I mused. Sam continued to snuggle in closer. "Maybe it's just the viciousness of the attack yesterday coupled with my getting a new partner. Too many thoughts and memories."

I gave him a slight nudge to move him off of my legs and stood as soon as he was off. "Let's see if some milk and cookies will help me get back to sleep," I said heading for the door.

At the word "cookies", Sam became a 150-pound guided missile. I bounced slightly off of the doorframe as we went through it together.

I knew from past experience, that it would be a while before I'd be able to even try to get back to sleep, so I took my snack back to my room and reached for the novel that I'd left on the bedside table and tried to lose myself in a turn of the century romance.

Three hours later, it was apparent that I was not going to be going back to sleep, so I hoisted myself out of bed and crept to the kitchen. I'd made it to the bedroom door when I heard the faint click of nails on wood floor as Sam followed me.

Sitting at the breakfast bar, I sipped my tea and pondered everything that had been thrust onto me yesterday. The case wasn't exactly a run of the mill type, but it was something that I fully understood. The steps that were to be taken, the chess game that would be played by the police department and the perpetrators and the leads that had to be followed.

No, the case was something that I understood. My angst was with Gannon.

Not with her, personally, but with what she was. Commander Willoby had given me a fresh partner to work with. My job was not only to solve the high profile cases, but now I was supposed to train her how to do that as well.

I wasn't sure that I was prepared for this part of the job yet.

It sure looked like both Jackie and I were going to be getting some real on-the-job training over the next few days.

By the time I left the house at six-thirty, I'd done a yoga workout, taken Sam for a walk and had run two loads of laundry. I'd run out of things to do to take up the time, so I decided to head into the office.

I detoured from my normal route to drive by the scene this morning. Someone had affixed sheets of plywood over the broken windows, and a cruiser sat in front of the building.

I guided my Honda over to the edge of the road and looked at the surroundings. The flashing red light high up on the light pole gave me what I wanted to know: this area had traffic cams that might be useful.

I walked over to the cruiser, and was glad that I recognized the driver. "Sargent Langly, how'd you get so lucky to pull this duty?"

The squashed face broke into a smile, "Well, well, well. If it ain't detective Dietz. I like working nights right now. Let's me have the house to myself during the day. How's it going with you, Monica?"

I shrugged. "Same old, same old. You know how it goes, Charlie."

"Yeah, I do," he replied. "I'm guessing since you're here at six-forty-five that you must have caught this one, huh?"

"Yep. Got this one thrust on me only a few hours after I got me a new partner."

"Ohhh. Sounds like you're getting all the fun," he said with a smile. "So how's the new guy working out for you? Getting him trained well?"

"She," I emphasized the word, "jumped right in yesterday. She's doing her darnedest to swim even though she got thrown into shark infested waters."

His face softened, "I know that you'll do well with her, Monica. Just like I know you'll do right by the people involved here."

"Speaking of the people involved around here, have you seen anything that would be helpful?"

"Naw. Had a couple of college aged kids come around about two-thirty, but they didn't linger or anything. Looked like they might have been walking home after hitting one of the local watering holes. Nothing real exciting. The lady that lives in the apartment above the shop over there," he pointed to the building across the street, "she waved at us last night when we took up the patrol. That's it. Been real quiet here."

"Thanks, Charlie. See ya around," I said as I headed back to the car.

I pulled into the parking lot of the police station ten minutes later. After a quick run to the traffic division to see about the cameras that lined the street, I made my way to my desk. Someone had dropped a few files on my desk somewhere between when I left yesterday to go to the scene and now. I flipped through the files.

Armed with a fresh cup of tea, I selected the top file and began reading.

Jackie found me there fifty minute later with one leg propped up on the lower desk drawer and my glasses on the desk. A note pad was covered with my scrawl of questions or special notations that I wanted to follow up on.

"Sorry," she said. My eyes tracked up to look at her. "I didn't realize that we'd start so early in the morning. Captain Willoby didn't mention that we were on a different shift, so I thought we went on at eight."

I dropped the file on my desk, "Jackie, relax. You're not late. I ended up getting up early this morning and decided to come in and get a jump on what's going on." She smiled and pulled out her chair.

The woman who was taking her seat across from me looked much different than the one I worked with yesterday. Gone were the ankle breaking high heels, fancy sweater and the skirt. Today, she was dressed in a more business casual attire. Tan slacks with a black blouse and a blazer. Her badge and weapon secured on her waist.

"So, what have you found so far?"

"Well, we've got a background on our victim. Looks like he was a customer at Cathy's yesterday. From what the uniforms found when they talked to a few of the witnesses, he apparently came into the store about ten minutes before everything went ballistic."

"Has anyone talked to his family yet?" Jackie asked.

"Figured that's going to be our second stop this morning. You have breakfast yet?"

"Yeah. Why?" she asked in a cautious tone.

"Well, lets hope that you don't see it again. We're heading to the morgue right now."

I noticed her color change slightly as I stood, but she maintained her facial expressions and followed me out.

For some reason, it always seems that I end up at the morgue in the early mornings. Maybe that's why I never seem to eat a big breakfast. Or maybe it's just karma. Either way, I end up seeing the large white building more often than I'd like to.

Jackie followed me in, never voicing her concerns, trusting me to lead her in the right way.

We stopped just outside the examination room. "Okay, Gannon, before we walk through this door, let me just say a few things. What we're likely to see here isn't exactly pleasant. If at any time you feel like you need to get some air or whatever, you go. I promise, if you do, I won't give you any grief about it." What the techs would do was something that I couldn't control.

She took a deep steadying breath. "Okay. I think I'm ready."

With that, I pushed through the doors and entered the sanctum of the county medical examiner, Dr. Wayne Rollins.

Wayne had been the medical examiner for nearly twenty years. I'd first met him when Bill took me on as a protégé. We were friendly, but only in a work sort of way. We knew the basics of each other's lives, but we didn't socialize off hours.

Wayne's head turned at the sound of the door. "Figured I'd be seeing you this morning, Monica."

"Well, it always seems that the dead don't pick the best times to go, do they?"

"Never seem to." His attention quickly focused on Jackie. "Training somebody new?"

"Wayne, this is my partner, Jackie Gannon. Jackie, this is Wayne Rollins, the ME."

They exchanged quick greetings and then it was time to get to why we were here. "What have you got on our vic, Wayne?"

He walked over to the drawer unit, and pulled out the slab that held the remains of Toby Williams. I snuck a glance over at Gannon when I heard her quick intake of breath. But she was breathing through her mouth now, which would alleviate most of the smells.

"Mr. Williams was shot seven times in the back. I've extracted three complete bullets, and the remnants of a fourth. Three were through-and-throughs. Cause of death was actually this one here, one of the through and throughs," he said as he pointed to the exit wound on the center of the chest. Somehow the projectile missed everything but the aorta. Poor guy was dead before he hit the floor.

"The other shots hit several vital organs including the lungs, kidneys and spleen. If the fatal round hadn't taken him out, odds are high that he would have bled out before help could have gotten to him."

"Any thing else that we need to know?" I asked.

"Other than being hit with seven rounds, this guy was in fairly decent shape. Liver and kidneys looked good. He didn't have much plaque buildup in the arteries, which leads me to think that this guy watched what he ate. Tox screen came back clean. The only problem he has, is he was shot." Wayne said shrugging his shoulders.

"I did collect a few unknown fibers off of his pant legs. And I sent the rest of his clothing over to the crime lab for analysis.

"Okay, thanks, Wayne." I glanced at my partner. She was still standing stoically trying not to let the obvious nauseousness that she was feeling become too prevalent. "Come on, Jackie let's go see his family. Bye, Wayne."

"Take care. Oh, by the way, I'm going to release the body if you don't have any objections."

"Can't think of anything." I waved as we left the room.

Once in the hall, Jackie started breathing a little easier. I made my way over to the vending machine and ordered up two waters. Handing one to her I said, "You held in there, but I can see that it cost you."

She looked a little embarrassed, "Thanks for not making a big deal about it. How long does it take to get used to going there?"

I started walking and took a long pull from the bottle before I answered her. "Guess that depends. Getting past the smell is one thing. I remember the first time Bill took me there, I did okay with the smell, like you did today, but when I saw the body on the slab that was a whole new ball of wax. I saw that body every night for the next week."

She looked surprised that I'd admit a weakness like that. "What happened that made it stop?"

We were back to the car by now, so I leaned on the roof before answering. "Another body ended up down there. It's no place for an eight year old boy."

"That made you stop seeing them at night?"

"No. I just stopped seeing that first one. I see him. I really don't know how to say this," I said suddenly at a loss for words. "You see, Jackie, part of what makes me good at what I do is that I don't forget. I can't claim to have an eidetic memory, but it's pretty close. That memory means that I see things that others miss. I never stop seeing those bodies that I've looked at there with Wayne. But because I don't forget them, and I know that I'll always see them, it forces me to work to the best of my ability to get justice for them."

"That's heavy," she said. "I mean, that's a big burden you work with everyday." She hesitated for a minute, "Thanks for telling me that."

I smiled at her, "It's going to take me a bit to figure out the partner routine, but I figured you needed to know that."

Toby Williams' house had started off as a basic Cape Cod, but along the way several additions had been made to it. As we pulled up in front of it, I looked at the house carefully. The original house was centered on the lot. It appeared that the first addition would have been added when an almost duplicate of the house was created just to the right of the main house, creating more living space and a garage.

The larger, more recent addition, was off of the back. The structure now stood a full two-and-a-half stories high, and was as wide as the combination of the main house and garage.

"Looks like somebody sunk a bit of cash into this place," Jackie commented.

"No question there. Wonder if it was worth it. Well, let's get this over with," I said as I pushed out of the car.

A young woman, perhaps in her mid-twenties, five-two with shoulder length blonde hair answered the door. "Good morning, Ma'am. I'm Detective Dietz, with the Blackberry Creek PD, and this is my partner, Detective Gannon. We'd like to speak to Mrs. Angela Williams."

"I'm sorry, but my mother isn't taking visitors right now. Her doctor gave her some tranquilizers to help get her through. They make her quite loopy. Might I be able to help?"

"You'd be?" I asked.

"I'm Katie Williams. My dad was the man that was killed in that shooting yesterday. Please come in, and I'll do whatever I can."

She led us to a small sitting room, "Can I get you anything?" she asked.

"No thank you. Ms. Williams, do know why your father would have been in Cathy's Collectibles yesterday at eleven-fifty?"

"No I don't. He should have been at work at that time. He works— sorry, worked for Brewster Industries. He was a sales rep there, and had been there for more than thirty years."

I glanced over, and Jackie was taking copious notes. "When was the last time that you talked to your father?"

"It was a few days ago. I don't live here anymore. After I graduated from Boston College, I took a position with Placard Pundit up in Boston. I'm a commercial artist. I came back when Lena, that'd be Lena Hornberg, called me. She's our next-door neighbor. She stayed with my mom until Russ and I got here."

"Who's Russ?" Jackie asked.

"He's my fiancé. Can you tell me what happened? Please. It would make things so much better if we knew."

"Right now, all I can tell you is that we are investigating several leads. I can't give you any more until we know what happened ourselves and we've got the guilty parties where they belong," I answered her.

"Ms. Williams, to your knowledge, did your father ever go to Cathy's Collectibles before yesterday?" Jackie prompted.

She thought for a minute, "He might have. It seems to me he said that he'd found this antique table that my mom had been looking for at some shop downtown. It might have been the same one."

"Okay, Ms. Williams. Thank you for your time," I said rising. I handed her one of my cards. "If you'd please have your mother call when she's feeling a little better, we'd really like to talk to her. And the sooner, the better."

"Why do you say that?" she asked in a defensive tone.

"Right now it's been less than twenty-four hours. The longer we wait, the more likely it becomes that the perpetrators get away. They have access to different modes of transportation and it makes our job that much harder."

"Okay," she said. "I'll have her call you when she gets up."

"Thanks for your time." I said again as she led us out.

Back in the car, I looked over at my partner. "What do you think?"

"They strike me as a nice, upper middle class family." She hesitated. "You think something's off don't you?"

I nodded. "I'm thinking about the house. At a conservative guess, I'd say it's going to be around two-and-a-half, maybe three million. How does a sales rep make enough for that? Gets my senses tingling and makes me think that we need to do a bit more research on Brewster Industries and start following the money.

My phone rang, "Dietz."

"Um, good morning. I was given this number by Commander Willoby. This is Andy Carson from the Crime lab. You're handling the Williams murder, correct?

"Yes. What can I do for you Mr. Carson?"

"It's Dr. Carson, and I'd rather not talk about this over the phone. Could you possibly schedule a visit here to the labs so I can go over what we'd classify as 'interesting material'?

I sighed. I really hadn't planned to make a trip to the lab, preferring to just have them shoot me the report. "Okay, Doctor," I emphasized the title, "Carson. My partner and I can be there in about twenty if that works for you."

"That'll be fine. I promise you, this will be worth your time."

"It'd better be, Carson. See you in twenty."

I sat there staring at my phone. "This could be interesting," I finally said.

CHAPTER 3

Bickford County's Crime lab was located in Midboro, the next town over. "Wonder what's so important that the guy couldn't tell me over the phone," I grumbled to Jackie.

"Don't know. Have you ever been here, I mean to the crime lab, before?" she asked.

"Not really. When the new lab opened, a few years back, I took a public tour. That's been the extent of it."

We pulled up to the limestone block building, and followed the signs to the visitor parking behind the main building.

"You okay?" Jackie asked as we made our way towards the main doors. "You look a bit frazzled."

I stopped on the path, let out a sigh. "I've got this weird feeling. The guy who called? He said his name was Dr. Andrew Carson. When I was at Boston College, I dated an Andy Carson. He went off to grad school and I went to the academy. I've thought about him on and off for the past ten years, but never tried to follow up. Now, here I am walking up to a meeting with someone with the same name, and I'm wondering if I'm going to end up going back in time."

"Odds are it's not even the same guy," she said. "He's probably sixty years old has been married for thirty years and had five kids and a dozen grandkids."

"Sure," I agreed as we started walking. With the way my luck had been going, it would be the Andy I knew and I'd make a fool out of myself.

The large glass doors opened automatically. "Really?" I muttered as we walked through and spied the large metal detectors. Reaching to the waistband of my slacks, I pulled my badge out and flashed it to the guard.

"Morning, Detective. If you'd please step into the ante-room, we'll secure your side arm and cuffs."

I shrugged, "This is a little over the edge, don't you think?" I whispered to Jackie.

"I agree with you. Wonder why they're so anal about letting officers in."

The guard chuckled. "Guessing this is your first official visit to the crime lab. The work that we do here is responsible for linking suspects to specific crimes, and often times is the key piece of evidence that leads to a conviction. Now, what would happen if somebody decided to come in here with a gun and cause a little havoc?

"The chain of custody would be jeopardized. And once the chain is broken, or even brought into question, the relevance to that piece of evidence is gone."

"But we're cops," Jackie moaned as she dropped her Glock into the lock box and removed the key.

"That's true," the guard answered. "But isn't it possible for a cop to be bought off? Not saying it's likely, but all it takes it one. And if it happens once, anything that our lab touches is forever tarnished."

"Okay, you win," I agreed securing my own Glock and the Berretta from my ankle holster into another box. "Now, can you point us towards the lab of Dr. Carson, please?"

"You're here to see Andy? He's a great guy. Smart, with a wicked sense of humor."

"Great. Wonderful. Is he paying you for the advertisements or what? Where do we find him?"

The guard led us to the back hall. "Take the elevator to four. Andy's in room four-oh-three."

"Thanks," I said as we strode towards the elevators.

Stepping off at four, I wondered if we had inadvertently taken a time machine instead of an elevator. Where the lobby had several potted plants and a welcoming look to it, the fourth floor reminded me of a hospital. Tiled floors, thick windows and heavy doors, but it was the smell that reminded me most.

"Can you imagine working in a place like this?" Jackie asked.

"Not really. Can't believe any one would, but it takes all kinds, right? Well, lets see what this guy wants. Here we go, four-oh-three." I stopped and looked at the door.

It looked like every other door on the floor. Beige in color, the numbers on it were engraved on a small plastic badge. A keypad sat to the right of the door.

"How do you suppose we get in?" I asked Jackie.

She looked at the keypad, shrugged and shook her head, "Don't know. Maybe we knock?"

I rapped on the door three times. "If this nut case doesn't have something that—"

The door opened a bit and a bespectacled man looked out. His face went from questioning to a wide grin of understanding. "You'd be Detective Dietz and partner, I presume?"

"Bingo, Stanley. We're looking for Dr. Carson."

He opened the door to let us in. "I'm Jake Steele, one of Dr. Carson's assistant, not Stanley," he said.

I shook my head, "I was referring to H.M Stanley, who was credited as saying 'Dr. Livingston, I presume.'"

"My apologies for not getting your reference right away. I'm sorry about the non-descript request for your coming here," he said as he moved toward a second door. "This is a clean lab. Before I can take you in, we'll need to put on protective garments. Please follow me," he said as he led us down a short hall.

At the far end, sat yet another door. This one looked a bit more serious than the first two combined. Beside the numeric keypad there was a screen, which appeared to be for palm prints.

Our host turned back to us, holding out two small packages of what appeared to be paper scrubs.

"What are these going to protect us from?" Jackie asked.

Steele smiled, "These are not to protect us. These are to protect what's in the lab from us."

"Okay, you've lost me now. Why don't we just cut through the charade and tell us what the heck you've dragged us down here for?"

"Detective, I'm going to beg your indulgence for just a few minutes more. Dr. Carson normally doesn't bring people to this lab, but this time we've come across something that is entirely unique, and you need to see it to fully understand. Please," he said as he motioned to the scrubs.

"Okay, but this had better be worth it," I grumbled as I fought to pull the paper booties on over my shoes.

I finished pulling the stupid scrubs on and went into the hall. Steele then handed each of us the matching paper cap and mask. Once these were on, he handed us the safety glasses. At this point, I wasn't sure what to expect.

Here we stood, with literally every part of our bodies covered either by the paper suits, booties and cap, or by the plastic of the goggles and gloves. I turned to look at Jackie and a laugh slipped through my clenched teeth. "We look like extras from some alien movie," I joked.

"This is no joking matter, Detective," Steele assured me. "Are you ready?"

We nodded that we were ready, and Steele passed us through into the interior of the lab. My eyes were assaulted the minute that we stepped through the door. Bright lights from overhead shone down on the lab tables, which in retrospect looked like OR tables. It wasn't making me feel any better.

In the back corner, was a solitary figure decked out in scrubs and a lab coat that was covered with smiley faces picking their noses. This guy has class.

"Dr. Carson," Steele called as we entered.

The figure turned, "Ah, Jack, thank you for bringing them in. I'll take it from here."

Steele nodded and then retreated through the door.

From what I could see, Dr. Carson was roughly six-two and not-exactly bulky, but he wasn't thin either, and he had the bluest eyes I'd ever seen. There was no way that I could have ever forgotten them. They were killers, even through the safety glasses.

"Detective Dietz?" he asked looking at me and I nodded. "I'm Dr. Andy Carson," he said holding out a gloved hand.

"It's Monica. Pleased to meet you," I said as I shook his hand. "This is officer Jackie Gannon, my partner."

"Thank you both for coming down. I normally don't bring non-scientists back here, but under the circumstances I think it best for you to see this." He turned to walk away, then spun around. "Do either of you have a cell phone or any other electronics with you right now?"

"Yeah," I answered, wondering where this was going.

"Please," he said grabbing another lock box, "put them in here. You'll be happy you did."

After dropping all of the electronics, we followed Carson to a section of the lab that was void of any electronics except a single free-standing computer. On the lone table, lay the suit coat that Williams was wearing when he was shot.

Dr. Carson stepped to the side, picked up a magnifying glass and handed it to me. "Before I explain what we found, I'd like you to examine the bullet holes first."

Taking the hand lens, I bent down over the coat and held it up to the first hole. The fibers were ragged and sticking out in every direction. I tried to look for something that shouldn't be there, and was coming up empty. "I'm not sure what—wait. There's something metallic here." I compared the small thread of what appeared to be silver with the rest of the fibers.

On the black fiber of the jacket, I could make out individual strands. I understood the basics of how cloth was made, so this made sense to me. It was the silver strand that didn't follow procedure. It was thin—no thicker than a human hair—and it was a single strand. I looked closer, and saw that there were several single silver strands in the cloth, but they weren't woven in.

When I looked up, Dr. Carson was smiling. "What is this, Doctor?" I asked.

"I believe that we are looking at a state of the art suit coat, Detective. These silver strands are actually thin silver wires. The entire coat is lined with them."

"Who would line a coat with silver wire?" Jackie asked.

"Perhaps understanding what the wire does first, might give us an indication of who and why." Dr. Carson said. "We noted that the coat has these wires in a pattern through only the body. They do not appear in the sleeves or cuffs. To be honest we didn't even notice them until we'd brought the coat into one of the labs. The computer alarms suddenly started going off indicating a computer breach.

"When we realized what was going on, we boxed it up and brought it here, into the clean lab. Going through it we discovered this," he said pointing to a small plug that was embedded in the lining of the pocket. "When we ran through the possibilities, we came up with the improbable, but it ended up being spot on."

He flipped the computer monitor on, and the data flashed on the screen.

"Are those, credit card numbers?" Jackie asked as we scanned the data.

"What we are looking at here, is a smart suit," Dr. Carson said. "Why don't we go back into my office to discuss the rest of this?"

I was glad to be rid of the scrubs and other gear, and was trying to fight with my hair. On a good day, my mass of mahogany hair is a challenge to control. After wearing the cap for the past half-hour, it looked like the aftermath of tornado.

Jackie walked out of her stall, took one look at me and broke out in hysterics. "Keep it up, Gannon, and you'll be riding the bus back to the station," I growled.

"I'm, sorry," she gasped out while fighting to control her breathing. "It's just your hair looks like it's ready for some bird to come back to nest in."

"Thanks. How about I taze you, just for kicks, and then your hair will match?" I joked and we both shared a laugh.

"If you are both ready, I'll escort you to Dr. Carson's office," Steele said popping his head through the doorway.

"I'm about as ready as I'll ever be," I said as I followed Jackie while wrestling my hair into a very messy ponytail.

We went back into the hallway, and turned left to the end of the hall. "This is Dr. Carson's office," Steele said as he knocked and pushed the door open.

We stepped inside, and I was amused. There was no other word for it. "Is this the doctor's office or a toy store?" I whispered to Jackie.

She too was looking at the massive toy collection that was prominently displayed on the wall shelves. There had to be at least a hundred different toys here.

"I was thinking the same thing," she whispered back.

The door on the opposite side of the room opened, and my mouth went slack.

"Ladies, please, won't—" he said stopping mid-stride. His gaze fixed on me for a few seconds before the smile reached his eyes. "Please have a seat," he said motioning to the two chairs in front of his desk.

I could feel my mouth still hanging open, but couldn't remember how to make it close. He. Was. Gorgeous.

My original take was spot on. He was about six-two, and the blue eyes were even more potent without the safety glasses. He wore a shirt that matched his eyes exactly. The short sleeves gave evidence to well-toned biceps, and his ebony colored hair was long enough to drape over the back of his collar, but well trimmed.

He looked as though he'd just stepped out of an ad for men's wear instead of that ridiculous lab coat and scrubs.

His eyes met mine, and I watched as the edges of his mouth turned upwards.

He reached out and took my hand and wrapped it in both of his, "Monica. I should have made the connection before. I'd apologize, but you'd remember that I forget almost everything when I get into the lab. It's great to see you again."

I could feel the heat in my face and my heart was beating in an irregular pattern. What the heck was going on with me? We were done. We'd broken things off ten years ago, and now he's been thrust right back into my life and I'm reacting like a teenager.

"Ahem," Jackie cleared her throat. "Just wondered if we might get back to that pesky business of the smart suit?"

Both Carson and I looked over at her, and realized that our hands were still interlocked. Quickly, we pulled our hands free. I sank into the chair as if the bones in my legs had dissolved, while he went behind the desk, pulled out his chair and conveniently tripped over the base.

It caused us all to laugh, and broke the moment of intensity.

"I'm sorry about the distraction," Dr. Carson said taking his seat. "As you saw in the lab, the suit coat is unquestionably unique. It appears to have been specially made. When—"

"Hold on a sec, Doc. What would indicate that this is anything but a specially made coat?" I asked.

"What I mean is, it's not an add on. Whoever made this coat didn't begin by purchasing a suit and then retrofit it with the electronics. No, this coat was modeled after a ready made coat, but was made, most likely by an expert tailor, and the electronics were integrated directly into the manufacturing process."

"How can you be sure that it wasn't retrofitted?" Jackie asked. She glanced at me, "I mean, it had an Armani label on it."

Dr. Carson took the question from there. "We can be certain that it wasn't a retrofit for several reasons. First, the quality of the coat. Looking at the exterior of the coat, there is no way to tell the difference. But when we look at the interior hems, we can see the differences," he paused as he swiveled to his computer and began tapping on the keyboard. Moments later, several pictures popped up on screen.

"Okay," he continued. "The picture on the left is from the coat in question; the one on the right is from an exemplar Armani. If you look at the stitching, here," he pointed to the photo on the left, "we see that the stitches are about an eighth of an inch apart, with a slight slant to the right. On the exemplar, the spacing is three thirty-seconds. Not much of a difference, but it is there and the stitches are straight up and down.

"The next indicator is the material itself. When we looked at the coat," he pointed to an enlarged view on the screen. "At first glance it looks like a standard wool blend, however when you look at the individual breakdowns, we find that whoever made the smart suit used a blend that is only available here in the states. Not something that you're likely to find in an Italian garment."

"But isn't all manufacturing done in Asia?" I asked.

"Oh, a fair amount of it. But they still determine what blends are to be used, and what processes need to be followed."

I thought for a minute, "So what we've got is a specialty suit that was likely made for a single person with the explicit purpose of stealing credit card information. Is that correct?"

Dr. Carson thought for a minute. "I don't think I'd want to go on record as saying it was only for the reason of the credit cards. I think, and right now this is just a hypothesis, but I think that that suit would absorb information from any electronic source."

"What difference does that make?" Jackie wondered aloud.

"It's not about credit cards," I blurted out. "Or not only about credit cards. If I'm following you here, Dr. Carson, this suit would strip out the data from any computer, cell phone, tablet or any other electronic device, right? That would give them a way to obtain company secrets, pending contracts, internal memos, contacts and a whole lot more."

"Why would some one want all of that? And who would want it?" she asked.

"The first question is to work on the what data they were after. As for the why, that's really going to depend on the what. Perhaps it was a specific competitor trying to get a leg up in a specific industry. Or maybe they're simply a clearing house; go out collect all of the data they can, separate it and sell it off to interested parties." I looked back to Dr. Carson, "Would I be correct that you have copies of all of the data that had been collected by the suit?"

"Yes. Once we understood what we were dealing with, we did download the entire contents of the memory. I'll burn it to a CD for you, but I have to ask that you be extraordinarily cautious with this data." He let out a long sigh, "It took us a bit to catch on to what was happening, despite the alarms. So, some of our files—"

"Are you telling me that that suit broke through the firewalls that protect the crime lab computers and transferred data from here?" I demanded.

Dr. Carson deflated. "Yes, Detective. That's exactly what I'm saying. Director Jacobs is working with the IT team on it right now, but the simple fact is that the data that you will be getting has information on several cases that we would prefer to not have made public at this time."

"You've got my word on that, Doctor. I'll need that data, along with the photos that you took during the suit-opsy." I hesitated for a minute, "I probably don't need to tell you that that suit should be keep separate from everything else and under heavy security, do I?"

"No," he shook his head. "Whoever is working on the suit has to be logged into the room. As you saw, there are several fail-safes to keep unauthorized people out. There is also a special vault in the lab where the coat is secured when it is not being worked with right now."

"Thanks for your time, Doctor," Jackie said as we rose. He shook her hand briskly.

"The pleasure was all mine," he said, again taking my hand in both of his. He didn't seem to want to let go. "I hope we meet again, Detective."

There was a look in his eye that should have had klaxons going off in my head, but I think I was just mesmerized by his face.

Out in the car, Jackie looked over at me, "You okay?"

"Huh? Oh sorry, I don't know. I'm still trying to take it all in. Everything that he told us in his office just seems too unbelievable. It's a bit much to accept."

"Oh," she exaggerated the word. "I thought you were still mesmerized by his charisma."

CHAPTER 4

Back at the station, I called Commander Willoby to request an appointment to bring him up to date with what we had found out. "Thank you, Sir, we'll be there at three."

Hanging up the phone, I glanced across the desks at my partner, who was laying out what appeared to be a twelve-course meal for lunch. "Hungry today, Jackie?"

She looked up at me, the open bag on her desk surrounded by the six Tupperware containers, and flushed. "No. I'm just very specific about what I eat. You know, making sure everything is healthy and all. What about you? Aren't you planning to have lunch?"

I shrugged. "I'll probably get around to grabbing something from the sub-shop across the street when I'm ready. They deliver, so it works for me."

As she began to fork up some fruit, she asked, "So, what happens next? I mean what's our next step?"

I leaned back in my chair and propped one foot on the bottom drawer handle. "Well, the first thing that we need to do is figure out who would be able to create a suit like that. I'm going to start by doing a quick read-through on the material that Dr. Carson sent over. Maybe there is something there that we can trace that will lead us to our mysterious tailor.

"Once we have that, we'll proceed by tracking down who the suit was made for. I mean, did Williams commission the suit or was he working for someone? That information should give us some basic directions. Maybe after we see Commander Willoby, something will shake loose there."

"Just kind of guessing, but don't you think that Williams had to be on the take a bit? We recognized that his house was valued at more than he could afford—"

I put a finger up, "Hold on, Jackie. We observed that the house would be valued at more than it appears he could afford. Until we run his financials, we won't know for certain." Knowing how much I hated following numbers, I made a split decision, "In fact, I think you can start there once you've finished with your entrée."

"You're mean, but you knew that right?" she asked. I was only guessing, but I had the feeling that she felt the same way about running financials as I did.

"Hey, it's got to be done. One question that we need to make sure that we don't lose sight of is, was Williams an intended target or innocent bystander?"

"If he was wearing the coat, he's no where close to innocent!"

"In one sense, you're correct. But was the shooting yesterday aimed at him, or was he merely caught in the crossfire?"

I ended up caving in and called the sub-shop to have an Italian Sub delivered as I was reading through Dr. Carson's report. "May have something here," I murmured to Jackie who was now searching the records for Williams' tax information.

"What's up?" she asked.

"Well from the metallurgy tests that were run on Williams' coat, it appears that what we have is ninety-nine percent pure silver that has been spun into a four-thousandths of an inch thick wire. Carson estimates that the total length would be about sixty feet of wire that are embedded in that coat."

"How's that going to help us?" Jackie asked, rubbing her eyes trying to relieve the strain.

"Well, I think I'm going to begin tracking down just who has the capabilities of making that kind of wire. Maybe they can tell me about who bought that much wire."

I turned to my computer and began my search. It took nearly an hour before I found what I was looking for, "Got something here," I said softly.

"Glad one of us is having luck here," Jackie retorted.

"I found a manufacturer for jewelry wire, who will custom size silver wire. I think this deserves a little more research."

The alarm on my iPhone went off, and I glanced at the time. "Well, let's go. We've got to see the commander about this in ten." I stretched after I stood trying to work some of the kinks out of my back before I shrugged into my blazer. "How are you making out with the financial search?"

Jackie just gave me a blank stare. "You knew that it was going to be layered under mountains of false accounts and shell corporations, didn't you?"

"Not for certain, but I had a good suspicion. If it gets too much, we can always call in a drone to run it for us."

She stretched a bit before she answered. "No, I don't think that we need to do that. I'm making headway. The more turns he throws at me, the more determined I'm becoming. Nobody goes through this much trouble unless they're trying to hide something. He's piqued my interest. Now I'm going to find it."

"That's the spirit," I said as we entered into the Commander's outer office.

Like magic, his door opened, "Perfect timing, Detectives. Come right in," the commander said.

We followed him into his office. I was a bit shocked. Three other people sat in chairs already. "Detective Gannon, Detective Dietz, these are Special Agent Tom Weine," he pointed to nearest man who had skin the color of hot chocolate. He shifted his point towards the skinny golden skinned man, "Special Agent Hector Immentz". With a casual gesture to the tall black haired man he finished, "And this is Deputy Director Mark Shuman. They are all from the Boston branch of the F.B.I. Gentlemen, Detectives Monica Dietz and Jackie Gannon.

"The detectives are heading our part of this investigation. Detective, please give us your report so far."

I sighed. I didn't exactly like working with the F.B.I., but I could. It was kind of like cleaning your room as a kid: you'd do it when you absolutely had to, and there was no other choice.

"The deceased male has been identified as Toby Williams who lived on Weston Woods Drive. We went by the house to speak with his widow, but she had been sedated and we are awaiting an appointment with her. ME confirms that Williams was shot seven times, all in the back. The surprise for us thus far came from the guys over at the crime lab. They discovered that the suit coat that Williams was wearing at the time of his death was part of a 'smart-suit', which contained wires and a series of electrical components that enabled the coat to get by any firewall and copy all information from any electronic devices.

"At this time, it is unclear whether Williams was acting independently or working for someone at the time of the shooting. Based on the information obtained from Dr. Carson—"

"Andy Carson?" Agent Weine asked. "Son of a gun, he used to be one of the best we had up in Boston. I'd heard that he'd made his way out to the Cape. He's good people."

"Thanks for that tidbit," I added self-consciously before I continued. "From what Dr. Carson has given us, it appears that the suit was lined with a very thin wire that was made from silver. The coat also contained several microprocessors which again were embedded into the coat in hard to find locales. These processors were triggered by a proximity switch when the suit was near to specific frequencies of electromagnetic fields. When turned on, they collected all data that was stored on any electric device such as computers, phones, tablets or credit card readers. The consensus is that the coat was specially made for the client. At this time it is unclear who that actual client was, if it was Williams or an employer.

"We are also awaiting a full detail of the data that the coat had already downloaded. Dr. Carson and his team were working on that this morning, and when he sent the photos and basic tech points to me, he stated that they hoped to have that completed by the end of the workday."

Everyone was scratching notes down on their pads. I was wondering what Jackie was writing down, but figured that I'd talk to her on the way back to our desks.

"Detective," Agent Immentz began, "what reason would someone have for wanting a coat like this?"

I didn't follow his line of thinking, but decided that I wanted to keep my answers guarded until I knew what game we were playing. "Sir, at the present, the best guess is that Williams, or his employer, were using it to copy credit card information along with other data that may give them a heads up on what certain companies are pursuing."

"So you think that this is being used for identity theft?" he asked.

"That's one possibility. Until we see Dr. Carson's full report, we won't know for sure."

When no other questions were raised, Commander Willoby nodded to Director Shuman.

Shuman cleared his throat. "We've been looking into the potential kidnapping of the owner of the store who has been identified as one Catherine Evans. This is unusual for a kidnapping since at this point, there have been no ransom demands. We are tracking down some leads based on the car that was used; a group in the Boston office is working with facial recognition software and the traffic cam videos to see if we can make any identification. The plates were camouflaged, so it's taking a bit of work to uncover things."

"Has the second victim been identified yet?" Weine asked.

Commander Willoby took that question. "Not yet. When he was shot yesterday, he was carrying no identification, so currently he is being listed as a John Doe. We've put an announcement out to all agencies with his description. About all we can hope for is that someone reports him as missing."

"What about the hotels?" I asked. "It's possible that he's here on vacation and is staying at one of the local hotels. Maybe someone should run over and start flashing his picture around to the desk clerks."

Several more ideas were bounced around before the meeting was adjourned. As we were walking back to our desks, Jackie asked, "What if there's a connection between Williams and this John Doe?"

"What do you mean?"

"Well, we know Williams because he's a local and he had ID on him. So far we've considered that Williams was using the coat to steal information. What if he's selling the coat?"

"Why would he want to sell that coat?"

"Monica, think about it for a sec. If you've got some new idea that you're going to market and sell, you need to prototype it, right? Once you've got the prototype, you've got to show it to people, advertise it. How can you guarantee that your product will do what you say it will? You hold demonstration. What if Williams was demonstrating his product?"

I thought about what she was saying. We were back at our desks, so I flopped ungracefully into my chair to think. At this point in the investigation, it was as plausible as anything else. "Okay, it's definitely a possible avenue. I think the best course of action right now is for us to continue on what we were working on prior to our meeting. But now you've got something to really look for."

"I do?"

"If you're right here Jackie, Williams would have needed to fund the experiment and paid for the prototype. With either, there is going to be a record somewhere."

She leaned back in her chair, "Makes sense. Do you think it would be under his name or a company name."

"Making a guess, I'd say company name. I'm going to see what I can do about tracking down our wire and head in that direction."

Twenty minutes later, we were both engrossed in our own searches. Jackie was apparently getting serious about her computer work, as she had slapped a barrette into her hair to keep it from falling into her face. The sleeves of her blouse had been pushed up to the elbows and she was muttering to herself.

I simply grinned. I was glad to see she was totally absorbed in the work. I checked the number that I needed and dialed.

"Manson's Jewelry Supply, how can I help you?"

"Good afternoon. This is Detective Monica Dietz from the Blackberry Creek Police Department, in Blackberry Creek, Massachusetts. I'm hoping that I could speak to Ms. Janet Manson please."

"One moment," the receptionist said and then elevator music filled the earpiece. I tapped my unpainted nails on the desk impatiently.

"This is Janet Manson," a crisp voice said.

"Ms. Manson, I'm Detective Monica Dietz from the Blackberry Creek PD. I'm currently investigating a murder here, and was wondering if you might be able to help with a few items."

There was a long silence before she spoke, "I guess so. I don't know much about solving murders."

"That's okay, Ms. Manson, I do. What we're interested in is a length of silver wire that was recovered at the scene."

"Well we do sell wire, but how will that help?"

"This wire is unique. It is four-thousandths of an inch in diameter, and about sixty feet in length. Can you tell me if you've sold a length of wire like that say in the past year or so?

There was a light tapping in the background, "Um, it appears that we did custom make a wire of about that thickness, but it was for a much larger quantity than just sixty feet. Our records here indicate that it was for one-thousand feet."

"Okay. Would you happen to have the name of the individual or the company that commissioned that order?"

"I do. But I'm not sure that I should give it to you. We have customer confidentiality that we have to consider."

"Ms. Manson, I'll get a warrant if I need to, but it would be a huge help if you'd just give me the name."

"I tell you what, I'm going to call my lawyer. If he says it's okay to give it to you I will, but I've got to do what's right by my clients."

"I understand. I'll give you my number here and when you know, you can call me, okay?" Once she agreed to that, I gave her my direct line and hung up.

"How are you making out, Jackie?"

"I can't pin him to any purchases, but I'm still digging. It doesn't look like his financials are consistent. Maybe we want to have a professional take a look. I see what looks like tax evasion in a few of his companies here."

"Did Williams own the companies solely or did he just own shares?"

"From what I'm seeing here, it looks like it was solely."

"We'll look at it to see if we can find any links, but it's hard to prosecute a dead man for tax evasion."

Noise from the changing shifts carried in. I'd spent the last part of my day calling a judge that I knew, and trying to wrangle a warrant out for a guaranteed way to get Ms. Manson's client list. Until something changed, I was a bit stuck.

"Excuse me?" a voice said drawing me out of my brainstorming session.

I sat upright and spun the chair around so I could see who had intruded into my quiet time.

And there he stood.

He looked as he had this morning, with the exception of two features. The windswept hair hinted that he'd likely driven over with the top down on a convertible and the smile that was now fixed on his face looked like he's just won the lottery.

"Dr. Carson. What a surprise," I managed. I noticed Jackie's surprised look, and figured that she was going to want me to tell her what was going on here. I was just hoping that I was going to get a chance to figure it out before she asked.

"Detective," he said nodding at Jackie. Turning back to me, his voice became a little sultrier, "Detective. I took a chance that you'd be here right now, and brought these over for you." He pulled out a small stack of CD's from his coat pocket.

"Thank you, Dr. Carson. You didn't need to do that. If you'd called, I could have come over to pick them up."

"Yes, you could have, but that would have deprived me the opportunity to see where you work."

"Typically, cops and criminalists don't congregate. You science folks tend to stay in your labs and we stay here in our squads. So what is it you really came over for, Dr. Carson?"

"Please, call me Andy."

"I hate to leave when the show's getting good," Jackie said, "but I've got a date. See you."

"Bye," I called to her as she headed out, looking back at us and smiling. Looking now to my visitor, "Okay, Andy. What can I do for you?"

He sat on the corner of my desk. "When you walked into my lab today, you nearly killed me. I haven't seen you for at least ten years. After you left, I just sat there and wondered what had happened. It took me some time to realize that when we split years ago, that I never truly got over you. I didn't even know that you were working here when I took the job. I just needed to be out of the big city, and this seemed perfect. Everything was going perfectly, and then, you walked into my lab. And," he paused and frowned. "I'm not mad at you. I realized that I missed you. So, I was getting ready to go home and prepare a single serving of the Swanson Hungry Man meatloaf, when I decided to go with impulse and see if you might like to join me for a meal out and we can catch up a little with each other."

He looked at me through those ridiculously sexy eyelashes. I really wasn't ready to go anywhere. But at the same time, the idea of spending a little time reacquainting myself with the transplanted Dr. Andrew Carson would probably be a much better use of time than sitting home by myself with a Lean Cuisine dinner, watching a DVD.

"How about we split a pizza?" I offered.

"That sounds perfect. We can get a chance to catch up with each other. It's probably a good thing knowing that we'll have to work with each other on the job.

"I'll tell you what, Andy, I've got to log this new evidence in and secure it in the vault here before I can go. Shall we meet at Donetello's in say an hour?"

His eyes sparkled as he stood. "I'll look forward to seeing you there." He took my hand, lifted it to his mouth and kissed the back of it ever so gently. "I'll be waiting for you."

I just nodded. My heart was still running laps and my legs felt like they were going to collapse. How could one little kiss on my hand upset my tranquility so bad?

I had to be out of my mind. Saying that I'd meet him in an hour. It was too reckless for me; too fast.

I couldn't get there quick enough.

CHAPTER 5

Donetello's sat just off of the coast road, near the old pier, a squat little brick building, with a faded façade and bad lighting. But it served the best pizza in town. I glanced at the clock on my dash as I pulled into the small lot behind the pizzeria and noted that I still had ten minutes before I was to meet Andy. Pulling into the first open slot I found, I tried to relax by focusing on my breathing.

At thirty-two, there should be no need for me to be getting concerned about meeting someone for pizza. It's not that I hadn't dated over the past ten years; it's just that I hadn't found anyone who really did anything for me.

Until I'd responded when Andy kissed my hand.

Now I was sitting here wondering what was going to happen. I felt my pulse begin to race again. I closed my eyes and concentrated on the rhythmic crashes of the surf pounding on the jetty.

I felt calm enough to go in after three or four minutes, so I climbed out and started for the door. As I walked around the building to the seaside, I kept doing the breathing exercises that I'd learned in my yoga class, hoping to keep myself calm . I rounded the last corner, and stopped dead in my tracks.

He was there leaning on the split wood fence staring out over the ocean.

I stood there for a few seconds, and he seemed to sense me. His head came up slowly, and he turned in my direction. The smile took ten full seconds to totally reach his eyes, but when it did, oh my.

"Hello, Monica," he almost purred.

My legs felt like they were going to melt on me. "Hi, Andy. I'm not late am I?"

He pushed off of the fence, "No. I got here a few minutes ago, and became mesmerized by the ocean. Shall we?" he asked opening the door.

It was still early in the evening, so Donetello's wasn't packed yet with the after-dinner crowd who habitually came it to watch whatever sporting event was playing that night while nursing a few beers. We stepped up to the small podium, and waited for the hostess to seat us.

I felt him slide closer to me. "You smell great," he murmured.

"I think that's the pizza," I remarked, trying desperately to keep my footing.

"No. Pretty sure that's you. It's like a cookie on warm spring day. And since you look as pretty as a flower, I guess that makes me the luckiest guy in here."

"Andy, I don't know how to break this to you, but I think you're a bit deluded. We're just here to share a pizza. We already know each other. I'm not sure—" the waitress came over to escort us to our seats.

"Hi! Welcome to Donetello's. I'm Tracy, and I'll be serving you tonight. If you'd please follow me," she chirped as she led us to a small table in the back corner.

I sat across from Andy, looking at him instead of the menu, and wondered what I'd gotten myself into. I'd almost always been someone who needed to have all of the facts in place before I'd make any kind of move. The facts were he'd broken my heart when I was not quite twenty-two. Now ten years later he suddenly gets dropped back into my life and I'm agreeing to go to dinner. What is wrong with me? Maybe I should excuse myself and head to the nearest hospital to have my brain scanned.

Before I could convince myself to go, Tracy was back to take our order. We'd asked for a couple of glasses of water and ordered a loaded pizza with everything but anchovies and olives.

"Now, what was it you were saying?" he asked.

I made the mistake of glancing up, and he was looking at me with those eyes of his. Oh, boy. "Andy, it's just that you're, um, I don't know how to say this, you seem to be in a different place than I am, I think."

"No. No, pretty sure you're at Donetello's and that's where I am. Seems like the same place to me," he said with a smile. He reached out and placed his hand over mine, "I'm going to take a stab in the dark here, but I need you to know something before I do. When you walked into my lab this morning, you took my breath away. I wasn't able to do much this afternoon after you left. I capped it off by putting two teaspoons of salt in my coffee.

"But I also know that I've spent way too much time locked away in my lab, and my relationship skills are quite rusty. So, I had to follow my instinct and brought you the data earlier as an excuse to see and talk to you again. And now I'm guessing I'm making you feel uncomfortable right now, and I'm sorry for that. We used to be really close."

I smiled a bit. "I'm not exactly uncomfortable, Andy. It's just that you totally caught me off guard. It took me a fair amount of time to get back to an even keel after you walked away at Boston College. When you called this morning, it totally threw me for a loop, just the possibility that it might be you. I recognized you the moment we walked into your lab. I think your eyes should be on a deadly weapons list. They were potent when we were at school and now every time you look at me, they make my bones feel like jelly. I know what you mean about not being able to focus."

I hesitated and decided that I needed to be as honest as I could. "To tell the truth, I'm afraid. Afraid that I'd like to take this companionship somewhere further. I knew the boy that you were. I don't know the man. And, I'm afraid that you could hurt me again"

"Monica, can we try it this way? How about we share some stories over our pizza. It'll give us a chance to catch up and get to know each other and we can see what happens after that. If we want to take this further, we can begin taking those steps. If we think it's best if we just stay as work-friends then that's okay too. But at least we can say that we didn't sit around and wonder what might have happened."

"I don't know what else to do, Andy," I admitted. "I'd given up on relationships and then you called me into your lab. Now I need to see it through."

"Here you go, guys," Tracy said as she brought our pizza over. "Anything else I can get you?"

"How about a bottle of Merlot, and a couple glasses?" he looked at me with a raised eyebrow.

I was breaking all of my personal rules tonight anyway, so why not one more. "Sure, that'd be great."

Tracy returned a moment later with two wine glasses and our bottle. She poured while Andy struggled to get the slice of pizza onto plate without leaving the toppings behind. "I've got Ph.D.'s in criminalistics and physics, yet I can't keep a slice of pizza together," he mumbled.

"It's okay, Andy. Nobody here is going to dock you any points."

When he'd finished, I raised a glass, "To new beginnings." Our glasses clinked and we began eating.

"So," he said between mouthfuls, "tell me about yourself, and what's happened over the last decade."

I swallowed hard. This was the part of getting involved with somebody that always drove me nuts. Telling about myself. I sighed, "Well I'm thirty-two, five-ten green eyes and mahogany hair. After Boston, I went to the academy and I've been a cop for the last ten years, and made detective three years ago. I've been going to St. Gregory's Catholic church and try to get there every week. Unfortunately, my job sometimes gets in my way there. My older sister, Amy, is out in California and my brother, Phil, is a lawyer in Michigan. My parents still live in the same little house in Burlington where I grew up. Right now, I share my apartment with Sam." I took a sip of wine and checked my watch, "He'll be wondering where I am shortly," I added.

"So, you're living with a guy and came out with me anyways?" Andy asked.

"Jeez!" I palmed my forehead. "Not exactly." I looked up to see his pained expression, "You see, Sam is my Newfoundland. My dog," I said with a smile.

"Your dog? Okay, now I feel better. I may get bit, but he most likely won't be pounding my face in because I took you to dinner," he said as he saluted with his wine glass.

"What about you? I've told you the basics, so don't you think it's fair that you reciprocate?"

"Not much to tell really. As I know you remember, I was the head nerd at Boston College for the entire four years I was there. After BC I did my masters at Dartmouth and then did my doctoral studies and post-doc at Harvard. I was recruited by Boston's crime lab, and spent too many years up in the big city. I decided that I wanted to try a smaller setting and when the opportunity arose, I ended up here.

"My mom moved to Arizona last winter. It suits her. My sister, Anna, is out there with her family. So it's just me and my cat, Fred."

As our conversation continued, I noticed that the flow of people coming in was beginning to pick up. Most of the customers who were in small groups and took seats at the tables and booths, while those that were solo, tended to stay around the bar.

Except one.

He was a well dressed man in his early forties, I'd guess, who was sitting alone at a small table in the corner. I didn't mention anything to Andy, but made a few mental notes. He looked to be roughly six-two, dirty blond hair, and brown eyes. Eyes that seemed to be looking through us.

The man sat at his table with his elbows propped on the table and his hands clasped in front of him moving only to take a drink. There was a glint of gold on his right pinky, that appeared to be a large ring.

Waiting for someone? I wondered. But, if he was waiting for a dinner companion, wouldn't he be watching the door?

"So," Andy continued with our conversation, "what do you think?"

I froze for a second and recovered as quick as I could. "I'm sorry, Andy. What was the question?"

He smiled, "I thought I'd seen your eyes glaze over from my babbling. I was thinking maybe we could go for a walk on the beach before we called it a night."

I reached over placing my right hand over his left, "That sounds terrific. It also will give me a chance to explain why I missed the question the first time, and it wasn't because of your babbling." I gave his hand a squeeze and smiled at him. His face lit up with its own smile.

Fifteen minutes later, we were on the beach walking side-by-side, with our hands tucked into our pockets. "So, are you going to tell me what caught your attention in there?" Andy asked.

"It's probably nothing. But there was a guy who was sitting alone in the opposite corner from where we were—"

"Looking at other guys while you're out with someone?" he quipped.

I spun around fast and looked him square in the face. I was ready to be mad at him, but then I looked at his eyes. They were smiling the way they do when you play rough with a puppy. The smile on his face matched. "Occupational hazard?" he queried.

"Yeah," I sighed letting my head droop. "I can't say why this guy caught my attention. He wasn't doing anything that he shouldn't have been, but he stood out, you know. Everyone else who was solo in there was up at the bar. So I wondered why he wasn't."

"Monica, Monica, Monica," he said. "So what you're telling me is that this guy triggered some instinct in that serious cop brain of yours and that's where you went?"

"Yeah. I can't tell you what it is, or was, but yeah, it's along those lines."

He gently raised my chin so he could see into my eyes, "Don't fret about it. I fully understand getting totally absorbed in a hunch. You may be a cop, and I may be a scientist, but we both operate in spaces where we have to follow our hunches. It's how we work." He smiled cannily, "So, I'm going to follow another now."

I realized what he was going to do a milli-second before his lips touched mine. What I didn't see coming was my response.

As soon as his warm breath caressed my face, it was as if my brain switched gears and went on auto-pilot. By the time our lips touched, my hands were entwining themselves in his hair, and I was pressing in closer.

I don't know how long we embraced, since time stood still for me. Then, as slowly as he'd begun the kiss, he backed out. His eyes had to be reflections of mine; crazed with desire, but restrained by control. "Sorry," I whispered.

"I'm not," he said breathlessly. "I started that, and I'd gladly do it again."

"I've never ... this is so unlike me, I'm not sure what happened."

Andy smiled, "It looks like another one of my hunches paid off. I figured you'd still do that to me after all that time," he said as he rubbed the back of his hand over my cheek. "And, it looks like we have something else to talk about, unless you intend to tell me you reacted like that out of the goodness of your heart," he challenged.

I shook my head, "I try very hard to be honest. It's a quirk."

"Then we'll talk about it. Later." He took my hand and led me back to the parking lot.

That night I lay awake in bed, and replayed the whole evening over in my head. There were definitely some high points. The companionship that I hadn't realized that I was craving, his kiss. "I'm not sure how I feel about this, Sam," I muttered as I lazily stoked his thick fur. I moved my hand to scratch his ear, and he rolled into my side and emitted a small moan. "Puts you in puppy ecstasy every time, doesn't it?"

I jumped when the phone on the bedside rang, "Blast it all! All I'd really like to do is have a night where I get some sleep," I moaned to Sam while I reached for the phone. "This is Monica Dietz," I answered fully expecting someone from the department to be on the other end of the phone.

"Well, Detective Dietz," a man's voice drawled. "I thought I should let you know that it would be in your best interest to let Mr. Williams' passing go."

"Who is this?"

"I'm just someone who's trying to look out for your welfare. I don't want to see you get hurt or nothing, so you'd best let Toby go."

"Are you threatening me?" I asked while I grabbed for my cell to place a trace on my line.

"No. We'd never want to threaten a police officer. We just want you to let it go so … you know nothing bad happens to you."

"Are you going to try and harm me if I'm just doing my job?"

"Hey! No way! We just heard on the streets that if some badges keep pressing into things that don't concern them, that this real bad guy has promised to send 'em to sea. Now we don't want nothing like that to happen to you, so we're just, uh, passing the message along."

While he'd been talking, I'd texted the alert room at the station, and was hoping that they were tracing the call. I reached over to the nightstand again, and had to stretch to grab the notepad and pencil that were there. I started jotting down notes about the phone call, what the caller sounded like, key phrases that he might use and any other piece of data that might be useful.

"So is there a name that you'd like to pass on to me? Let me know who might wish to do me some harm?"

"Nah, nah we can't do that. If they ever found out that we'd given you a name, then they'd be after us. And we don't want that. So anyway, you just let this all go and we can all forget about it," he said just before the line went dead.

"Dang!" I shouted at the phone that was now telling me that if I wanted to make a call I needed to hang up and redial. I slammed the phone back onto the receiver and snatched my cell from the bed. I swung my feet off the bed while I hit the speed dial.

"Blackberry Creek Police Department, control room, Officer Ben Adams."

"Hey, Adams, it's Dietz. Any luck with the trace on the call that just came into my personal line?"

"Just a moment, please," I heard the audible click and then the strains of music filled the phone. I rubbed the bridge of my nose hoping that it would ward off the headache that was forming there.

I went back to petting Sam, drawing as much stress relief from the act as I could, "What happened to my peaceful night, Sam?"

Sam just looked at me with those huge brown eyes of his, and then proceeded to move so that he was sitting on my lap with his head on my shoulder.

The phone clicked back on, "Detective?"

"Yes?" I answered.

"This is Bart Schafer, I'm working the communications station this evening. "Unfortunately, we weren't able to nail this guy's location. Probably wouldn't make any difference anyway. The number pinged back to a pre-paid cell, so it'd be likely that he was moving so that we couldn't get a fix on him."

"I'm just having no luck at all tonight. Okay, do me a favor and see if we can find out how the phone was paid for. Maybe it will give us something on the Williams case."

"Yes, Ma'am. I'll send whatever we pull tonight to your desk."

"Thanks, Schafer." I hung up the phone and cuddled Sam a little closer.

I'd just turned off the lights and snuggled into the covers when the phone rang again, "Oh for the love of Pete," I snarled as I grabbed the cell this time and glanced at the readout. "Why's he calling me now?" I asked Sam who had come back to the head of the bed. "Dietz," I said answering it.

"Monica, it's Andy. Andy Carson from the crime lab. There's a problem."

"Don't tell me, you missed me, right?" I asked sarcastically.

"No. Well, yes I do, but that's not why I called. Somebody broke into my lab and torched it."

My eyes shot open wide. "What was that?" He repeated himself before I was able to get my emotions under control. "Okay, where are you right now, Andy?"

"I'm at the little coffee shop across the street from the lab. The fire department is there now, but they won't let me go in. I-I don't know what was taken or damaged. Oh, God," I could hear the panic and despair in his voice.

"I'll be there in fifteen minutes, Andy. Just hang in there."

CHAPTER 6

It took a bit more than the fifteen minutes that I'd promised Andy, but I pulled up less than a block away from the scene.

The streets were crowded. Two large pumpers stood just in front of the crime lab shooting streams of water from the ladder tops. Smoke billowed out from multiple windows and flames were still visible in a few others. Over the noise of the trucks, I could hear the yells of command from the various fire chiefs sending their crews to specific vantage points to battle the blaze.

I scanned the crowd. There were a few faces that I recognized, but most were strictly on-lookers who were there to watch the show. I slipped out my phone, and turned it to the video setting and shot a few moments of video, getting as many of the on-lookers in the frames.

When I finished, I walked over to the first two faces that I'd recognized. "Lieutenant. Keri," I acknowledged them.

Walker looked at me, "Don't tell me that you've been given this case as well," he said.

"Not that I'm aware."

"Then why are you here?" Keri asked. "If I had the choice of being home in bed right now or here, I'd be in snores-ville, you know what I mean?"

"I can definitely relate. Not sure how this is going to affect my case. The items that I was here to see today were in the labs on the fourth floor." I turned and looked at the building. "And it looks like that's where the major action currently is."

"Yeah," the Lieutenant observed, "this is sure going to complicate lots of things for many departments, ours included. This lab processed the majority of evidence from most of the high profile cases around here. The fire has the potential to destroy the chain-of-custody for that evidence, which could lead to many of those cases being thrown out." He looked back at me. "Now, if this isn't your case, why are you here?"

I could almost feel the blush heating my face, but this was my commanding officer. "Well, Sir, I met Dr. Carson earlier today. He called my cell number around ten-forty-five and told me that the lab was on fire. I came down on my own."

"Is Dr. Carson here?" Keri asked.

"He said he was. My plan was to find him and talk with him."

The Lieutenant looked at me with an upraised eyebrow. "You go ahead and find him. But, we'll talk to him."

I found Andy about five minutes later. He was standing at the back of a crowd of people who had assembled on the corner to watch the fire. Andy was leaning on a lamp pole, and looked miserable. "Hey," I said as I came up to him. "You okay?"

When he looked towards me, I could see that his eyes were brimming with tears. My heart went out to him, this funny guy who had entertained me all evening, who had kissed me silly was now leaning on a pole almost in tears.

I reached out to him, and pulled him in for a tight hug. I was surprised at the ferocity of his response. He gripped me in a bear hug so tight that I thought that there would be bruises where his arms encircled me. "Thank you," he whispered in a rough voice.

We stood there for a long minute. The two of us embraced, my left hand rubbing in circles on his back.

When I felt the hug loosen, I leaned back so I could see his face. "Come on, let me buy you a drink," I said sympathetically. He nodded, so I took his hand and led him to a small diner just around the corner.

Inside, we sat across from each other, and I reached out and took his hands. "Do you want to talk about it?"

He didn't exactly smile, but the grin was better than the dour look he had had previously. "I'm not sure what to say, Monica," he began. "I was at home and the phone rang around ten-ten tonight. The caller identified himself as a guard here, and said that there was a problem in my lab and I would need to report here at once.

"I told them it would take about twenty minutes for me to get here. It ended up taking me nearly half an hour. I was walking up the front walk when there was an explosion." He paused and looked out the window and shook his head.

"All of my work. All of the evidence that we process for the various town police departments. It's all ruined," he said.

"Andy, I'm going to call my Lieutenant. He and his partner are the ones that are assigned to this case, so they're going to want to talk to you. I think that there may be some carryover from the case that I was working today to what happened here. I'm going to have them meet us here, and we can both talk to them."

It took them ten minutes to fight through the crowds to get to the diner. I'd moved over so I could sit next to Andy, and currently had my arm around him while his head leaned on mine.

"You sure know how to keep a secret, Monica," Keri said with a smile and a nod. "Nobody in the department even had an idea that you two were seeing each other."

I gulped. Honestly, I hadn't thought of that, but that was the least of our problems right now.

"This is a very recent development," I said squeezing Andy's hand. It was probably easier to run with what they thought, and not get overly excited about things.

"Okay," Aaron said, taking over the conversation. He shocked Andy when he began reciting the Miranda rights.

"I didn't do anything," Andy nearly pleaded.

I squeezed his hand again, "Andy, it's okay. It's standard procedure to protect everyone involved."

"I'm going to record this conversation," the Lieutenant said and looked at his watch. "Interview begins May fifteen at oh-twenty-eight. Please state your names for the record," he said as he motioned to Andy.

"Doctor Andrew Carson, Criminalist with the Bedford County Crime Lab."

I was surprised when the Lieutenant motioned for me and prompted with "And?" I shrugged, "Monica Dietz, Detective, Blackberry Creek Police Department."

"Can you tell me what happened tonight?" the Lieutenant asked.

Andy gave him the same story that he'd told me. "Why did you call Detective Dietz, Dr. Carson?" Keri asked.

Andy's face flushed slightly. "I met Detective Dietz this afternoon when she came to my lab at my request. While there I showed her some unusual evidence that related directly to her current case. During the time that she was there, I, uh, recognized her. We had dated for a time when we were both in college. When the opportunity presented itself to see her in her squad room, I delivered the data that she'd requested personally.

"During that visit, I asked her about the possibility of going to dinner this evening. She accepted and we dined at Donetello's. When I got the call about the lab, and then witnessed the explosion, I didn't want to be alone. I'm relatively new in the area, and have almost no friends outside of work. I called her and asked if she'd come."

"Detective," Keri said, "Do you wish to add anything to Dr. Carson's statement?"

"No, I think Andy has it pretty tight."

"Is it your policy to have personal relations with people who are working on various parts of your cases, Dietz?" the Lieutenant asked.

I glared at him. "Lieutenant Walker, there are no regulations on whom I am allowed to see on my personal time. Yes, Andy, I mean, Dr. Carson and I met in an official capacity today, but the fact is, as he already said, we dated when we were both at Boston College more than a decade ago. We are both adults, currently unattached, who felt some attraction to each other. If he hadn't felt it, he never would have approached me, and without it, I never would have accepted.

"I also know, thanks to our date this evening, that Andy has no family in the immediate vicinity. He cares intensely about his work, that's what pulls him. Watching something that is precious to you being destroyed makes you crave those little personal connections. He called and I responded. I'd do it again in a minute."

Keri looked over at her partner and he nodded.

"Dr. Carson, could you please describe the voice of the person who called you?"

Andy closed his eyes thoughtfully, "His voice was kind of rough, nasal. It almost sounded like he was using something that would mask his real voice. His accent almost sounded like something from the south—"

"Like a southerner?" I interrupted.

Andy's eyes opened a bit, "Yeah, I guess. What's the big deal about the caller having a southern accent?"

The Lieutenant beat me to the explanation. "It might be that the same person who called you about your lab called Detective Dietz regarding the case she is currently working on. Do you remember when you got your call, Monica?"

I pulled out my phone, and scrolled through the outgoing texts. "It would have been around ten, perhaps a few minutes after. I texted to dispatch at ten-oh-three to have them put a trace on it."

"Do you think it was the same guy?" Andy asked. He turned so he could face me, "He didn't threaten you, did he?"

"Relax, Andy," I said. "He said that if I didn't let the Williams case go, that there would be someone who wanted to do me harm. He didn't—"

"That can't happen!" Andy nearly shouted causing the other six occupants of the diner to look at him. "Oh, God, that can't happen. You've got to let it go."

I put my hand on his arm, looked into his blue eyes and felt a tug-of-war. Something in his eyes made me want to give him what he asked for, but I had taken an oath years ago to protect others. For the first time in my career, I realized that I'd have to scuff one to protect the other.

"Andy, listen to me," I said gently. "Right now we're all dealing with an influx of information and it has our nervous systems hyped on adrenaline. As cops, we get the crank-pots who call in to give us different kinds of threats. Most of them are just talk." I placed two fingers on his lips to prevent him from interrupting me. "We've been warned on this, so there will be people watching my back through the rest of the investigation. I need you to let me do my job here. Okay? Besides, he lured you here prior to the blast. Did you ever stop to think that maybe the intended target tonight wasn't the evidence in your lab? If you'd gotten here a few minutes earlier, you would have been in there."

I moved my fingers from his lips, but continued to stare into his eyes, hoping that I'd see some kind of message there. I did see emotions: anger, fear and concern.

"Oh, God. I hadn't thought of that." He rubbed his hands over his eyes and before he took a deep breath. Moving his hand to my cheek, "Take care of yourself. Please. There are feelings that I can't explain right now as tied up as I am. I need time with you."

Oh-boy! I thought. It figures that the first time I've got a guy who's really interested in me in more years than I care to admit, we'd have my superior officer and a colleague with us.

"Ah-hem," the Lieutenant faked a cough. It was enough to break the spell that Andy and I were currently sharing. "What is your read on this, Monica?" he asked.

I tried to refocus my brain on the topic at hand, and not worry about Andy. It was pretty hard. I'd looked back to the Lieutenant and Keri, but Andy was still holding my hand under the table.

"My best guess it that the caller was the same. The timing works out, the basic description of the voice patterns are similar." I paused for a moment, "And I think the case is the same."

Keri looked at me, "What do you mean the case is the same?"

I looked over to Andy, "How many cases are you working on right now?"

He shrugged, "I'm not really sure. I oversee the entire lab, and at a guess right now we were probably running tests that related to maybe eight, ten, cases. What does that have to do with anything?"

"We need to find out if anyone else received a phone call," I stated. When the others looked at me, I tried to slow my though process enough that I could relate my thoughts. "Look, I don't believe in coincidences. But it's strange that both of us received calls only minutes apart from what is very likely the same person. But what ties us together? Yes, we went out tonight for dinner. Is the caller likely to be one of the people in either of our past relationships?

"I don't think so. I think that the answer lies in what we share professionally. I'm the lead investigator on the Williams murder. There are many other officers, and even other agencies, involved with the various angles of the case, but I'm the lead on the homicide.

"Andy is the lead on the scientific research for that case. He heads the lab, yes, but his focus today was with the unique coat that Williams was wearing at the time of the shooting. There's our link. We share that case, and that case alone."

The Lieutenant sat quietly, rubbing a swizzle stick between his fingers thoughtfully. "I think you're right, Monica. So this case will connect to yours. We'll need to work on the chain of command, because with this attempt, it puts several agencies together working in close proximity."

"We'll also most likely be coming at things from multiple angles," Keri added.

The Lieutenant nodded. "Yeah, we're all going to be in for some fancy footwork with this one." He gulped at his coffee. "Doctor, what are the odds that Detective Dietz's case will be compromised with the attack on you lab?"

Andy thought for a minute, "We may have gotten a lucky break." He looked up with a grin on his face. "When everyone was leaving, the coat was in the small secured storage room in the fourth floor lab. But, I was concerned about several things with leaving it there. Albeit, sabotage wasn't among the list.

"While I was finishing some paperwork, I realized that I just didn't feel comfortable with it in the storage lockers. We had secured it away from any other electrical devices, but I don't know how powerful the sensors in that coat are. So, before I met with Monica to give her the most recent data, I decided that to have that coat secured in the high-security vault in the basement. I placed it there around five-ten, went back to the office grabbed what I wanted and left."

"So the coat is in the basement vault," the Lieutenant asked.

Now Andy smiled, "Yeah. It's in a climate controlled waterproof and blast proof vault. So that would be secure. As for the other pieces of evidence, there wouldn't have been much on the top floor. It's mostly my lab and office that is up there. It should have all been secured in the secure rooms on the lower floors. This attack may not have hurt as bad as I first feared."

"Lieutenant," I spoke quietly. When he looked over I continued, "I think we need to consider that the attack was directed at that coat and at Doctor Carson himself. Only his offices and the area where the coat was appears to have been targeted. Might mean that the organization that is behind this, has somebody inside."

"These are definitely angles that we will need to coordinate on." He consulted his phone, tapped out a few keys, "I'm scheduling a conference tomorrow at nine. Bring your partner with you. I'd suggest that you both go home and try to get some sleep. It's going to be a couple of interesting days. End interview, oh-one-forty five," he stood and chugged the last dregs of his coffee. "Thanks for the help, Detective, Doctor," he said.

He'd made it two steps before he turned back, "Doctor, out of curiosity, can you keep the coat's location a secret for a while?"

"Sure. I've finished running all of my test on it, so there would be nothing else that I can do. Nobody knew that I was taking the data over to the squad room tonight after work, simply because our protocol is for it to go through interdepartmental mail, and more importantly, I didn't decide to do it until I was ready to walk out the door."

Keri looked from Aaron to Andy, and then smiled, "So they don't realize that we have the information. They think that it all went up in smoke, but it may just be the fact that smokes them out."

I eased back into my house at three-fifteen, and Sam met me at the door as if to say, "What took you so long?" I reached down and stroked his silky fur. "Come on, boy, let's head to bed."

As I walked towards the stairs, I noticed the light on my answering machine blinking. "Okay," I said aloud, "this wasn't here when I left to go to meet with Andy about the lab fire." I pressed play.

"Detective Dietz, we have taken action to ensure that the death of Toby is let go. There is no further need of your services on this matter. Follow our advice, let this go and do not endanger yourself or of your partner. This matter no longer concerns you," the rough voice said through its southern accent.

Using my cell, I called dispatch and got worked around until I was with communications again. I heard the voice come through, "This is Bart Schafer."

I smiled, "It's Detective Dietz. I received a message on my home machine that will need to be entered into evidence, but I'm not sure how you want me to do it." It took Schafer about ten minutes to walk me through the process of downloading, saving and sending the message.

By the time I finally fell back into bed, it was almost three-forty-five. I was out almost as soon as my head hit the pillow.

CHAPTER 7

"Morning, Jackie," I said as I rushed into the squad room and dropped my bags onto my desk.

Jackie sat at her desk with an apple slice in her hand staring at me. "Running late this morning, are we? Did you have such a good time with Dr. Cutie that it kept you up all night?" she asked with a twinkle in her eye.

"I ended up spending quite a bit of time with Dr. Carson last night as we were watching the fire company put out the blaze in his lab," I shot back.

"His lab?" her hands were waving like she was trying to fend off an angry swarm of bees. "You went out with Dr. Carson back to his lab?"

I sighed. The whole story was going to be out soon, so I may as well be the one to tell it. "Andy asked me to go for a pizza last night. We had a very nice time, and there were some—" I hesitated, not sure how far I wanted to go with this. I finally gave in, "There were some serious tingles before the evening was out. We said goodnight, and I was home well before ten.

"Then I got a phone call from someone who is still not identified, that delivered a minor threat. I ended up spending almost an hour working on the trace of that call. I was just getting ready to call it a night when the phone rang again. This time it was Andy. His lab was on fire, and he was in shock.

"I ended up meeting up with him, and eventually Keri and the Lieutenant, and spent the next few hours going over the events of the day, and getting Andy calmed down enough to handle things. Satisfied?"

"Oh, I have so many questions. First, Dr. Carson is now Andy, huh? How strong were these tingles? Oh, and how did you calm him down? And finally—wait! His lab was on fire? What about the evidence?"

"Glad to see that you've managed to keep things in perspective," I joked. Taking my seat, I filled her in on what had happened and that, for the immediate future, we were keeping it quiet about the suit coat.

"Dietz, Gannon," the Lieutenant said as he strode across the room. "Just got word that we're on for nine. Sounds like some of our friends from the FBI will be joining us. We're going to be in conference room C, on the second floor."

"We'll be there, Sir," I said, still unsure of how to proceeded with everything.

He turned back to me, sighed, "Monica, I know that last night put you in a sticky spot. I thought about it when I finally got home. Julie was sound asleep, and I realized that it was only by Providence that she and I haven't gotten caught up in the same scene. The fact that I married the Assistant District Attorney as opposed to a criminalist slipped my mind. I didn't mean to give you a hard time about Dr. Carson last night. He seems like a real nice guy."

"He is. I don't know how far things will go with him, but I promise, Sir, I wont let it derail my focus on this matter."

"What's going on at nine?" Jackie asked as the Lieutenant walked back to his desk.

"We're meeting with the Lieutenant, Keri, the commander and several members of the FBI to go over things. We have a feeling that all of these events are tangled together."

"Why do you think that they are all linked?" she asked.

I ran through the list that we had come up with at the diner. By the time I'd finished, it was time for us to head to our meeting.

I returned to my desk ninety minutes later with a splitting headache. The annoying side effect of dealing with so many law enforcement agencies in one case. The only new information that I came away with was that our John Doe was now awake in central.

I popped three ibuprofens and chased them with a slug of tea, and was massaging my eyes when Jackie made it back to her desk.

"Feeling okay?" she asked.

"Just peachy," I snapped. Taking a deep breath to calm myself, I tried again. "Sorry, Jackie. Not enough sleep, the case feels as though we're wading through a bog and if that's not enough, my emotions are all over the board due to a threat and a kiss. Right now, it's a fifty-fifty toss up as to which one has me more worked up."

She laughed, which eased the tension around us. "Do you want me to take John Doe solo?"

"No. I want to check my phone messages to see if we've got our warrant yet to access the shop record to find out who bought that sliver wire. Once I've got that set, we'll head out to Central and see Mr. Doe.

"Depending on what we hear, maybe after lunch we'll take a drive into Boston. Personally, I'd like to get to the bottom of this as soon as possible."

Fifteen minutes later, we were in the car heading for the hospital. "What's the word on the warrant?" Jackie asked.

"It should go through this afternoon, but it's only for the list. Since the State Police have gotten involved, they're going to serve it, and the results will be faxed down to us. With a little luck we'll have another thread to pull on today."

Central hospital was situated on the west end of town, just before you headed off of the Cape. It wasn't a large hospital, but was staffed with some excellent doctors and nurses who could handle just about anything. This was a huge benefit when it came to dealing with people who had multiple injuries and were key to an ongoing investigation.

Simply put; it saved me a two hour drive to Boston.

We walked into the ICU and quickly noted the uniform standing guard on a single door. "This the John Doe from the antique shop shooting?" I asked him.

"Yes, Ma'am."

"Any body been in to see him today?"

He checked his log. "His case doctor was in at eight-fifteen, a duty nurse went in to change the I.V. bags at ten-twelve. Another doctor came in to check on him, I believe it was his surgeon, at ten-forty-three. He's had no other visitors."

"Okay. Has he been talking much?

"From what I've heard, they've had him pretty much doped up on pain meds, so he's not saying much. I think I heard that one of the nurses got his name out of him overnight, but that was before I came on."

"Thanks," I said as I walked in.

Something was off. I couldn't place it, but I sensed it.

I scanned the monitors, nothing seemed out of place to me, but then again, I'm a cop not a doctor.

"Monica, is it me or—"

"My spidey sense is tingling too." Leaning towards the door, "Officer, please call the nurse!"

I heard the call go out, and within seconds the sounds of feet slapping the floor could be heard.

"What seems to be the problem, Detective?" a heavyset nurse asked.

"Not sure. I'd like you to take a look at everything and tell me if something is off. Both my partner and I just have, you know, a feeling."

"I'm not paid to jump at your feelings, but if it means I can—okay, now that's interesting," the nurse said as she followed a cord. "This isn't hooked up correctly. In fact it's not hooked to Mr. Jenkins at all!"

I shot a look over to Jackie and then back to the nurse, "What's it hooked to?"

She was busy tugging at the cable, and when the end came free a small black box swung at the end. She dropped the cord and ran to the bed. She pressed the emergency call button on the wall. "It appears that Mr. Jenkins is dead. Please have Doctor Evans paged."

An hour later the ward was still crawling with cops. I wandered over to where the Commander and the Lieutenant were standing and watching their team.

"The second doctor who went in to see Mr. Jenkins used an alias. Hospital records don't have any information on a Dr. Ralph Fitzsimmons," I said as I leaned against the wall next to the Lieutenant.

"Nobody saw this guy and realized that he didn't belong here? How could he just waltz into ICU and into a guarded room without raising suspicion?" Commander Willoby asked.

I shrugged, "To be honest, Sir, I'm not sure that they know everyone on staff. I mean, this hospital is associated with three teaching colleges, so I'd have to guess that the interns and residents are changing every few months. If I'd have to guess, the guy came in wearing the standard lab coat with the hospital emblem on it, had what looked to be the appropriate identification tags, and walked in like he belonged here."

"That's just what we need," the commander said. "Any chance we have him on video surveillance?"

"Jackie's with the hospital security staff right now. They were going over all of the video from the various cameras from around the ICU at approximately the appropriate time frames. Right now, it' going to take a stroke of luck to nail this guy here."

I thought for a minute before I added my next thought. "Just a hunch here, but when we find this guy, we're going to want to run his face through the software. If he knew how to get the appropriate identifications that he would need, he most likely has some intimate knowledge of the hospital layout. Meaning that he most likely also knows where the cameras are.

"If I was going to go in and commit a deed like this, knowing that my face was going to be captured on video, I'd show them something other than my own face. We'll need to look at the possible prosthetics and stage costumes that may have been employed. We're also going to want to focus on attributes that can't be easily hidden," I finished.

The Lieutenant looked over at the commander, "She's right, Eric. Whoever came in here had more than a working knowledge of the security that is in place. They'd be aware of the cameras, and most likely how to bypass them."

Commander Willoby, shook his head. "You two aren't making my morning any better, but I agree with this assessment. I haven't been out of the detective bureau that long that I forgot how the job is done. The only questions I still have are, how do you propose to proceed from here and what do you want me to do?" he asked looking between the Lieutenant and me.

"I'm going to get Jackie and head back to the station. We can use the computers in the AV lab to clean what ever she finds. We should be able to get a fairly accurate height range from the videos. If their arms or hands are visible, we'll be able to get close ups there. Perhaps a scar or a tattoo will peek out from somewhere. I think until we get a clear picture of what and why, that's the best that we can do."

"That's going to have to be good enough for now," the commander said as he pushed off of the counter he was leaning on. "I'll go and brief the mayor and our friends at the FBI and see if we can't come up with some kind of plan to work with."

He turned and began to walk away, stopped and turned back to me. "Dietz, we need to figure out the connection between these bodies. Somewhere out there is the answer that tells us the why."

"Yes, Sir. I agree. The State police should be executing the warrant on the vendor who sold the wire. That should give us something to take the next step with."

"Get it done," he said as he walked away.

Turning to the Lieutenant I asked, "Have we heard anything new on the girl, yet?"

He shook his head. "I'll let you know as soon as we hear. Something needs to break in this case soon."

My phone signaled an incoming text from Jackie. "Jackie thinks that she found something. We'll be back at the station," I said before I pocketed my phone and headed for the door.

"Let's run it again," I stated. My eyes were already screaming in protest from the amount of effort that I'd put in straining to get a glimpse of the so-called Dr. Fitzsimmons.

Jackie sighed, "Monica, we've already run it twelve times. We've run it forwards and backwards, in slow motion and double-time. What do you think you're going to find?"

"I don't know, but there is something that we're missing. And since I don't know what it is, I want to run it again. This time, let's do it at three-times zoom and in slow motion."

The frames of the video slowly scrolled by. I strained to see, hoping that something would pop for me. A glare caught my eye.

"Stop!" I yelled. "Back it up three frames." I stared at the screen. Was I imagining it, or was there actually something on his arm? "Look there," I pointed to the subject's right arm on the screen. "Looks like some kind of jewelry. Maybe a watch or a bracelet?"

"I don't know," Jackie said squinting at the screen. "Yeah, maybe it does. Let's see if I can clear it up some." Her fingers flew over the controls of the console.

Ten agonizing minutes later, the image was in much better focus, and we enlarged just the section that we wanted. "Okay, this is interesting," I commented.

"What am I missing?" Jackie complained.

"Look carefully at the watch. Describe it to me," I commanded.

"It's elegant, small mother of pearl face, appears to be silver or platinum. So?"

I used another monitor and reran the first part of the video and stopped when it showed one of the security guards. "Look at him, and at his watch."

"His arm is bigger. And so is his watch. So what?"

"It's a matter of perspective isn't it? How many guys would wear a watch like this?" I asked pointing at the suspect's. "Not many. Why? It's too feminine. That's what we were missing. We saw a person dressed as a male, but the movement and body language was off. Why? Because unless someone is a fantastic actor, our own habits tend to override what ever else we're doing. What we've got here is a woman who is trying to pass as a male to throw us off her track."

Jackie's eyes flashed from bewilderment to realization. "That's why the facial recognition program wasn't helping! We were looking in the wrong section." She paused, "Why would a woman want to ensure that this guy was dead though?"

"That's a question that I'll be sure you get to ask her when we've got her in holding. Why don't you try running her through the right data base now, and I'll go update the Lieutenant?"

"Sounds like a plan to me," she said.

I was almost back at my desk when the communications officer came in. "Excuse me, Detective Dietz, this package just came in for you. It's marked priority, so I thought I'd bring it down."

"Thanks, uh," I looked at her name tag, "Rollins." I took the package and ripped it open as I went to my corner.

"Well, well, well," I muttered as I slid out the sheet that the State Police had obtained for me. I spun to my computer and utilized the search program there. "Okay, who are you J.T. Lewis?"

As I was searching the databases, Jackie rushed in. "We may have hit on something. When we refined the search for females, the recognition software spit out—"

"A J.T. Lewis?" I interrupted her.

Her face fell, "Well actually a Juliet Teresa Lewis, but yeah. How'd you know?"

Turning my chair so I could face her I said, "It seems that we may have our first real connection here. The warrant the State Police executed in Boston for us turned up a J.T. Lewis who bought the wire. Hitting on the software gives us something that we can work with."

"I'd guess that we're heading out to nab her then?"

I shook my head. "We've got a few issues first," I stated. "To begin with, we only have proof that she bought the wire. There's nothing illegal with that. For that matter, I'm not even sure that making the suit itself is illegal.

"The surveillance video doesn't show that it is her conclusively. At this point, any competent defense attorney would blow us out of the water. No, what we need to do now is to find some real connections. Connections between her and our two vics.

"The final problem we have, is that we don't know where she is. The last address we have is from when she left county lockup two years ago after serving five for running a confidence game. She kept in close contact with her P.O. for the first six months, and then she disappeared. When I brought up her driver's license info, the address there cross checks to a cemetery on the edge of the county."

Jackie slumped down in her chair. "What do we start with?"

"Let's take a few different angles," I said after a few seconds. "Why don't you try to track her down? Start by going back to the hospital, and going over the surveillance videos from their entrances and then the parking garages. Perhaps we can find out how she got to and from the scene this morning.

"While you're doing that, I'm going to keep following the line I'm tugging at now. I've been running known associates and comparing with any links that we might find between the two vics."

Jackie pushed up from her desk, "Alright, I'll head back to the hospital. Do you think the department is going to pay for my vision correction? After watching this much video, my eyes are going to be shot."

"Welcome to the wonderful world of being on the detective squad."

As she walked out the door, I fiddled with a pencil trying to get my thoughts to align. I was sure that I was missing something, but what? I needed a link.

I decided to try a new direction, and grabbed the phone.

"Midboro Crime Lab," the voice answered.

"Um, hi. This is Detective Dietz, from the Blackberry Creek Police Department. Could I please speak to Andy," I did a mental head slap, "I mean, Dr. Carson?"

"One moment please," the smooth voice said.

"Monica?" Andy's voice came through the receiver a moment later. "What can I do for you today?"

When I heard his voice, it was as if some unknown weight had been lifted off me. "Before I go into that, how are you guys doing there, after last night and all?"

There was sadness in his voice, "There was a tremendous amount of damage. What the fire didn't destroy, the water did. It's a real mess up on four. But, we've got some crews coming in shortly that specialize in this kind of stuff. Thanks for asking. Now, what can I do for you?"

"We've made progress on our favorite case and I've got a question that I'm wondering if you can help me with."

"Shoot," he said, "and I'll see what I can do?"

"We've identified the person who bought wire that matched what was in the coat as a Juliet Lewis. Unfortunately, we have nothing to bring her in on other than that. We need some physical connection. I was thinking, that if she had purchased the wire that was in the suit worn by Williams, her fingerprints might be on it somewhere."

"Hmmm. That's an interesting idea. With the technology of the suit, it was likely assembled in a clean room, so we may not find anything, but we can check. When should I expect you?"

I glanced at the clock on the wall, calculated in my head how long it would take to get the necessary materials and travel. "Why don't we plan for about an hour?"

"That'll work on my end. I'll make the necessary preparations here, and Billy, the guard, will know where I am. And," he hesitated for a moment, "would I be out of line to inquire about the possibility of having dinner with you when we are done?"

CHAPTER 8

I pulled into the parking area by the back of the lab building. I needed to get to the bottom of this case as fast as I could, but it seemed that with every step I took there was an obstacle in the way. An obstacle named Dr. Andrew Carson.

Slamming the door of my Honda, I glanced up to the top level of the building. Plywood now covered the broken windows, while the yellow crime scene tape snapped in the brisk sea breeze.

It was a reminder of what perils we faced.

I went into the main entrance, this time greeted by a different guard than the last time. Pulling out my shield, I set it, and my two weapons on the counter along with the bag I was nearly dragging. "I'm here to see Dr. Carson," I said.

The guard eyed the large black nylon bag that was embossed with the BCPD symbol. "Would you kindly open the bag, Ma'am?" he asked nervously, his hand moving to the grip of his own Glock.

I sighed, and carefully undid the zipper and exposed the layers of Plexiglas. "It's a portable fuming station used for collecting fingerprints on oddly shaped pieces of evidence. Dr. Carson and I found something unusual in some evidence that was previously brought in, and we are trying to tie it to a specific person of interest."

He looked at the odd assortment of materials, shrugged, and then collected my weapons and placed them in the lock box for me. "I'll call Janice to escort you to the room where Dr. Carson said that he would be waiting for you," he said and pulled out his walkie-talkie.

I'd never been in the basement level of any major government building, but I was surprised. The other levels of the labs that I'd seen had been very practical, but there had been some attempts at making it look comfortable. As I followed Janice down into the bowels of the lab, I had the ominous feeling that I was walking into a dungeon.

We rounded a corner and Janice stopped to point at a door. "Dr. Carson is waiting for you here," she said as she knocked on the door.

Andy opened the door and a smile erupted across his face that reached his eyes. "Monica. You're earlier than I expected." He turned to my escort, "Thanks, Janice."

She nodded, turned and headed back the way we had come.

"Please come in, and welcome to the dungeon," he said. A snort escaped my mouth before I could get my hand over it. Andy looked at me quizzically. "Okay, I'll bite. What joke did I miss?"

I shook my head and worked to catch my breath. "I'm," I gasped from the hysterics I was fighting. "I'm sorry. It's just as I was walking down here, I kept thinking to myself that this place looked like what I'd expect a dungeon to look like. Then to hear you call it that. It was too much."

"Well, I'm glad to have provided the nightly entertainment for you. I do ask that you kindly remember to tip your servers tonight," he said with a big smile and a bow. I lightly tapped his shoulder, and the smile grew. "I like it when you play rough."

Suddenly his eyes changed and he stepped back. "I'm sorry, I didn't mean it—"

I reached out and took his hand, "Andy, I understand humor. You didn't offend me, or make me think that you're planning something else. You made me laugh today, which thinking about it now, makes me feel good."

"You had a hard day today, huh?"

I nodded. "Yeah I guess you could say that. I overslept, had to explain to my partner why I was with you until early this morning. She thinks of you as Dr. Cutie, by the way. I thought we'd made some progress with the case, but as we got to the hospital, we found out that our suspect had been murdered. Right under the noses of the guards."

Andy pulled me into his arms and his hands gently traced circles on my back. I thanked my lucky stars that he wasn't a patter or a there-there-person. He just gave me the support that I was craving right now. I let myself relax in his embrace, and I felt the tension that had been camped out in my shoulder blades pack up and move on.

"I've got faith in you, Monica," he said before he gently kissed my forehead. "You'll figure this out. So, if you're ready, we can leave our electronics here and go and see what we find on your wire."

Ninety minutes later, I was disassembling the fuming station. We'd found four different fingerprints, and were now running them through the Integrated Automated Fingerprint Identification System's database. "How long before you know anything?" Andy asked.

"Depends," I answered. "If the print is from someone that has a criminal past, it'll take about a half an hour. If it isn't, we won't know for at least an hour. And that will only be if the person has gone through something that requires their fingerprints to be in the database."

"What do you mean, done something? Wouldn't that make them a felon?"

"No. Let's say some one has applied for certain licenses or work in specific jobs, like working in a crime lab or a casino. Or perhaps they have a pistol permit. These people wouldn't have broken the law, but because of some activity, either job or hobby related, their prints would be on file."

Andy thought for a moment, "Okay, I guess that makes sense. Well then," he looked at his watch, "it would seem that we have about—"

The beeping from the computer cut him off. I rushed over to look at the screen, which was now flashing "POSITIVE MATCH". "Interesting," I mumbled.

"What'd you get?"

"Well, we now know that the only people who touched this wire besides the manufacturer were in the system."

"That's good, right?" Andy asked, and then hesitated. "Wait. You said people. Are your saying that you got hits on more than one?"

I looked up at him, "Bingo! It appears that one set belonged to our friend Mr. Williams. But the set that I'm more interested in right this minute belongs to one Juliet Lewis."

"But how would both of their prints end up on this wire?"

I'd already pulled out my phone and held up a finger to him. "Special Agent Immentz? Hi, it's Detective Dietz from the Blackberry Creek PD. Need a favor."

"Okay, Detective. I'm not sure what the F.B.I. can do for you, but let's hear it and we can see what happens."

"We may have had a break in the Cathy's Collectibles shooting. When we went into interview the survivor, we found him murdered."

"Detective, that doesn't sound like a break at all."

"I'm getting to the part that is the break, Agent. When we ran facial recognition on the hospital security video, we identified Juliet Lewis posing as a doctor who went into room shortly before we arrived.

"Earlier today, we discovered that a J.T. Lewis had purchased one-thousand feet of the exact sized wire that was in the coat that Toby Williams was wearing when he was shot. Dr. Carson and I just finished processing the wire from the coat, and isolated prints from Juliet Lewis. That means that she was involved in someway in the deaths of two people.

"Lewis has a rap sheet and is currently out on parole. When I checked with her P.O., he said it's been a while since he's heard from her. We need to find her as soon as possible. I figure the F.B.I. has better resources to find someone who doesn't want to be found."

There was a silence on the other end of the phone before Immentz's gruff voice came back on. "Okay, Detective, I've just sent out the request and the pertinent info. We'll do what we can."

"Thanks," I said as the line went dead.

"Sounds like you've made some real progress to me," Andy said walking over to me. He stepped behind me and began kneading the tensed muscles in my back.

"Listen, Doc, I'm going to give you two years to stop that before I get mad."

"I'll take my chances," he said with a chuckle. "Now, how do you feel about surf and turf for dinner?"

The phone rang at three-eighteen. I cursed Alexander Graham Bell as I fumbled for the receiver. "Hello?" I muttered.

"Dietz? This is Sergeant Jacobs, Ma'am. I'm sorry to call you at this hour, but the Commander requested that you be notified."

I huffed out a sigh, "What's happening, Jacobs?"

"We've located a body, Ma'am that matches the description of one of the men that was involved in the shooting at Cathy's Collectibles. You, and your partner, have been requested to report to the scene at 174 Macaroon."

"Okay," I said rubbing my eyes trying to wipe the sleep out of them, and the fog out of my brain. "Have you notified Officer Gannon?"

"She is the next call."

"Very good," I said as I hung up the phone.

Sam was stretched out on the bed, his ears perked up and his eyes intently watching.

"You're lucky," I told him as I rolled out of bed.

I made my way to the valet that sat in the corner. Here I had a top and a pair of slacks set out. It was a habit I'd gotten into after being on the force for less than a month. When a call came in in the middle of the night, having your clothes ready gave you one less thing to worry about.

Before I left the room, I crossed to my dresser and unlocked the box that sat on top. Pulling the slide back a little, I checked the condition of my Glock and my little Beretta before holstering them and heading for the door.

Sam accompanied me as far as the door. "No, you're going to stay here tonight. I don't know how long I'll be," I said as I scratched his head and then headed into the night.

I made it to Macaroon Street in just less than five minutes. Finding the scene was simple. I just looked for all of the flashing lights.

I parked behind one of the cruisers, and headed to the scene. I palmed my badge toward the nearest officer as I ducked under the crime scene tape.

"What's the story?" I asked the officer.

"Got a call from a neighbor around two-thirty. She said there was a bunch of yelling going on here. While the nine-one-one operator was on with her, they heard the shots. My partner and I responded along with two other cars. We got here at two-thirty-seven. As we pulled up, a figure took off running down Macaroon and then ducked into the alley behind the SuperSaver there. Two officers followed on foot, but weren't able to apprehend him.

"Dickenson, that's my partner, and I went into the building here. Several residents were in the halls as we went up. Found a body in apartment 304. We didn't get an ID on him, but his picture is very close to the one of the pictures that the F.B.I. released of the suspects in the shooting the other day."

"Thanks," I glanced at his nametag, "Kilpatrick. I'm heading up there now. When my partner gets here, send her right up."

I walked through the single wide glass paneled door and looked at the lobby of the building.

It wasn't ornate, but I wouldn't call it plain either. It was clean and well kept. There were five doors besides the one that I'd just come through. Four were numbered; most likely being apartments and the last had an exit sign hanging over it. An elevator sat with its doors open, cordoned off with yellow tape while an investigator was dusting for prints.

Climbing the stairs, I kept my eyes open for anything that might be of help, but found nothing.

The third floor lobby was set up almost exactly the same as the ground floor one was. However, this lobby was not empty. I counted six different police officers, four crime scene investigators, two members of the coroner's staff and in the middle were two members from my division talking with two civilians.

Adam Westly looked over and motioned me over.

"What do we have, Adam?" I asked.

"A mess inside." He turned, "Mr. Tifton, Mr. Howard, this is Detective Monica Dietz. She will most likely be the detective in charge of this case. Monica, Mr. Hugh Tifton is the owner of the building and this is his lawyer T.J. Howard."

"Why will she be the detective in charge?" Tifton wanted to know.

It was the other detective, Nate Martin, who answered. "Detective Dietz is the lead investigator on another situation that appears to tie in with the shooting tonight. If the two cases are linked, she'll be in charge of both."

This seemed to satisfy both men.

"Do we have any idea who the victim is?" I asked.

"I was just going over the rent rolls with the other detectives. The apartment is leased to a Julie T. Louise. But that's not her in there." Tifton said.

The stairwell door opened and Jackie walked though. She headed right for the group of us.

"Mr. Tifton and Mr. Howard, my partner, Jackie Gannon," I said.

Howard's eyes looked intently at Jackie. She smiled demurely at him and then turned away.

"Jackie, we're going to need to—" I stopped mid thought.

"Mr. Tifton, you said that the lease was to Julie T. Louise, right?"

"Yes. But that's sure not her on the floor in there," he protested.

"Sir, by any chance would you have a picture of Ms. Louise?" I asked hoping against hope.

"Sure. I take a picture of each of my tenants for my files. Here we go," he said opening the folder he held.

"Holy Cow!" Jackie exclaimed. "That's Juliet Lewis!"

I smiled, "Bingo! Looks like we've got another connection. Jackie, call this in. Let them know that she is now wanted for questioning in connection with three murders."

"Okay. Wait! Three? Did you and Dr. Cutie find prints?"

"I'll tell you what Dr. Carson and I found. Right after you take care of the call."

Jackie headed towards the door by the stairs and pulled out her phone to update dispatch. I drifted towards the windows on the opposite side of the hall. I needed time to think.

What was the connection? How did Juliet Lewis factor into this? From my research, I'd discovered that she wasn't well educated, but the suit design was top notch, both in style and function. My intuition said that there had to be someone else involved, but right now the big question was who?

Jackie came up behind me, "Monica? Are you ready?"

"Yeah," I answered glumly. "I think that we're going to need to go back to the beginning and start over with this, Jackie. We've missed something fundamental, but right now I don't know what."

I stepped back from the window and made my way into the open room.

The crime scene photographers had finished taking their pictures, and the coroner was now in with the body. I stood in the doorway and took the scene in.

It was definitely a woman's apartment. The flowers, knickknacks and shelves full of little figurines and perfume bottles said that. The shrapnel that covered the floor said that what ever had happened in this apartment had been more than a happy visit.

"Okay, so this is Juliet A.K.A Julie's apartment. Who is the guy?" I asked.

Jackie shook her head. Wayne spoke up, "As we prepared to move him, we did a quick search of his pockets. Found a wallet here, and bagged it already, if you want to take a look. Otherwise, I'll send it along with the rest of his clothes and stuff tomorrow after I post him."

"Thanks, Wayne," I said crossing the room and accepting the bag that he held out. Extricating the wallet from the evidence bag, I flipped it open. "Massachusetts driver's license. Picture matches the vic. Says that his name is Leo Spiro."

"Leo? Did you just say Leo Spiro, Monica?" Nate asked.

"Yeah, Leo Spiro. Why?"

"I believe that you may want to talk to either Sylvia or Bill. Seems to me that they busted good ole' Leo a couple months back. Think it was on possession with intent to sell, or something. Anyway, as I recall, seems that Leo got some big-time lawyers to come in to the rescue. They were bigger than he could afford on his own. Bill thought that perhaps he was involved in some mob action, but we really don't have much of that going on around here. Maybe he's got some more info for you."

"Thanks, Nate. Did you know Leo at all?"

Nate looked back at me with a thoughtful expression. "I think it was about four, maybe five, years ago I had a couple run-ins with him. Mostly it was petty theft. Last I'd heard, before, Bill and Sylvia collared him, was that he was doing time in the county jail." Nate slumped against the doorjamb with his hands in his pockets, "You know, it's funny. I can't ever remember hearing about Leo being a violent one."

Jackie and I left the scene at just before seven, and headed for breakfast over at Shirley's Diner.

Shirley's was an old fashioned diner that served excellent food at a reasonable price. It had been a favorite of cops long before I joined the force. I led Jackie in and we found a seat near the back exit. It took less than two minutes to order so we began to lay out the plan for the day.

"I figure that our first stop today is to check in with Bill and Sylvia," I said as I sipped my Earl Grey. "From there, we're going to hit the morgue." At the mention of the morgue, Jackie's face turned slightly ashen. "I wished I'd known that we were going back there today. I'd have ordered some dry toast."

I smiled a wry smile. I'll take my enjoyment where I can. "After we hit the morgue, I think we'll need to—"

My voice trailed off as I watched Andy come through the door.

CHAPTER 9

Andy stopped at the counter, and then his eyes found me. A smile curved on his lips. He nodded to the waitress by the counter as he walked back to where we sat.

"Fancy meeting you two here," he said.

"Hi, Andy. What brings you in this morning?"

"Other than my legs? " he asked jokingly. "I've about run out of things to fix for breakfast in my apartment, and I've got the feeling that I really didn't want to be alone, you know? A couple of the cops that have come through the lab have mentioned this place. Figured I'd stop, have breakfast at the counter, and then head out for the day. What about you?"

"We got a call around two-thirty this morning. Just finished processing the scene. Time to fuel up before we go at the rest of the day."

"Yikes! Two-thirty? Monica, you keep some really lousy hours, hon."

I could feel my face flush.

"Dr. Carson, why don't you join us for breakfast?" Jackie asked sweetly.

His eyes flashed from her to me, questioning.

I reached over to the chair next to me, "Pull up a chair, Doc."

He signaled to the waitress and sat next to me. Jackie's eyes were flashing from him to me and back again.

I looked over at Andy, "Anything interesting on the docket this morning?"

"Not really. I've got to testify this morning. This afternoon, I'm going to be pawing through the wreckage of my lab. The crime scene group has finally released the scene, so we can go in. I'm…" his voice trailed off.

"What was that?" Jackie asked.

The waitress delivered a bowl of oatmeal and a cup of coffee for Andy. He no more than glanced up and gave her a smile. She smiled back and then headed back to the counter. There was an emotion in his eyes that he was trying to keep out of his voice.

He slugged down a gulp of the coffee, let out a long sigh, and tried to answer Jackie's question.

"I've been thinking about the fire at the lab. A lot. That place is secure. I don't see how anybody could have gotten through all of the checkpoints to get up to the lab floors without somebody noticing. It makes me wonder who it was."

Jackie looked at him, but I could see that she wasn't following his line of thought.

"Do you really think that it was someone that you work with?" I asked.

"You mean you think that this was an inside job?" Jackie gasped.

Andy nodded. "Nothing else makes any sense. That would be the easiest way for someone to get to that level and not raise any suspicion."

"Have you mentioned this to anybody yet?" I asked thoughtfully.

He swallowed a spoonful of oatmeal. "Not yet. I was going to call over and speak with either Detective Marsbury or Detective Walker."

I popped a piece of French toast, thinking while I chewed.

"Let me tell them," I volunteered. "Actually, why don't you write a note and I'll deliver it."

Jackie stared at me open-mouthed. "Why the secrecy?"

"I'm playing a hunch. If it was someone from inside the labs, they're either going to be hanging around to keep tabs on what's happening, or they're going to split as soon as they discover anything that might point back to them. By Andy not saying anything directly, it should give us a little bit of a lead so we can be ready before anyone makes a move."

"But what if people see the two of you sitting here having breakfast?"

Andy looked over at me, and I could feel the heat on my face. "Actually, what Monica said makes sense. And there are enough people who've now seen us together outside of the labs to propagate the rumor that we are seeing each other romantically. They may not take any notice of that."

I tried to hide my face in my tea, but Jackie kept staring at me with a big grin on her face.

Andy had finished his oatmeal and coffee. He dropped a ten on the table as he stood. He leaned down and gently lifted my chin and kissed me gently. "Since we're seeing each other, let's plan for lunch around one, okay?"

I was so befuddled; all I could manage was a nod. His kiss had me going faster than any cup of tea could ever do.

By the time Jackie and I got back to the station, my mind was beginning to work again and I was wondering what I'd done. Agreeing to meet Andy for lunch? Was I really trying to keep our cover? I knew I'd never cancel. Was I ready for the rumors? Did I care?

"Dietz. Gannon," the Lieutenant called out as we walked into bullpen. Detouring from the main aisle, we went to his doorway. "Yes, Sir?"

"What's the current status with the victim from last night?"

"Nate and Wayne called us in. The vic there ended up being Leo Spiro, apparently known to Bill and Sylvia. We'll be checking in with them in a few. We ended up being tagged since the vic matched the description for one of the shooters from the Cathy's Collectibles shooting.

"The part that really sealed our involvement, is that the apartment was registered to Juliet Lewis under an alias. Yesterday, Dr. Carson and I verified that her prints were on the wires that had been embedded into the suit coat that Williams was wearing when he was killed. And we also positively identified her as the "doctor" who went in to Jenkins room just before he died. We need to find her."

"You're darn right you need to find her!" he nearly screamed. "You're telling me that this woman is still running around after being directly tied to three dead bodies? Let's get everybody cracking on this. Now," he added sternly.

I took two steps out of his office and then spun on my heels and went back. "Sir?"

"What is it, Dietz?"

"I had a conversation with Dr. Carson this morning. I wanted to update you on it, since part of it concerns your case."

He waved me to a chair, and for the next fifteen minutes we talked about Andy's concern about the fire being an inside job, some of the staff members that I'd met at the lab on my last few encounters there and about the amount of time that Andy and I were spending together.

"When it comes down to it, having you and Dr. Carson "seeing" each other may prove to be a major coup for our intelligence gathering."

"We'll keep it as professional as we can, Sir."

He chuckled. "Monica, have fun with it. When Keri and I saw the two of you together the other day, it was the first time in over a year that I'd seen any life in your eyes. Enjoy this. Explore it. Be open to it. You know better than most, life is too bloody short. Live to enjoy each day."

I walked back to my desk with my head spinning. I wasn't exactly used to my immediate superior telling me to get involved with someone on a personal level.

"You okay?" Jackie piped up from her computer.

"Yeah. At least I think so."

She smiled. "While you were in with the Lieutenant, I saw Bill and Sylvia. They're sending over their file on Leo. Maybe we'll finally find the missing link."

I nodded and picked up the pile of paper that someone had dumped on my desk.

"Why do people think that my desk is the clearing house for unwanted paper?" I grumbled.

Jackie looked up. "I promise, I didn't see anybody in here. What'd they leave you anyway?"

I started flipping through the pile. "It appears to be old circulars, past public notices and—"

"What's that?" Jackie interrupted me.

We both stared at the sheet of paper that I now held between my thumb and forefinger. Letters had been cut out from either magazines of some other source and arranged and glued in place.

I read the message aloud.

"You have been warned. Forget Cathy's Collectibles and the other collateral damages. Disregard and die."

"Boy, that sounds enticing," Jackie murmured.

"Grab an evidence bag, Jackie and let's get this into questioned documents ASAP. Maybe our secret admirer left us something more than a simple message."

Gingerly, we slid the document into the bag and sealed it. While I filled out the label for the bag, Jackie got the Lieutenant to fill him in on the situation.

"You two have had an exciting morning," he said as we sat around his desk twenty minutes later. "I've already called Willoby requesting someone to go over the security tapes of the entrance. We'll be going over anyone who came in carrying anything that maybe called a package."

"We've got to be closer to this than we think," I stated. "There is no reason for someone to take this kind of risk unless they are really afraid that we are about to put the final nail in their coffin. Why threaten a police officer?"

"What are you thinking, Monica?"

I looked back at Jackie, "We are only making the assumption that these crimes were linked. We don't have any physical proof. Lots of circumstantial, but nothing concrete. It could be a series of unrelated coincidences, and a lawyer is likely to try that approach."

I paused to let my thoughts straighten themselves out before I went on.

"We haven't made any public statement that Jenkins' death, or Spiro's were linked to the attack at Cathy's Collectibles. So, why would someone leave us a letter like this? The only way that they would know that they were linked, was if they themselves had been directly involved.

"They intentionally brought up the original shooting, and then called the other incidents 'collateral damages'. They're trying to cleanup their own mess here, and they keep getting deeper in."

"Do you think someone in this department has a hand in this, detective?" the Lieutenant asked.

I shook my head. "Right now, sir, I really don't know. To my knowledge, the department has sat on the information about Juliet Lewis' involvement in Jenkins' death. The report from this morning's murder hasn't made the news yet, and even so, the apartment was rented to a different name. Yet someone knew. Somehow, the fact that we were looking in that direction got out to the perpetrator."

Jackie blanched. "And they did it between the time that we made the connections yesterday and the time that we were at the scene this morning."

Lieutenant Walker paced from his desk to the window and back. "I hate to think that there is even the slightest chance that we have a mole in this department, but you are both correct. Information that we haven't released is being used and the source has to be close to the detective's bureau. What's your status with the Leo Spiro Investigation?"

"We're planning to head down to the morgue after we finish here," I announced.

"Okay," he said turning to stare out the window. "I want the remainder of this investigation to be quiet. We don't talk to anyone not directly associated with the case. Your updates will be to me, possibly commander

Willoby, here in this office in person. No papers. Is there somewhere else that you could do the majority of your work?"

"Hadn't really given it any thought," I said while Jackie just shrugged. "Sir, what about people that we will have to communicate with?"

"That can't be helped much. You'll need to follow protocol with them, but again, request no paper trail other than the formal reports. Also, try to deal with only one person at each of the labs."

"You can talk to Dr. Cutie, um, oops, I mean Dr. Carson when you get together for meals and other recreational activities," Jackie said.

Walker laughed, "Actually, that will be a perfect cover."

Sure I thought, and maybe Jackie could start dating the ME?

We were driving along the Shore Line Highway, which, as its name suggests, follows the shoreline from Cape Cod down the spit of land.

"Any ideas on where we should go to find a place to work?" Jackie said breaking the silence.

"The more that I think about it, the more I like the idea of not having any particular fixed place. If we're constantly in the same location, it's easy for someone to tap a phone line, bug an office or any number of other things that they could do to figure out what we're looking at. I'm kind of leaning towards the idea of using my personal laptop and just pulling into random restaurants. Sit at a booth have a cup of tea, and do a little work.

"The less structured we are, the harder it is for anyone who is trying to chase us down. Since we can't use the office, we'll just have to improvise."

Saying this, I pulled off at the next exit and into the parking lot of Panda's Chinese Buffet. "I think that this should suffice for now."

"Aren't you supposed to meet Dr. Carson in less than an hour? Are you really planning to eat here? Now?"

"Relax Jackie. I texted Andy earlier and told him I'd let him know where we should meet for lunch. His reply stated that he was out of court earlier than planned, so I told him to head out this way. Now, I'll just tell him where to get off."

I punched a few buttons on my phone and sent the text on its way.

Andy arrived less than ten minutes later.

"So what's with all the cloak and dagger stuff? I mean, I get you're detectives, but can't you have lunch like a normal person?"

When I didn't smile, he looked at me more intently.

"Monica, what's going on? Are you in danger?"

For the first time in longer than I can remember, someone was actually shaken by the fact that I might be in danger.

I motioned to the door, "Let's talk about it inside."

Inside, Panda's appeared to be doing a great business. I smiled as I estimated at the number of guests that were utilizing the buffet today. I was counting on being invisible by being part of the crowd. When no one turned to look at us, I relaxed slightly. "So far so good," I mumbled.

We were seated at what I considered to be the perfect table—in the far back corner with a clear view of the door.

I set my plate down and began picking at the snow peas and General Tso Chicken. Andy quietly slipped in next to me.

"Okay, I've been patient long enough, Monica. What's going on?"

I looked over at Jackie, sighed and then filled Andy in on the whole story.

"So, if I've got this right, you're now suspecting that someone from within your division is selling you guys out, too?"

"It may not be exactly from our division, but it seems that there is someone in the department who is transmitting data," I countered.

"So how do you guys solve this, as well as the original case?"

Jackie answered while I finished chewing.

"Basically, what we've been more or less ordered to do is not to use the office for the next few days. We're going to have only limited contact with anyone from the labs—"

"I'll work directly with you two. You know that, right?"

I nodded. "That was part of our plan. You and I'd meet, and then I could slip you evidence. When we met the next time, you'd give me the results."

Andy sat staring off into space for a minute. The only movement that he made was gently swirling his drink.

"Andy, what are you thinking about?"

"I'm wondering what the connections are. We know that we're connected because of the case. But what evidence connects everything."

Jackie's eyebrows shot up. "We've been looking at the people. Juliet Lewis to each of the vics. Is that the kind of relationship that you're talking about, Dr. Carson?"

Andy smiled at her. "First off, Detective Gannon, I'd like to think that we're beyond the formalities. How about Jackie and Andy?" Jackie smiled and nodded, and Andy went on. "What I'm thinking of isn't exactly like those relationships. I'm thinking more along the relationship of Locard's exchange principle."

As soon as I heard the words I nodded, "Right."

"Locard's exchange principle? What's that?" Jackie asked.

"Dr. Edmond Locard stated that whenever a person does anything, they leave a bit of themselves and take a bit with them. In other words, there is always trace that will link a suspect and the crime scene. Think about the first link that we got between this Lewis character and your first victim. We pulled her fingerprints from a wire that had been embedded into the coat. What does that tell us?"

When she didn't answer immediately, he told her. "Those fingerprints only could have gotten there by direct contact. We know that she was involved in the making of the coat.

"By applying the same idea we can evaluate the evidence that has been collected at the other scenes. We may be able to find some trace that is unique to both scenes that might give us something to work on."

Jackie looked less than sure. "But if we already know that Lewis is involved, how will this new information help us?"

I beat Andy this time.

"What Andy is suggesting, is that we're not looking to link Lewis to our vics, but can we link a piece of evidence to her. For example, can we find a specific type of fiber on all of our vics. It may not solve the case outright, but it should provide a few more pieces of the puzzle."

"Exactly. Also, as an afterthought, I'm going to compare the evidence that we find on the note that you received this morning to everything as well. Let's see if there are any links there," Andy said.

CHAPTER 10

We lingered over our lunches, talking making extra trips to the buffet, or in my case visiting the desert bar. Andy walked with me as we headed back to the cars. In front of my Dodge, he turned so we were face to face. "I'm not going to deny that I'm concerned about this whole mess, Monica." His thumb brushed my cheek.

I reached up, and held his hand there. "Believe me, I'm worried too. But we're taking precautions to make sure that nothing happens."

He leaned in, and gave me two light kisses before he turned and walked to his car.

"It must be nice to have someone care about you like that," Jackie said from somewhere behind me.

"Hmm?" I managed as I turned. She had detoured on the way out to grab a copy of today's paper, which she now had tucked under her arm.

Jackie laughed lightly. "What I said was that it must be nice. He's got you all mushy right now."

My brain was beginning to function again. She was right, he'd done it to me again. "Oh, what am I going to do, Jackie? Every time I'm near him, I lose my focus."

"If I said enjoy it, would you be upset? He flusters you, but you'll figure out how to work through it in no time."

"Hope you're right," I said as I climbed in.

"What's next?" she asked as I pulled back onto the highway.

"Well, seeing as we're already out, why don't we go back to the Williams' residence and see if Mrs. Williams can spare us a few minutes?"

We pulled up outside the Cape Cod fifteen minutes later. Katie Williams, dressed in a black dress and heels, answered the door.

"Oh, hello, officers."

"It's detective. I'm Dietz and this is my partner Gannon, Miss Williams. We'd like to speak with your mother."

"All right, I suppose. Please follow me," she said backing into the foyer. "She's still shaky right now. My Dad's funeral was this morning, and we just had a family lunch here. Almost everyone has gone now. Mom's in the back, sitting on the deck with her sister and Russ."

We followed her through the set of French doors that led to what looked like a small, enclosed courtyard complete with in-ground swimming pool and elaborate gardens.

"Mom? These are the police. They need to talk to you about Daddy's..." her voice trailed off.

Angela Williams turned in her seat. I knew that her file had her listed as being fifty, but she looked as though she was my age. Her platinum blonde hair was braided and fell to her mid back. Only her hazel eyes conveyed her sorrow.

But it was these hazel eyes that scanned me from head to toe.

Suddenly I felt embarrassed by the condition of my skin, and wondered how many wrinkles my line of work was going to etch before I reached the age where I should have to worry about them.

I spoke first. "Mrs. Williams, I'm Detective Monica Dietz and this is my partner Detective Jackie Gannon. I'm very sorry about your loss, ma'am, but we need to ask you some questions about Mr. Williams."

Her body seemed to deflate when she answered. "I know," she sighed. "Why don't we go into the study?" She detoured to the kitchen to pour herself a larger mug of coffee from the stainless steel carafe. "Would either of you care for a cup of coffee or a soda?"

When we shook our heads, she led us to a room in the front corner of the house. Two shelves of books lined the outside wall, while a large desk sat directly in front of the windows. A few armchairs were stashed into the corners.

Angela Williams made her way to a chair behind the desk and motioned to the two nearest chairs for Jackie and I.

"Now then, what can I do for you?" she asked.

"Mrs. Williams, could you tell us about Mr. Williams? What his interests were, who he associated with?" I began.

"Toby was a good provider, a devoted husband, and a committed father. He worked hard at Brewster, and was one of their managers. He specialized in manufacturing, so he often made trips overseas to work with their facilities in other countries."

"Did he work with a specific team of individuals?" Jackie prompted.

"Oh, no. He didn't work with any particular group. His job was to go from group to group and work out any problems that they were having with their facility. He was real good at his job. No one ever gave him any trouble."

"Can you think of anyone who wanted to hurt Mr. Williams?"

She closed her eyes, shook her head. "No. That's why this is so devastating. Toby never did anything to hurt anyone else, so why'd they have to hurt him? I keep wondering if perhaps he wasn't the target, and those people were after someone else and he was just in the wrong place at the wrong time."

Now the tears started to fall. Big, fat, heavy tears eroded the perfectly done makeup and left watery trails down her cheeks while here shoulders rocked. "Please find whoever did this to my Toby," she sobbed.

"We'll do everything that we can."

Back in the car, I looked over at Jackie. "You okay, Gannon?"

"Yeah. It's just rough when you meet someone whose life has been completely destroyed by somebody else just because they happen to be at the wrong place at the wrong time."

"Maybe. Maybe they were collateral damage, or maybe they were the intended target."

Jackie thought for a moment. "Now what?"

As I pulled back on to the street, I gave a cursory glance at the clock. "Think maybe it's time we went for a cup of tea and some computer time. We need to finish our background on Brewster Industries and do the complete financials on Toby Williams.

Randy's Coastal Café was a little block building that sat along the south shore of Cape Cod Bay. Several picnic tables dotted the grounds stretching from the edge of the drive to the beach. When we pulled in, three cars sat in the parking lot, close to the tables. I guided the Dodge to a space that was at the far end of the lot, and parked right in front of the last window.

"Is there a reason you parked so far away?" Jackie asked.

"I've been here before. This window is aligned with the corner table, which means that we'll be able to see who is coming and going and watch the car at the same time. Theoretically, we shouldn't be able to be surprised."

Pulling the door open, I had the pleasure of watching the lone dining room waitress jump at the sound.

"Oh, hello," she said standing and walking towards us. "Will it just be the two of you?"

I nodded. "And we'll take the table in the corner."

She shrugged, "One in the back has a much better view."

"This one has exactly the view that we're interested in," I commented.

Five minutes later, we were settled in, Jackie sipping a latte and me, a chi tea. The table between us was covered with our laptops, files and notepads.

"What do you want me to look for?" Jackie asked.

"Why don't you run William's financials? I'll start looking into Brewster Industries."

Her frown about digging into the financials made me smile. Little did she know that I'd given her the easier of the tasks.

"This is frustrating," Jackie whined nearly an hour later.

"What's that?" I inquired.

"Williams' finances. I'm looking at his tax records, bank records, companies and investments, but nothing seems out of the ordinary."

"Let me see." I pulled her laptop around so that I could see the screen. "From this, his income shown on the taxes coincides perfectly with the company documentation." I scowled. There was something here that just wasn't registering with me, and I was frustrated that I was missing it.

"Jackie!" I said excitedly. "How do your expenses compare to you income?"

She looked like a deer in the headlights.

"What? I thought we were looking at his financials, not mine."

"We are. But look at his numbers." I spun the computer back towards her.

"His income and expenses are the same. Nobody spends exactly what they make!"

"Bingo. This tells me that he's got accounts hidden somewhere. Ones that he isn't claiming anywhere."

"Let me guess, I get to keep digging, right?"

"For the moment, yes. I want to finish following a line at Brewster."

"What have you got there?"

"I'm trying to find out who actually owns it. All I've come up with thus far is a list of shells. I'm playing a hunch, but I'm thinking that there's a reason that the actual individual who owns the company doesn't want to be known."

"Makes sense." She let out a sigh, "Well, I guess I'd better get back into the grind."

We worked in companionable silence for nearly another hour, only talking when the waitress came to refill our drinks.

"Gotcha," I murmured.

"What was that?" Jackie asked.

"It seems that Brewster Industries is owned by one Albert Griffin. If I'm right, this would be the same Albert Griffin who happens to be the head of one of the biggest crime syndicates in Massachusetts"

"Well, that sure makes this whole wild goose chase more interesting."

"Sure does. We can run Lynch's financials tomorrow as a follow up. Did you get anywhere with Williams'?"

"I do find it interesting that although he is an employee of Brewster Industries, that he owns so many companies himself."

"Does he own them outright, or just shares?"

"Almost an even split. The ones that he only owns shares in though, he owns a controlling percentage."

"What kind of companies does he own?"

Jackie referenced her notes. "Okay, he owns Cod Publishing, a coin operated Laundromat and a computer sales/repair store outright. There is also something called TKA Enterprises, which he owns as well. He's a majority shareholder in a car dealership, two jewelry stores and a boat charter service."

"Am I correct that he doesn't work at any of these places, he just owns them?"

Jackie nodded her head again. "Yeah. As far as I can tell, he owns them, but has other people running them." She paused, "Let me amend that to almost all of them. I can't find anything out about TKA Enterprises."

I thought about it for a moment. "I think that we've made significant progress on things here. Why don't we send our reports in, and lets have one of the drones pick up where we left off. They can scour the records and compile the rest of the info for us, and we can hit it fresh in the morning?"

Rubbing her eyes, Jackie smiled. "I can get behind that totally. I think I'm going to be having nightmares about dancing numbers tonight."

As we loaded up our computers, my attention went to a car that had slowed down near the entrance. It wasn't the first time that I'd seen this car this afternoon.

"Hey, Jackie. Check out the blue Lincoln that just slowed down."

She looked out the window. "Yeah what about it?"

"It's the fifth time that car has gone by. Twice in the opposite direction, and this is the third time this way."

"They probably just live close by, you know. They need to pick the kids up from school, take them to dance class, run to the store, that kind of stuff."

"I don't think so. There isn't a house with in five miles of here, and even for those houses, there are much more efficient ways in and out of town. Somebody has a keen interest on something here."

She nearly dropped the computer bag she had in her hand. "Do you really think that they've tracked us down?"

The car had picked up speed again and was rounding the curve just east of the café.

"I'm not sure, but I don't like taking any chances. Let's get out while the coast is clear."

Dropping a few bills on the table, I waved to the waitress and we hurried out to the lot. Twenty seconds later, I was accelerating westward down the road.

"Why are you going this way? The station is the other way," Jackie commented.

"Let's just say, I'm playing a hunch."

Less than a mile from the diner, we passed the Lincoln. It was sitting on the edge of the road, it's driver on a cell phone.

I glanced in my mirror as we sped past and was able to see the passenger point. Seconds later the Lincoln was following us.

Jackie was also looking back. "Uh, Monica, he's behind us. But does it really prove anything?"

"Not yet, but this might," I said as I threw the car into a tight spin and floored it. We'd passed the Lincoln before the driver could react. "Keep your eye on 'em, Jackie," I called as I watched the speedometer get closer to 90.

"He's behind us, and nearly holding pace."

"Okay, I guess that confirms that he is following us," I mumbled as I threw the car into left turn onto Bay Street. "Jackie, can you get his plate number?"

She grabbed the binoculars that we kept in the center console, "I'll try."

As a precaution I hit the lights hoping that I could keep the road ahead clear as we neared town.

Jackie turned around in her seat, picked up the microphone. "Dispatch, this is K-one-eighty. I need a plate check on two-oh-four-victor-alpha-tango."

"One moment, K-one-eighty," the female voice responded. "That plate is registered to a two-thousand-twelve Tahoe that belongs to a Samuel Knight, last know address six-two-four-zero Wilshire Boulevard."

"That's no Tahoe behind us," Jackie said crossly. Keying the mic again she said, "Dispatch, thanks for the check. We are currently on Bay Street heading north, requesting backup. Suspect vehicle is a blue Lincoln, two occupants."

"Are you in pursuit, K-one-eighty?"

Jackie shook her head, "Negative, Dispatch. Subject vehicle is following us at high rate of speed."

"Roger, K-one-eighty. Aerial-two has you in sight and is vectoring in cars twenty-six and thirty-one. You are requested to keep the chase clear of town limits."

"Roger," Jackie responded. "Where do we go from here?"

"There's a road that runs near the beach. It's late in the season and too cold for too many people to be out right now, and this area isn't known for its surf, so we'll try there." I stated. "There's one of our backup crews," I pointed out as we went tearing down the road.

And that's when everything went wrong.

Bay Street is pretty much a straight run from the Atlantic to Cape Cod bay, and is lined with mostly empty fields and dunes. Unfortunately, people seem to love playing with their motor toys in those areas.

The first backup unit had just pulled in behind the Lincoln, and the siren was just screeching out its first tone when a dune buggy came over the embankment and onto the road. The officer now behind the Lincoln reacted like almost anyone would when a car came careening in from the side, and tried to pull over to make room.

That was when the passenger in the buggy opened fire.

The radio crackled, "Shots fired! Shots fired!"

"What?" I asked glancing in my mirror just in time to watch the patrol car hit the opposite embankment, go airborne and then land on its roof before it rolled three times.

Jackie was already on the radio. "Dispatch, K-one-eighty. Officers down, Bay Street just past Sand Pit Road."

"Roger K-one-eighty."

"Keep your eyes open, Gannon," I snarled. "They were ready for us, somehow they—"

A sharp crack interrupted me as the rear window splintered.

"K-one-eighty, we're taking fire!" Jackie reported in a now hysterical voice.

I could see the blue-green water of the bay just ahead. "Hold on," I told Jackie as I swung the car into a hard right turn. Tires squealed and I heard the metallic pings of at least two more rounds hitting the car.

I kept my eyes focused on the road as I pushed the car to the limit. Bullets were hitting the frame now and then. Suddenly the sound of automatic weapons rang out.

I chanced a glance out the side window, and breathed a sigh of relief. "Looks like we've got some aerial support," I noted.

Jackie was still facing forward, one hand on the dash and the other holding the microphone. Her eyes were wide with shock, and she had lost all color. Definitely in shock.

Getting shot at for the first time could do that to a person.

I gritted my teeth and concentrated on keeping the car on the road.

"K-one-eighty, Aerial-two reports that your tail is clear, but suspects fled scene. They are on patrol to do search, backup is enroute. What is your status?"

I looked over at Jackie. Still frozen like a statue.

Grabbing the microphone, "Uh, Dispatch, K-one-eighty. We are on the way in. Please have medical personnel meet us. My partner is currently is dazed."

"Dietz, you get her to the hospital for an evaluation, understood?" Commander Willoby's voice blared over the radio.

I sighed. "Roger, Commander."

Two hours later, we stood in Willoby's office. Jackie's color was much better. It was amazing at how well some smelling salt worked for bringing her back to the present.

"Any idea who was following you?" the commander asked.

I shook my head. "No, sir. I never got a good look at either of the men in the car. It looked like one had dark hair and a blue ball cap, the other one I just saw a dark colored hat and sunglasses."

"I'm sorry, sir," Jackie repeated for what had to have been the fifth time since we had gotten there. "I didn't get a good look either. And once the bullets started hitting the car, I kinda blanked."

Willoby waved his hand in a dismissive gesture. "Relax, Gannon. It happens to all of us at some point." He leaned back in his chair and scratched his chin in thought. "Not much else we can do tonight. Your shift ended ninety minutes ago, the evidence is locked up and you're both moving under your own steam. It seems that you've made some real progress today. So, let's call this a day.

"Both of you go home and get some rest. Gannon, you take those meds that they gave you, you hear?" He waited for her to nod her agreement. "We'll pick this up in the morning."

"Take care of yourself, Jackie. But be on your toes and stay alert," I said as we walked into the parking lot.

"Why do you say be alert?"

"I've got a feeling that we've either gotten too close, or we've already stepped on somebody's toes. The way they followed us out there today? That wasn't an accident that they had people there. They were hoping to ambush us and get us off the case permanently. So, take care of yourself."

Jackie's eyes were as wide as saucers, but she nodded and got into her car.

I watched her pull out, scanning everything. What I'd said had made her nervous, but I hoped that it would keep her alive.

Pulling into traffic myself, I too kept a close watch. I'd been here before, knew to be wary and was sure I could protect myself. What I didn't think I could handle was losing another partner.

CHAPTER 11

I had finally settled in for the evening and was trying to relax and unwind by reading a novel. Sitting in my favorite rocking chair, my foot dangled over the arm and my toes glided over Sam's luxurious fur. It made us both feel good.

At least until the doorbell rang.

Sam responded like a shot, dashing through the house barking and then taking a stance by the front door.

Cautiously, I walked to the door. I rarely use the front, and I've repeatedly told everyone to come to the side. So I was apprehensive about going to the front at this hour.

As I passed the hall table just inside the small entryway, I eased the drawer open and checked the spare 9mm that I kept there. If someone tried to force their way in, I had an equalizer within reach.

Stepping to the side of the door, I peered out into the black night.

A lone figure stood on my steps, a package in his hand.

The figure turned and in the moonlight I saw his face.

"Andy! Hold on," I said as I worked the deadbolt.

I swung the door open and Andy took one step inside.

"WOOF!"

"Dear God! Monica, there's a bear in your house," Andy whispered, frozen in place.

I turned and looked where he was pointing, and laughed.

"Andy, this is Sam. My dog."

"Dog? Are you sure? That thing's mammoth!"

Sam trotted over and nuzzled my elbow. I ended up tossing my arm around his neck. "They claimed he was a dog when I adopted him." I ruffled his fur. "What he is, is really a big baby. As far as he's concerned, he's a hundred and fifty pound lap dog."

Andy cautiously held a hand out to Sam. Sam sniffed him twice and then slurped his big tongue across Andy's cheek.

"Oh! Yuck!"

I just laughed. "He likes you,' I said sweetly.

I hung Andy's jacket in the closet, and then Sam led us back to the sitting room.

Andy sat on the sofa, and patted the seat next to him, hoping that I would take the seat.

Sam beat me there, and leaned heavily into Andy.

I sat in my rocker again, and smiled over at Andy. "I think he likes you."

"Well, that makes me feel better. Now if I can just keep him from crushing me." He grimaced, but his hand began stroking the silky fur, and Sam's eyes closed as he lapsed into doggy ecstasy.

"Anyway," I said with a smile. "What can I do for you, Andy?"

"Well, I guess you already have done two things that I was hoping for. You've given me somebody to talk to, and, you've reassured me about your safety here.

"Andy, I'm a cop remember. I've a gun and everything."

Fatigue shone on his face, and I wanted to go to him.

He leaned forward resting his arms on his knees. "Monica, I don't doubt that you can take care of yourself. But I worry. With everything that has happened over the last week, somebody's got it pretty hard for you. Or, maybe more to the point, they've got a reason why they don't want these murders solved. They're playing for keeps here."

I reached over and placed my hand on his. "Andy, everybody is taking this seriously. No one is ignoring the threats that this guy has sent. As far as we know, he's already responsible for three deaths; we don't want him to get a chance to increase his numbers."

Andy interlaced his fingers with mine. "I've never been in a situation like this before. My life for the last ten years has been in the labs. If I ever saw the suspect, it was at court. Now, whoever is responsible for this, has come into my sanctuary and attacked me on my home ground."

He let out a shaky breath. "My sense of self is shaken from all of this. Everything that I thought I knew? Useless." He dragged his fingers over his face.

"Andy, he only wins if we give up and stop. If we keep poking into those dark areas, looking at the points of intersection, then at some point we will find the guy. That's my job. I'm going to nail the bastard, and throw the bloody book at him."

Andy smiled wearily. "That's just what I needed to hear. I guess I just don't want to be alone tonight. Too many thoughts running through my head. I also," he paused as if trying to figure out how to say something. "I also realized how special you were to me. When I came to that conclusion, I realized that I didn't want you alone over here." He looked over at Sam, who had maneuvered himself onto his back and was sleeping with all four paws pointing up.

"Thanks for the concern, Andy. I'll admit, there have been a few nights in the past that have given me serious cases of insomnia. This one hasn't done that. Yet. But it makes me feel good to know that someone else out there cares."

This time, he interlocked his fingers through mine. "I don't think that I ever truly got over you. When we called things off and went our own ways, I was too intent on my studies. But whenever I had time alone, my mind drifted to you. I'm afraid that I may do more than just care for you, Monica. I think I may be falling in love with you."

I'm not sure which sound Andy laughed at. It could have been the startled snort that came from Sam, who appeared to be running in his sleep or it could have been the "Wha…wha…what?" that was combined with my stunned face.

Either way, he laughed. "I know. I was a bit surprised to hear me say that as well, but now that I have, I feel better."

"Andy, we don't really know each other. We are different people than we were back in college. We only ran into each other a few days ago. We can't be talking about falling in love right now."

"On the one hand, you're exactly correct. We haven't known each other, in the mature adult roles that we've grown into, that long. But, we've known each other much longer than a couple of days. It seems, to me at least, that we meshed like pieces from a puzzle. Besides, my Mom always said that when I met the right girl, I'd know it almost from the start.

I think," he hesitated. "I think I knew it way back when, but I was too scared to admit it to myself. I'm so glad that we found each other again."

We sat quietly both of us lost in our own thoughts for a minute or so.

Our fingers were still laced together, so I squeezed his hand.

"Andy, I agree that these feelings are different. It's like we've known each other longer than we have. I guess my mind is still so tied up with everything with this case, that I'm not sure if my feelings are like, lust, love or because we've ended up going through some crazy scenarios very recently."

He smiled, "I'm a doctor; a trained scientist who specializes in extracting tiny bits of data from small samples. I'll help you with your experiment to determine that you're in love with me."

We both laughed.

"I normally don't drink tea or coffee this late, but would you like something?"

"Sure. I'll have whatever you're having. How's that?"

"Okay. Two cups of hot chocolate coming up," I said as I rose to go put the water on.

I had company. Sam heard me step towards the kitchen, and hoped that this meant there would be food or a treat for him. In his attempt to persuade me, he went and sat by the pantry door.

Andy followed a moment later, carrying the package that he'd brought.

"What've you got there?" I asked as I put the kettle on.

"A few things actually." He set the box on the counter and opened the lid. "First, we have the results from the letter that you found today. I ran it through electromagnetic imaging. Didn't find any fingerprints on the paper itself. However, we dissolved the glue and peeled the letters off the paper. We ended up with getting a few partials there. From sizing and angles, we were able to assemble two viable prints for you. Obviously, you'll need to take it from there."

I looked at him stunned. "You got partials off of the backs of the letters that were cut out?"

Andy nodded. "Yeah. Criminals figure that by wearing gloves when they assemble the letter that they deny us the opportunity to use fingerprints. However, they often forget the gloves when they are cutting the letters out. Pretty convenient for us."

"That's excellent! I'd call Jackie, but I don't want to screw up our evening by talking shop with her."

Andy smiled, slipped his arm around my waist and kissed my forehead. "Talking shop with me during our evening is okay, right?"

Now it was my turn to smile. "Yep." I stretched a bit and our mouths met.

It took another ten minutes for us to get back to the tasks at hand, and that was only because the shrill whistle of the kettle annoyed us.

As I stirred the cups of chocolate I asked, "So what else is in your box of magic?"

"Well, we've already gone over the prints. The second item that is in here, is a copy of our security camera footage. It hit me that when you said that you were suspecting someone from inside, and we are too, that perhaps they are contacting each other through a source that isn't always traceable."

My mind jumped to where Andy was heading. "You're thinking that they are communicating with somebody and using a courier service to get the messages back and forth, right?"

"It plays for me," he said.

"Yeah it does. Couriers come in and out of the building all the time. They sign in and out, but nobody really pays attention to them. If they meet with someone, as long as they deliver a package, nobody notices them. Smart."

"That was what I'd thought as well. I made copies of the tapes from the last two weeks. It's on the DVD. Lastly, I may have found something that gives us a place to start our search. The lab found traces of soil that was embedded on the clothing of Leo Spiro. I went back to the jacket that Toby Williams was wearing when he was shot. It was a long shot, but I figured unless they'd actually used a clean room when making the jacket, there might be some dust caught in the interior. Sure enough, there was an extremely small trace amount of something.

"I ran it through the gas chromatograph mass spectrometer. It turns out that the elements that were found in our dust sample on the inside of Williams' jacket matched the elements found in the soil on Spiro's pants. By itself, that isn't enough to do anything, but the ratios are the same. In fact," he pulled out a printout, "they are identical."

I studied the printouts. "Are you saying that Leo Spiro was wherever that jacket was made?"

"At this point, I can't say he was at the exact location, but I can tell you that you've got another piece of circumstantial evidence."

I turned and stared out the window into the darkness. "Is there anyway that we can isolate where these samples might have come from?"

"Actually, yes. I was going to ask if you and Jackie would like to accompany me tomorrow up towards Boston. I've got a friend who is an expert on soils, and has done soil studies all over the country, including several in the Massachusetts area. We probably won't get an exact location, but we should be able to get some ideas."

"That sounds like a plan. The nice thing is, that we won't have to find someplace to hang out tomorrow."

The chocolate was long gone, and this time, Andy and I had managed to cuddle up on the couch. We'd turned the lights down and watched the Music Man, one of my favorite musicals, as we enjoyed each other's company.

At the conclusion of the show, Andy stood and stretched. "I was going to try to give you some lame reason for me to camp out on your couch tonight. But seeing that you've got some pretty serious protection there," he pointed to where Sam lay on his back asleep. "I guess you don't need any further protection, do you my fair lady?"

"Your offer of protecting the fair lady is appreciated, but this particular maiden can defeat anything that happens to come at me."

I would later think that my timing was ironic.

The house pitched into blackness

Small arms fire rang out through the night and plaster from the wall exploded.

I'd already wrenched my hand from Andy, and was slowly opening the drawer next to the chair. I extracted my .357 magnum revolver.

I could see Andy in the moonlight. He looked at me with eyes as wide as saucers.

I didn't have any idea who was coming, but I was sure that we were in for one more visitor, and I wouldn't be unprepared.

I glanced over at Sam, and was dumbfounded that he was still sleeping. It wasn't until the door creaked open that his eyes flashed open and in a move that looked to be far too graceful for a dog that large, he was on his feet heading for the noise.

"Sam! Hold!" I whispered harshly, hoping that I could keep him from going out.

Thankfully he stopped just shy of the door.

I mouthed to Andy "Take cover by the wall and stay low."

He looked like he was about to argue, but followed me to a point that offered some protection.

I tried to control my breathing like they taught me in tactical school, but in those courses, you aren't expecting the armed bad guy to march into your own home. That tends to get the adrenalin moving.

I could hear someone moving quietly coming nearer to where we were. Every few seconds, the sound of a door being opened slowly echoed throughout the house.

"Do you think we got her?" a raspy voice asked someone.

"Would you just shut up?" came the answer in a clear tenor.

Okay, mental note to self, there are two armed intruders in my house. Why? At this point, my mind registered that I needed to get Andy, Sam and I out of here before this got any worse.

The moonlight illuminated a figure who now appeared in the door. His facial silhouette broken by the night vision goggles he was wearing.

My heart sank. He had a clear view of everything, and we were in the dark. Things had definitely gone from bad to worse.

"Hey, Alex, I think someone's in this room."

"Well there you go, thinking again, Derek. I told ya' before, let me do the thinking. Your brilliant plan got us into this situation in the first place. Now let's see if we can waste this cop and get out of here before someone else arrives."

I was trying to figure out how to maneuver myself into a better position to get a clear shot when the second shadow came to the door. I watched in horror as a gun appeared, anticipating the sting of the initial hit followed by the slow burning pain that would register the severity of the wound.

Instead I heard a loud bark, a thud followed by someone screaming in pain and very menacing growling.

"What the hell is that?" I heard the voice now identified as Alex yell.

It sounded like Derek tried to answer, but his voice came out as a hiss and then suddenly stopped.

Furious barking rang out, along with the sounds of nails on the hardwood floor.

"Holy crap!" Alex yelled. Now there were the sounds of someone running added to the sounds coming from a determined dog.

I didn't waste any time, "Andy, let's go. Out the through the garage and then we'll keep close to the house."

Andy hesitated long enough to grab the box he'd brought in before he headed in the direction that I pointed. I backed towards the door, the revolver still at the ready.

As I neared the hall, I could hear the faint moaning of the man that Sam had taken down. I didn't have the time to make sure that he was going to make it, but I did spare him a look and enough time to kick his gun away.

Sam was still barking, but there was no other sound, so I assumed that the other intruder had managed to get away.

I whistled, and Sam came running to find us.

We reached the door, slipped into the garage and headed for the door to the yard. Andy grabbed the knob.

I grasped his hand and whispered, "Wait a minute. Let's see if anyone is out there before we go charging out."

Andy nodded and stood still as I grabbed a flashlight from the shelf, and the garden rake. I laid the flashlight on the tines, turned it on, and then maneuvered the whole thing so that the flashlight was just in the corner of the window.

BANG!

The shot rang through the now quiet dark, and was only followed by the sound of breaking glass.

"Well, we know that someone is out there waiting for us," Andy said.

"Yeah. It also means that we're kind of pinned down here. And of course with the way my luck has been going, my phone is on my dresser on charge."

"I've got mine right here," he said pulling it out.

I was still on the phone with the 9-1-1 operator when I heard the sirens.

"Sounds like the cavalry is almost—" I broke off when I heard breaking glass followed by a muffled whoosh.

"Someone just tossed a Molotov cocktail through the window of the garage," I told the operator.

Andy had grabbed the fire extinguisher that my father had insisted that I always kept near and was working to put out the fire when two more crashes sounded.

Sirens wailed and then came to a sudden stop in front of the house. A moment later, two uniformed officers came through the back yard and announced that everything was clear.

We followed them to the safety of the patrol cars. Andy's free arm was around my shoulders as much in comfort as for guidance. Sam paced along on my other side.

I turned to look back at my little house. Flames leapt out of what had been the kitchen windows. I could feel the tears streaming down my cheek. Andy pulled me closer, and I leaned into him and pulled Sam along.

"What else is going to happen?" I asked.

An explosion rocked the house.

CHAPTER 12

At the sound of the explosion instinct kicked in, and I forced Andy to the ground and dove for cover myself.

Debris rained down on us like hail from some ill-fated storm.

"My house," I gasped. Slowly, I pushed up to look around.

Andy's head came up. Slowly he turned to me, "Are you hurt, Monica?"

"Not physically, no. But I, oh…"

Tears flowed down my cheeks as I fought to regain control over my breathing. No sound emerged only deep gasps for oxygen.

I felt Andy wrap something around me, and the comforting presence of Sam's weight as he settled his head on my lap. I knew that there were emergency personnel there, but my mind was so abused that I couldn't make any sense of what was happening around me.

I sat with my head resting on Andy's shoulder, wrapped in a blanket and cried until there was no more. Andy's arm held fast around my shoulders and Sam's head in my lap were the only indication that this was reality right now.

The next thirty minutes was filled with the activities of the fire department trying to save my house and the police doing what they could to preserve the scene. I didn't move except when the EMT's forced me to go into the rescue squad to be checked out.

After I was cleared I just sat on the stretcher and sobbed. Sam folded himself at my feet, and Andy took a seat next to me. We sat there for what seemed hours.

I heard the shuffle of feet, and felt the movement of my protectors. Slowly, my gaze lifted enough so that I could make out the shape of someone standing in front of me.

"You've had a rough couple of days, detective," Commander Willoby stated.

"Yes, Sir," I choked out.

"I'd ask how you're doing, but I can see that right now you're barely holding on. Unfortunately, I think that we need to talk about a few things immediately."

I felt Andy shifting, "I'll go."

"Don't leave me," I pleaded. Even I was shocked by how needy I was right now.

He turned to me, "Monica, I'm just going to go over and talk to the officer right there." He pointed to where the fire captain was standing. "I'll see if I can find someplace to get us a couple of hot drinks, and then I'll be right back."

I clung to his hand, as if it were my only lifeline.

He bent down, kissed my head. "I'll be quick. I promise."

I watched him walk towards the captain, and then clasped my hands to keep them from shaking.

"Would that be Dr. Andrew Carson?" Willoby asked pleasantly, watching Andy walk away.

"Yes. Andy—I mean Dr. Carson and I have started seeing each other recently."

"From what I know of him, he's a good man. I'm glad that he'll be with you to help you get through this."

It took over an hour to answer all of the questions. Commander Willoby's questions were followed by an interview with the Massachusetts State Police and finally the interrogation had ended with fifteen minutes with the county arson investigator.

"I need to figure out where I'm going tonight," I said as we watched the arson guy climb into his car.

Andy turned to me. "What do you mean?"

"Well, obviously I can't use my house. The motels in the area aren't exactly pet friendly, and even if they are, they have a thing about 150 pound dogs."

"You're coming with me tonight."

"Andy, do you think you're place is going to be any safer? Besides, you live in an apartment. What would you're landlord say?"

He smiled and draped his arm over my shoulder to pull me close.

"Monica, while you were talking with your commander, I spoke to the Kevin Watcovich. He's the fire captain, in case you didn't know. Anyway, Kevin is married to my cousin, Emma. He made a call, and we'll have use of their RV for the next few days."

I looked at him. "An RV? You want to go camping? Now? This may seem like a strange time to bring it up, but there's this whole murder investigation that I'm working on."

He smiled and pulled me closer. "I know. But if you're house moves around, it's harder to find you. Besides, it will give us all a place to work from for the next few days."

I sighed. I wasn't exactly looking forward to spending time in an RV, but it did seem like the only viable option I had at the moment. "Okay," I grumbled. "Let's go camping."

I roused up the next morning confused. It took a moment for me to remember the events from the night before and realize that I was in an RV, and not my own home.

I tried to get out of the bed, and literally ran into the wall. The so-called bedroom was barely the size of my closet at home. And they'd crammed a double bed and some storage space into it.

The lump next to me on the bed gave a snort and moved.

When the giant black paw stretched from under the covers, I gave a sigh of relief.

Slowly, I navigated my way down the narrow hall towards the cab of the RV. As I cleared the small galley, I looked up, and could just make out Andy's head poking out from under the covers from the bunk over the cab.

Looking out the windows, I could see that we were in some kind of campground, but I really had no idea where.

Turning back to the galley I tried the sink. Water spurted and splattered into the basin that was no bigger than a thick novel.

Sighing, I opened the cupboards and found a coffee pot and within a few minutes had it on the stove to boil.

"Now all I need to do is find what we've got to go with our hot water," I told the ever patient Sam.

"Morning," Andy's voice called.

I turned, to see him sitting crouched over in the bunk, scratching the head of an overweight white and orange tabby.

"It definitely is a morning," I agreed. "Where are we?"

"You passed out about ten minutes after we hit the road. I decided that I really didn't want to go too far at that hour, so I headed for a KOA camp that was about fifteen miles up the coast. Figured we wouldn't look too out of place here. It'll give us a chance to regroup, and do some planning of our own. We'll plan to move again tomorrow."

"How are we going to work?" I asked. "For that matter, how will I let Jackie know where to find me?"

Andy pushed off of the bunk and came to me.

"Things are going to be a bit challenging for the next few days. But what we have here is a travelling lab. We'll be able to do most of what we need right from here, as well as keep moving around. It tends to make it harder for the opposition to kill you if they can't find you."

I slumped onto the bench for the dinette. "Is that what this has all come to? Are we being forced to run because of a few threats?"

Andy sat across from me, reached over the table and took my hands. "A few threats are one thing. Sending you notes that speak of malice is another. But regardless of which one you want to focus on, right now, the fact is that last night someone broke into your house with the intent of removing you from the field of play. Permanently.

"Monica, you've come to mean too much to me to let you take chances like that. This seemed like the best solution to the dilemma. We can both work from the RV, so that's not going to slow either of us down. Plus, we get the added benefit that we can watch over each other. These guys are playing for keeps. I don't know who they are, or what they're after or why they're doing it. But what I do know is that they keep taking shots at the woman I'm in love with. And there's no way that I can sit by and not try to do something."

"Thank you," I finally managed. "I need to tell you something that you hinted at last night."

His eyes flashed up to mine.

I smiled demurely, "I guess I'm falling in love with you too. No one has ever stood by me this way before.

"I'm a cop, I'm trained to take care of myself and others without the need for someone else to protect me. But you've done that for me, and your actions have spoken volumes on this topic."

He raised our linked hands to his mouth, and kissed mine. "Now, what do we need to do today to nail these slimes who have sent us running?"

We were crammed around the dinette an hour later. Jackie had brought some extra supplies with her that made me feel more comfortable.

"I get the extra clothes and chocolate would make you feel better. But I'm not sure that I understand the spare gun and all the ammunition." Andy was sitting on the bench, but his eye kept going to the boxes that I was now storing.

"Actually, it's pretty simple. As a cop, when I'm on duty I'm required to carry a weapon. From past experience, I prefer to also have a back up piece. When they fire bombed my house, I left with only what I had on my back and the revolver that I'd pulled out of the drawer.

"Until the investigation is completed, I can't go in to recover my official side arm nor any of the other handguns that I kept. That's why I had Jackie bring me the new set. Besides, the revolver is really too bulky to carry concealed."

"But you have a badge. You don't need to keep it hidden," he pointed out.

"That's true, she doesn't." Jackie conceded. "However, the Smith and Wesson model nineteen only holds six rounds, where the Glock twenty-three holds thirteen in the magazine and the smaller twenty-seven holds nine and is easily carried as a backup."

"I always thought you women were supposed to consider jewelry as an accessory, not handguns."

Accepting the holster from Jackie, I replied, "To each her own".

Once my new sidearms were in place, I turned to the others. They were cramped at the dinette table, each looking over what I would only guess to be relevant reports for our case. "So, are we ready to do something?"

Jackie looked up. "What are we going to do? I mean, we're all but banned from being in the office, your house was demolished last night and now the two of you are hiding out in a camper. I've been relocated, under protest I might add, to keep the bad guys off of us. What do you propose we do? Personally, I'm about ready to turn in my detective badge and go back to traffic."

I pulled up a seat on the edge of the bench next to Andy and unconsciously began petting Sam's head. "Jackie, this whole thing is bizarre. No question about it. You got transferred into the group and within hours you've been called out on a big case. And that big case has some big teeth.

"The best thing that we can do right now, is to keep moving forward on what we have. We must be putting some major pressure on somebody, or else they wouldn't be taking the chances that they have. The attack on us last night doesn't seem like it was well thought out. Yeah, they had decent equipment, but they didn't do their research. They didn't know about Sam, or the fact that Andy was still there. They didn't even try to verify that I was asleep. What this tells me is that we've got them concerned. Very concerned.

"If we stop now, they win. So to answer your question, what we're going to do is follow the evidence. Andy brought some information over last night that he'd come across in the lab. That evidence is still in our custody, so the chain isn't broken. Before the excitement of last night, we'd planned that today the three of us would take a ride up to Boston to meet with another scientist who might be able to shed a little light on where whomever we're looking for is hiding.

"I think that is probably our best course of action for now." I stared over at her.

"We're going to go to Boston?" she asked timidly. "Why?"

Andy took the lead here.

"Basically, after we met yesterday, I went back to the lab thinking about Locard's principle. I carefully looked at the evidence that we had. We found soil samples, both in physical and elemental quantities, embedded in the evidence. Today's plan is to go see a friend of mine, Dr. Jared Simons. Jared and I did our graduate work together, and our labs were only a few doors apart. We're hoping that he can narrow things down for us."

"What are we going to do if they find us?" Jackie asked.

"With a little luck," I answered, "we're going to find them first."

Patrons were talking animatedly and loudly at the little diner we decided to stop in for lunch on the way back from Boston. I sat quietly staring at the wall, using my straw to mindlessly stir my drink.

"Okay, Monica. What are you thinking about?" Jackie finally asked.

My trance broke with her voice. "Huh? What was that?"

Both Andy and Jackie laughed. "Glad I can amuse you. What did you ask?" I tried again.

Jackie, still chuckling, answered. "I was wondering what you were so deep in thought about?"

"I was thinking about what Dr. Simons said. You know, that the soil had to be from somewhere near where sea water met with the ice sheet in the last ice age."

"Yeah, that's going to be a big help," Andy sighed. "I mean, let's face it. There's a pretty big section of Massachusetts that borders the ocean."

"That may be true," I said spearing a tomato. "But, it also eliminates a lot of land as well. Technically, we've narrowed our search by quite a bit."

They both looked at each other and then back to me. Jackie was the first to speak, "It sure must be nice to be an eternal optimist."

It was my turn to laugh. "Lesson six, or is it seven? Doesn't really matter. Next lesson in Detective 101, even a "no" is an answer. It's not so much being an optimist, but understanding the mathematics of the situation. We know that we are going to be looking for an area that meets certain criteria. If the area doesn't, we ignore it because its answer is simply "no". It doesn't mean that we don't at least glance there, but more that we can focus our energy on areas that are more likely."

"But how does that help us?" Jackie asked.

I was pleased that she wasn't being as negative now, and was willing to consider possibilities. I was even happier when Andy answered the question for me.

"Actually, Jackie, the process is relatively simple. The information that Jared gave us has us concentrating on waterfront locales. Next, we take a look at some other variables, areas that are restricted, State Parks, that sort of thing. Again, this will decrease our numbers. We can further this by comparing the tracking numbers off of certain packages that we know, using any data that comes from the print that we lifted from the letter that was delivered to the station, proximity to the crime scenes and other specific places.

"What we should end up with in the end will be between three and ten places where the variables all fit. That's when things become a bit more personal."

"Don't forget," I added, "Dr. Simons is going to be sending us a specific breakdown of the soils that were found. That gives us one more point to cross-reference with. Eventually, we're going to be able to bring our search into one specific area."

Jackie sipped her water.

"If that's true, then I'm not sure if I should feel better or be more concerned."

When I looked at her, she must have read my confusion.

"What I mean is, finding out where these guys are hiding will be great. But if they're already attacking us, what's going to happen when we get that close?"

"Fair question." I mused. "I don't have an answer for that—yet. That's the reason though that we've all changed our work schedules and habits."

"So we're being proactive, not reactive?" Jackie wanted to know.

"That's how I see it. The further ahead of them that we stay, the better chance we have of solving this before things get much worse."

Andy was about ready to take a bite of his burger, when he stopped.

"I know that we've got the basics with us to run a fairly sophisticated lab out of the RV. But how are we going to tie in to the rest of what's going on?"

"Well, even before they fire-bombed my house, Jackie and I were going to be staying in the field. What's the problem?"

Andy set his burger down. "I think we may have just inadvertently played right into their hand."

"What do you mean?" I asked setting my fork down before I dropped it.

"Think about it. If they've got someone into the department and the labs, they know that we aren't going in. Rumors about that will flow freely, so they'll have no trouble backing that up. The problem is we need certain pieces of data, so we're either going to have to go in and talk to people or we need to access it electronically."

"Exactly," Jackie said. "So what's the problem?"

Andy was turning a little pale, so I wondered what had him concerned or if it was lunch.

"They've already tried to kill Monica once. Now, by her being restricted on going into the office, they've only got to keep watch on one or two places, the Morgue for example, and they know where to find her."

Realization kicked in, and I sat stunned. "Andy's right," I finally managed. "By curtailing our daily activities, maybe we've helped them set a trap for us."

Jackie's eyes kept darting from Andy to me. "So what do we do?"

CHAPTER 13

Three days had passed since we'd made our trip to Boston, and the stress was starting to catch up with all of us.

Even though Andy's cousin's RV was a huge monstrosity, difficult at best to maneuver, and was abysmal when it came to gas mileage, inside was cramped. There just wasn't room for Sam, Andy, Fred and I. Life became real interesting when Sam and Fred decided to play tag—inside.

Normally, we sat out around the picnic table working on our various reports. But today was one of those wonderful days where the rain was cold and steady, so we were huddled around the dinette table.

Andy had been going over the videos from the security cameras. It had been a painstaking process, but he felt that he was zeroing in on something. I couldn't understand how he could keep watching the video feeds that carefully for that long. My eyes feel like they're going to fall out after two hours. He'd been at this nearly three full days. No wonder he was now staring out the window rubbing his forehead.

I leaned into him, and began rubbing his neck.

"Andy, you've got to give this a rest. You've got a boulder here."

I could tell by the way that his shoulders jerked, that he was trying to laugh it off.

"I'd take an hour off, Monica, if I felt that I was really getting anywhere."

"I thought you said that you'd found some irregularities. That's progress isn't, Doc?" I said hoping to lighten his mood.

"Maybe," he answered. "Yeah, I've got a guy that's come in at odd times. But he's wearing a uniform and the way that he angles his body, he distorts the picture. I just don't know what else to do right now. And," he let out a long sigh. "I hate to admit it, but I'm about camped out."

"Any word from Dr. Simons?" Jackie asked as she poured herself a cup of coffee at the stove.

"Not yet," Andy told her. "He figured that he'd have the results after three or four days, so he should be sending us something soon."

I looked back to the file on Leo Sprio, which I had finally received this morning.

After our realization about the possibility of a trap, the commander wanted us to stay out of the offices altogether. The only way that we'd been able to get any information was by using a very old fashioned system—the U.S. mail.

The basic procedure was for us send a request for information to the commander. We included a footer on the page so that it looked like a page number, but it actually corresponded to a point on a map. There were only two of these maps in existence, the commander's and ours.

The commander would act as the liaison between the different labs and us. When he had a report or other information for us, he'd address it to us at general delivery at the post office that we'd noted. He varied how the packages were mailed to us, hoping to keep our locations secure.

A pre-paid phone now allowed us to text information back and forth as well as providing a method for us to receive any emergency information that we needed to know. It was nice to have, but we used it as little as possible. We had no idea how much hacking abilities whoever was responsible for this had.

"Guys? I might have something here," I blurted out.

"What'd you find?" Jackie asked as she leaned over my shoulder.

"Well, it appears that our friend Leo had been observed palling around with several unsavory characters. Topping the list would be Derek Hanson." I dropped a photo of the two of them taken at a distance on the table.

"Whose Hanson?" Andy asked.

"Derek Hanson is one of the guys who was suspected in a triple murder two years ago. He's bad news. Rumor is that he's been working his way into some organized crime syndicates, but only on a contractual basis."

"A contractual basis?" Jackie asked. "What exactly is that?"

"Just what it sounds like. He goes in for a specific hit, and then moves on."

Andy closed the top of his laptop and leaned closer to look at the picture. "Who else has this guy been hanging out with?"

"Unfortunately, the list of his contacts is long and varied. The only quality that they all have in common is that they are all despicable."

"Monica," Andy closed his eyes and rubbed his temples. "Do we have any idea on where this Hanson guy is right now?"

"No. We'll have to put a request—"

"I know where he is," Jackie stated matter-of-factly.

I turned to where she was leaning against the counter, coffee cup in one hand and a printed report in the other and eyes as big as saucers.

"What was that Jackie?"

"We know Hanson's whereabouts. And we also know that he's not going to be of much use to us." She dropped the printed report down on the table.

My hand beat Andy's in the grab for it, but I held it so we could both read it.

"A coroner's report?" Andy asked wearily. "He's dead?"

"Sure looks that way to me," I mumbled as I began to flip through the packet. When I got to the cause of death I stopped and my hand began trembling.

"Monica? What's up?" Andy asked at the same time Jackie demanded, "What's wrong?"

I fought for control of my voice. "He was one of the two guys in the house the night that..." I couldn't continue.

"Oh, right. I remember someone called Derek was there." Andy's eyes flashed with anger. "They'd hired him to kill you, didn't they?"

My voice had deserted me again. I nodded and mouthed "Yeah," while I wiped the tears that were now streaming down my face.

Andy took hold of my other hand and squeezed it. "We're here for you, Monica. And don't you forget, you foiled their plan. You got all of us out of there in one piece."

I reached out with my free hand, this time ruffling it through Sam's thick black coat. "It seems that I had a lot of help. My gentle giant came to the rescue."

Andy and Jackie were both confused. Jackie looked at the cause of death, "Oh my!"

"I knew that Sam had attacked one of the intruders as we were trying to get out. I just didn't realize that it was Hanson, or that he'd broken Hanson's neck in the process."

Jackie bent down and hugged Sam's huge head. "You're one heck of a hero, Sam."

It was silent in the RV for a few moments; each of us was lost in our own thoughts. It was Andy who broke the silence.

"What does this information give us?"

I sipped my tea, and then began. "For starters, we now have identification of two of the men that were involved with the assault on Cathy's Collectibles. It's time to begin a thorough search of their lives over the past year or so. Somewhere in there is the connection that we are looking for."

Jackie interrupted me with a waving hand, "What are we looking for?"

"For starters, the third person on the assault team. We need to find some answers here, and perhaps we've been too mired in our own little thoughts to see the real issues."

My vision blurred.

"Welcome back," Andy said. He was standing in front of me, with his hands lightly on my upper arms. The front of my shirt was wet, and it felt like I was being prodded with a blunt object.

I looked down. Sam's s big head was bumping ruthlessly into my side.

"Okay, Sam. Settle down!" I snapped.

He dropped to his haunches, but he never left my side. It was then that I became aware of Jackie's face.

"Jackie! Are you okay?" I tried to get up, but Andy's hands kept me where I was.

"Am I okay?" she asked in disbelief. "I'm not the one who went into a trance five minutes ago. I'm not the one who has been totally unresponsive, to the point that her friends were about ready to call for an ambulance. No! I'm bloody well not okay! You just scared ten years off my life."

My eyes flashed from her to Andy. "I was in a trance?"

"You were somewhere." His face showed a level of concern that I'd never seen outside of an emergency room waiting area.

I sunk back into the seat. This was more disconcerting than I realized.

Andy leaned on the table, "You were in the middle of a conversation. It looked like you had a thought that you were pondering. But after thirty seconds or so, we started getting worried. You were totally unresponsive for probably three minutes or so, but they were among the longest three hours of my life." He flashed a comforting smile. "Apparently you had all of us worried. About the time that we realized that something was wrong, Sam here began barking and butting his head into you. That's how you ended up spilling your tea." He paused, arched an eyebrow and asked, "Can you tell us what happened to you?"

Unconsciously, I started petting Sam. "I knew that I was staring out the window as I started talking through things. I-I guess that my mind just started making all these connections. I didn't realize how far my thoughts had taken me apparently."

Andy reached over and gently angled my face towards him. "Our reunion only happened a short time ago, but you're already very important to me. Please be careful."

I reached up and took his hand. A shy smile formed, "You're important to me too, so I'll do everything that I can." We stared into each other's eyes, both of us smiling.

"Ahem. I hate to break things up, but I was wondering if there was any chance that we're going to get back to work on solving this crime or if I should go catch a movie or something?"

Andy rubbed my arm. "What connections were you thinking about?"

"I think that we need to go back to the beginning. We've overlooked something that is important."

"But we've been looking at everything that relates to Toby Williams' murder. We've got lots of links. What could we have missed?"

"I don't think we missed it," I stated. "It's more that we saw it, but didn't recognize it at the time."

Andy leaned back in his chair. "Why don't you tell me the whole story, and let's see if anything gels for you."

It took better than fifteen minutes for me to tell the complete story to Andy. As I finished, I looked over to him. He was staring out the window, scratching his chin. "What are you thinking about?" I asked.

"Trying to see things from your perspective. I figured that it might help to try and think like a cop and illuminate what was skimmed over."

"You're a scientist," Jackie pointed out. "You'd be likely to focus on those areas first. Is there some test that we forgot to look into?"

Andy shook his head. "No. Scientifically, we ran everything that we can. All that's left right now is to hear back from Simons. It's almost like—"

I slapped my forehead. "How could we have forgotten about that?"

"What?" Andy asked warily. "Care to share with the rest of us?"

I looked over to Jackie. "When we went to the scene, what information were we given?"

"Um, let me think. We got there, and they told us about the victims of the shootings. Both of them now that I think about it." She paused, closed her eyes. "We went back into the room, but that's about all I'm pulling out."

I smiled triumphantly. "What about the missing woman?"

"The missing wo—" Jackie stopped mid sentence. "Of course! Someone told us about the three men and that they thought that there was a woman missing. Why don't we have any information about her disappearance?"

Andy interjected, "Another thing. Why wasn't this in the papers anywhere? Wouldn't it be in the best interest of the missing woman if the public was aware that she was missing?"

"Now we're getting to the heart of the matter," I said. "We don't have any information on her disappearance because the F.B.I. was working that angle. They don't have to share information with us. Keeping it out of the papers? That may have been the decision of the F.B.I., or it may have been that we missed a small report. In any case, we need to start looking into the disappearance of Cathy Evans. I wish there was a way that we could use some of the resources that we normally have at the office to track her down."

"How do you want to proceed?" Andy asked as he twirled a pen through his fingers. "And, what can I do to help?"

It took us the rest of the morning to come up with a document that contained all of the important details that we needed answers to.

"So what do we do now?" Jackie asked.

"We need these answers immediately. Going through the mail is going to take a few days. Too long. Stopping at the police station is going to blow our cover. There has to be a way." I moaned.

"I think it's time for a good book."

I stared at Andy. "A good book is it? What? Has our little dilemma gotten too boring for you?" My voice was sharp, almost abusive.

"All set, Quick Draw?" he asked pleasantly. When I just stared at him, he shrugged and went on. "My thought is that many bookstores in an effort to bring in customers have small coffee shops and free Wi-Fi. If we go to the bookstore, you can keep your laptop in your purse until we're inside. Jackie and I can keep watch while you send it."

I thought about what he'd said. It started to make sense, but I thought perhaps a slight twist on things might be beneficial.

"Let's hold off on the bookstore until this afternoon," I said. "I think going to lunch may be a better option right now. Send the email from the coffee shop, or where ever, but we can have Willoby meet us at the bookstore with the data before dinner."

Andy, Jackie and I looked at each other. "That's a great idea," Jackie finally said. "I know that with the appropriate resources, we could have answers in less than thirty minutes, so the commander should be able to get it for us by dinner."

With that set, I made a few addendums to the email, and we headed out.

At six-thirty that night, I sat alone at a table on the edge of the bookstore's coffee shop fidgeting in the chair. A casual glance around the patrons of the store yielded Jackie sitting in a wing-armed chair reading a romance novel and Andy two aisles over perusing through a magazine about homebuilt airplanes. Homebuilt airplanes? Hmmm, I thought to myself, this could lead to a very interesting conversation.

A movement to my right caught my attention, and I used my peripheral vision to observe Commander Willoby walk in.

It was unusual to see him dressed in blue jeans with a polo shirt, but it definitely let him blend into the crowd. He looked like several other men who had come in and settled themselves into the crowded bookstore. Like many of the others, he had a black computer bag slung across his body. A woman with two small children followed him in and a well-dressed gentleman held the door for everyone.

My attention was drawn to the other man. I can't say why, but it was almost if I'd seen him somewhere before, but I couldn't put a finger on where.

In my job, I see so many people each day that it's not unusual for me to see a face that seems familiar. I turned my attention back to the job at hand.

Commander Willoby never turned to look at me, so I casually watched his movements as he strolled over and began to look at a display of nonfiction books just the other side of where I was sitting.

He glanced up once, gave a quick nod and then headed towards the business section located in the back corner.

I closed up my computer, stuffed it back into my oversized purse and made my way to the nonfiction section. Judging by where I'd been sitting, I started carefully going through the books on dog care.

Tucked in the back, behind a how-to-obedience training book, was a manila envelope. I glanced around to ensure that no one had taken undue interest in me, and then folded the envelope. Securing the envelope in the back cover of the book, I took one more look around and headed to checkout.

Andy had already made his way through the checkout, and was heading out to the car, and Jackie was meandering her way through the central displays heading towards the door.

A shiver went up my spine. It was my version of a sixth sense telling me that something was out of place. As I stood in line, I slowly looked around. I noticed that the man who had followed the commander in, was standing by a display next to the clearance titles near the checkouts.

He seemed to be looking at the latest thriller, but it could have been a set up.

The line snaked up through a series of racks. The moment that a display of gift cards was between the well dressed guy and me I carefully dropped the envelope out of the book and into my bag while I dug for my wallet.

When I looked up again, he was still there, but his attention was obviously on something other than a book.

That is, unless he liked reading novels upside down.

CHAPTER 14

There was no question in my mind.

Whoever it was that was holding that book upside down wasn't here for the reading value. He had a clear line on me. Of greater concern, he was directly between where I was and the only way out. I needed help.

Thinking quickly, I dropped my wallet.

Bending down to recover from my so-called accident, I grabbed my phone and typed "S.O.S." as a text message and sent it to the group. I could only hope that Jackie, Andy or the commander would pick up on what was happening.

While I was waiting, I let the cop in me take notes. He appeared to be in his early forties, around six-two, maybe two-twenty as far as his weight was concerned. He had a full head of blond hair, with light blue eyes. Dressed in a nice slacks, not a suit, but not too casual. The only piece of jewelry was a gold ring on his pinky.

My attention was diverted when the line moved again. Following the queue, I moved up one space, getting closer to the checkout—and to my mysterious observer.

Jackie strolled up the center aisle, looking at me questioningly. All I could do was roll my eyes towards our mystery reader.

I could tell when Jackie clued in on the problem. A slight bob of the head was the only sign that she could give me, but it was very reassuring to have backup.

I walked up to the counter to pay for my book, and tried to ignore the man standing only a few feet away.

"Have a great day," the cashier said gleefully. I turned to pocket my change, and noticed that the players were waiting for the cue.

Mystery man started to set the book back on the table. He was watching me through his lashes, while Jackie was standing to his right. The surprise came from the commander who had approached from the left.

"What the heck are you doing here?" he screamed at Jackie.

Jackie turned and stared at him. "You! You dirty old pervert! I've got a restraining order against you. You can't be here!" Grabbing a book off of the shelf, she hurled it in the direction of the commander, but there was nowhere near enough energy to get it there, so it hit Mr. Mystery on the side of the head.

"Oops," Jackie said raising her hand in apology when he turned towards her.

At that point, I could no longer make sense of the argument, but they had Mr. Mystery caught in the middle of their drama.

I could see store security moving in towards the ruckus, so I got out while the attention was on the melee.

Dashing out the doors, I was met almost literally at the door by Andy as he screeched the brakes to stop beside me. I must have been in shock, for it took me a few seconds before I could remember how to open the door.

"We've gotta go back!" I complained as Andy floored the car and headed towards the road.

"Nope."

Great! I thought to myself as we sped away. I've just abandoned my partner, we're leaving the scene of an incident and all I can get is one word out of him.

Andy kept his eyes focused and was weaving in and out of traffic as we sped along the road. I decided to keep my mouth shut about the driving and what was happening back at the bookstore—at least until we weren't doing ninety.

I heard the sirens blaring behind us, turned in my seat and cringed. Two police cruisers were gaining on us. "Oh, this is just great!" I snapped. Andy's eyes never veered from the road. "Andy, you'd better pull over. Things will go easier if you—"

The first cruiser went by us. The officer gave Andy a two-fingered salute before he pulled in front of us. The second car slid in behind us. As a three-car formation, we sped down the highway.

"Andy, why are we getting a police escort?"

"I'm not exactly sure. Right after you sent your S.O.S., your commander called my phone. Told me to be ready outside and get you out of there A.S.A.P. and to head to the Shoreline Expressway where two cars would take us to another secure location."

"Oh my gosh! Sam! What are they going to do about Sam?" I nearly screamed as the panic rose in my throat.

"I'm sure it will be taken care of, Monica. Try to take a few deep breaths."

The screaming of the sirens stopped, and the lead car veered off the highway. We followed him down a series of small, unmarked dirt lanes until we came to a small cabin. Once the officers had swept the cabin, they ushered us inside.

"Sorry about the confusion, Ma'am, the blond haired one said. We got a priority message from Commander Willoby stating that we were to escort you here."

"Where are we exactly?" I asked.

The dark haired officer spoke up, "Commander Willoby got permission for you to use this safe house for the night. It's the one that the F.B.I. keeps for their witnesses when there is a significant threat to their safety."

I nodded as I looked around the room. It was marginally better than the RV that Andy and I had been in for the past few days. The amenities were about on par with the RV, but it was the size of the place that gave it a leg up.

I turned back to the officers. "What about my dog? Or our other possessions that were in the RV?"

"Ma'am, Commander Willoby only gave us the orders to bring you here and get you clear of the situation at the store. It's my understanding the he will be joining you here shortly."

I didn't say anything, but crossed my arms and walked to the window and stared out at the landscape.

I didn't hear Andy come up behind me.

"It'll be okay, Monica." His arms came up around my waist.

Giving in to the sinking feeling that I was fighting, I leaned back into his broad chest. My hands covered his, and I tried to find some semblance of peace in the midst of the chaos.

My eyes slit opened when something cold and wet pressed into my cheek. Suddenly, my face was sopping wet and a low bark brought me back to reality.

I looked around, confused, as nothing seemed familiar.

Where was I?

My memory started to come back slowly. I was on the couch in the safe house.

A large dark shape moved in close, and again a large tongue covered my face.

I sat up, and was glad to see my 150-pound dog dancing joyfully.

"Sam!" I nearly squealed.

Sam responded with a hearty "Woof", as he dropped his chest to the floor while his butt stuck up in the air. His tail slashed back and forth with enough energy that papers were blown off the nearby table. He barked again.

"Go find your rope," I commanded. Sam bounded around the couch and headed for some unseen corner.

I peered up, and spied Andy sitting in an easy chair across the room, looking a little perplexed.

"He wants to play," I stated simply.

I must have looked dazed. Andy crossed over and sat next to me, and took my hand. "You had me a little concerned there."

"Why?"

"Well, one minute you were standing looking out the window, and the next you'd basically fallen asleep on your feet, leaning back into me. The two officers helped me get you onto the couch."

"How long was I out for?" I didn't like the idea of not being in control of myself to begin with. This made twice over the past few days that something had happened and I had no control over. Or any recollection of, for that matter.

"You slept for nearly two hours," Andy said while he played with my fingers.

"Two hours! How could I've slept for two hours?"

"I think that you've been pushing to the extreme for so long, that your body just decided that it needed a rest. Besides, you looked—"

The door slammed open, "Oh good! You're finally awake!" Jackie said as the commander followed her in.

"What's going on?" I asked. Sam returned and started knocking my leg with the knotted end of his favorite tug toy. Mindlessly, I grabbed the end and looked back to my partner and our commander.

"I was going to ask you, as you're the one who sounded the alarm," Commander Willoby said. "What happened that spooked you?"

"I'd noticed that guy walking in when you came in. Nothing really stood out, other than the way he was dressed. The first hint that something was off came after I picked up the drop and was over by the checkout." I paused, closed my eyes trying to bring the entire scene back into focus.

"I got that sense that I was being watched. Closely watched. When I turned to look around, I saw him standing by the discount books. At first glance, nothing was out of the ordinary. But then, I noticed that he was holding the book upside-down.

"His eyes never left me. I'm not sure what was the actual trigger. I guess I'm going to chalk it up to a heightened sixth-sense. Anyway, when I saw his stare, I knew he'd made me. I used the phone and sent everyone the S.O.S. hoping that a distraction would buy me the time I needed to get outside."

"Had you ever seen that guy before today?" the commander asked.

"No. The first time that I noticed him…wait," I said closing my eyes again. "I may have seen him before now that I think about it." I opened my eyes and looked at Andy. "And you may have too. The night we went to Donetello's."

The commander handed Andy a picture. "This was taken by the store's surveillance camera, so the quality isn't stellar."

"You think this guy was at Donetello's that night?" Andy asked. He looked at the picture again, and then his eyes brightened. "The guy by himself that sat in the opposite corner! I think you may be right, Monica!"

"I think he altered his appearance some how, which would explain why I didn't immediately recognize him."

Jackie looked over to me. "How could he alter his appearance? There hasn't been enough time for cosmetic surgery."

"I don't think he did anything permanent. He likely wore colored contacts to change the color of his eyes, and maybe a padded shirt to give the illusion that he was heavier than he really is. Subtle changes can hide you fairly well." I closed my eyes to concentrate. "Yeah, I'm pretty sure when Andy and I saw him before, he had brown eyes, and he definitely had blue today."

I looked over to Jackie and the commander. "What do we know about him?"

Jackie sighed, "Not much. When the security guys came, right after you left, they got between Commander Willoby and myself. While they were talking to us, he sort of snuck out. I saw him rush to the curb only a few seconds after Andy sped off with you.

"Almost immediately after that, he'd pulled out his phone and walked into the parking lot. I didn't see what kind of car he got into."

The commander spoke up, "I've got a few uniforms going over some footage from the store and the security tapes of the lot. We have a fair idea of the timing, but more than likely, we won't get much in the way of useful information."

I sat back on the couch. This guy had found us on more than one occasion. More concerning was that he had found us while we'd been off the radar.

"He has to be connected to someone high up. Someone who knew who we were, and who had access to how information was getting passed to us. He had to be watching you, Commander," I said.

"Thought of that as well. Just like I thought about the fact that whoever it is that is giving our friend his orders, wants you out of the picture."

The commander took a breath, exhaled it in a huff and then continued. "I'm getting more and more worried right now. They're escalating. At some point, they're going to determine that your demise is more important than keeping in the shadows. Get one guy, who is so committed to being 'made' that he doesn't even concern himself with the prospect of opening fire in a crowded area to take you out, and we're going to have a real mess on our hands."

Andy ran a hand over his face.

I looked closely at him for the first time in a few days. The time in hiding had been stressful to me, but I'm a cop so I deal with stuff like that. Andy's a nerd, a cute nerd, but nerd none the less. He's not a cop and he's not use to being under the gun.

"It's okay, Andy," I tried to reassure him. "We'll be there to protect you through all of this."

His head snapped towards me, his eyes full of fury.

"It's not me I'm worrying about, Monica! I'm worried about you. I'm falling in love with you, you nut!"

He got up and walked out of the room, leaving me sitting on the couch with my mouth gaping like a fish.

The safe house was relatively quiet at two-fifteen in the morning. Almost everyone else was asleep. I was awake because my mind wouldn't let me relax enough to.

I lay quietly on the bed in the dark room, listening to the chorus of snores that came from the others who had bunked here for the night, while my mind kept circling back to the discussion that we had had earlier this evening.

Andy had been so worked up, that he ended up going for a walk to calm himself. When he came back in, he didn't want to talk, and simply went to his room.

His profession of love had thrown me into a tailspin.

I wasn't ready for it, for one thing. My mind was too focused on what was going on with this case. I hadn't even let my mind take a look in that direction, let alone the leap that Andy had taken.

But, once he'd said that and stormed out, I closed up myself and thought.

I'd only known him a short time, but we'd already been through more intense situations than most couples would face in their lives. Did that affect the way that we felt for each other?

Honestly I didn't know. What I'd come to understand was he and I were going to need to talk about where we were going and how we'd get there.

I sighed. Apparently it was loud enough to wake Sam. He roused up, and carefully stepped onto the bed and curled his body so his big head rested on my lap.

I started running my fingers through his this fur, and he nuzzled into my hand more.

As we sat there, I tried to put away my personal feelings for Andy so I could concentrate on what was happening with this case.

When my attention made it around to focusing on the case I nearly jumped. "I never looked at the information that the commander brought," I said aloud.

Sam just opened his eyes, yawned and rolled over.

I crept out of bed and headed down the stairs.

Light spilled over from the kitchen into the hall.

I'd tried to be as quiet as I could, but one stair creaked. I froze in place.

A chair scraped followed by footsteps. "Hello?" a voice from the kitchen sounded.

"It's just me," I said solemnly. I crossed over from the hall into the kitchen door. "I forgot to look at the package that caused all of our troubles today. Figured I'd better do it in case there was anything important that would let us close this all tonight."

Matt had replaced the blond officer who'd escorted us in just before ten. Now he looked up. "Detective, it's pushing three. Why not sleep now, look in the morning? Nothing is going to get done until then anyway."

"I-I-I" I stammered, then sighed. "I can't sleep right now. Too many thoughts bouncing around and I don't know what to do about any of them." I leaned on the breakfast bar. "I guess I was hoping that I'd be able to do something about the one thing that I feel confident about my ability to handle."

Matt just smiled. "Pull up a chair. I'll put some water on for some chamomile tea. And," he looked at me with a sly grin, "I've heard a rumor that there is chocolate in the cupboard."

I could feel the muscles of my face tense as the smile developed. "Chocolate? Hmmm."

Matt, and his partner Charlie, turned out to be exactly what I'd needed. The information packet that the commander had delivered to me via the bookstore today had been placed in a time-locked safe, which couldn't be opened until the morning.

Feeling depressed, I popped a few squares of the giant Hershey bar that had been found. The constant banter between the two men had proved to be distracting, and they'd kept me involved with the conversation long enough for me to relax and feel ready to try sleeping.

Slowly, I made my way back up the stairs towards my room.

As I started down the hall, I noticed two things. Sam was sitting in the hall, looking intently at the door that was across from my room, and I could hear an unfamiliar noise.

"What's up, Sam?" I whispered to the big black dog. If it hadn't been for the moon light that was cascading in through the window, he would have been invisible.

His answer was that famous pose of all dogs. He tilted his head and cocked his ears while staring at the door.

"What's going on, boy? What do you hear, huh?"

I took two more steps and then stopped.

The sound that was coming out of the room wasn't in a language that I could understand. But the tenor of it was clear enough. Someone was audibly distraught about something.

Who and what? I wondered. Maybe the better question was why?

Well, whoever it was, was in the room right across from me. I hoped that they would be quiet enough for me to sleep through.

"Come on, Sam," I motioned to the door of my room. I followed Sam in, and then stopped with a disturbing realization.

Andy had taken the room across the hall.

CHAPTER 15

I'd hoped to fall asleep as soon as my head hit the pillow, but after hearing the mutterings coming from out of Andy's room, I lay there thinking for another thirty minutes. Apparently after that, I did end up sleeping fairly soundly. I didn't hear the chatter or the noise that came from the others setting up breakfast, nor did I hear the door click open when someone came in to call me.

I did however feel it when Sam jumped up to alert me that someone was at the door.

"Sam!" I choked as I pushed against his massive front paw, now positioned on my stomach.

He didn't budge, only barked again.

"Sam! Outside?" I tried again. This time he at least heard me, and gave me a big sloppy dog kiss before jumping off the bed and trotting over to whoever was at the door.

I rolled over and squinted towards the shape at the door.

Whoever it was had crouched down and was giving Sam a full body rub. I snagged my glasses from the table and looked again.

Andy was now sitting on the floor having his face cleaned by an energetic Sam.

"Andy, what are you doing here?"

He gallantly fought off Sam's advances and tried to get out of range of the big dog. "I came up to see if you were ready for breakfast. Your commander asked that I get you up."

I sighed. I knew that I needed to talk to him, but I wasn't quite ready yet. I'm sure that having only a few hours of sleep had something to do with how I felt.

"This is kind of weird, you know?" I managed. "I mean, we've been together in the RV, but we had separate rooms, and we didn't go into…" I motioned with my hands while trying to find the right words.

Andy laughed. "I know. It's a bit uncomfortable for me too. I see you sitting in bed, and I want to come over and sit with you, but chivalry demands that I let the beautiful maiden arise on her own."

I stared at him in disbelief. "Did you perhaps hit your head somewhere along the line, Andy? Yesterday you say that you're falling in love with me, and now you're coming up with lines like that. Maybe we should get you in to see a doctor or something?"

His smile reached his eyes, there was real humor there now. "No, it wasn't my head that got hit. It was my heart."

Oh boy, I thought. He continued before I could say anything.

"I think that you and I need to talk about a few things today, Monica. We've got to find a way to clear things up a bit between us." He took a deep breath and sighed. "I'm pretty sure that I screwed up my lines yesterday, but I was overwhelmed with emotions. This whole case has me on pins and needles, not because of what's happening to me, but because it's threatening you."

He stood there wringing his hands, and looking at the mass of fur ball that was now curled at his feet sleeping.

I went with impulse. I climbed out of bed and walked to him slowly. Without saying a word, I wrapped my arms around him and squeezed. "Let's plan to take a little time after breakfast and have that talk. We'll take Sam for a W-A-L-K," I spelled the word out. Andy raised his eyebrows in question. "If I say the word out loud, he'll be bouncing off of the walls until we are forced to take him now. I figure right after we eat, that way it will give us a chance for some time to work through things before we have to dive back into this mess."

"I can live with that," he said as his arms came around me pulling me in.

An hour later, Andy was walking on my right while Sam was on my left. I didn't know if I should bring up what I heard last night or not, so I kept quiet as we started around the cabin.

"Monica," Andy started, then paused. "I'm not really sure where to start this," he admitted.

"I Thought it was just me," I quipped.

"No, well, maybe I should say yes, it is you," he said looking at me slyly.

"Oh? So this lack of communications is my fault?" I snapped.

He stopped dead in his tracks. Surprise shone on his face. "No. I'm not trying to, oh blast, I'm really screwing this up."

I stopped and turned to face him. Sam sat at my side, looking at us with his head tilted and ears perked, almost as if to say, this should be interesting.

Andy took a long deep breath, and then almost stared into my eyes. "Monica, what I was trying to do was lighten the mood with a little humor. And like so much else, I've bolloxed it up."

"Andy, you haven't—"

"Shh. The way I feel about you makes me nervous. To the point that I can't think straight." He looked away momentarily, scanning across the small pond. "I know that I hurt you when I left you to go to grad school. I thought that it was inevitable. The idea of keeping up a long distance relationship while plowing through grad school didn't seem plausible, so I made up an excuse and left.

"Over the past few years, I've done well in my chosen field, but I always had this nagging feeling that something was missing. I could never put my finger on it, but I lived with the ever-present knowledge that there was a hole in me.

"When I decided that I needed to get out of the big city last year, I didn't even consider heading out to the southwest. Right now with most of the continent between us, my mom doesn't harp on my not being married, and we can all have a relatively normal life. When the opportunity presented itself to take over the Bedford Labs, I jumped at it. Never guessing that you'd be here.

"I guess what I'm trying to say is you have touched me in a way that no one else ever has. The boy I was years ago missed that. The man I've become misses that, or I should say missed it. That was until I saw you a week ago. Seeing you? Well, for the first time in a too many years, I felt whole again. I know that it's only been a few days since we reconnected, but I've never felt like this before with anyone else. Ever.

"And it only makes it harder to swallow, when I realize that people are trying to hurt you. It makes me want to protect you, and shield you. I," he fumbled for the words again. "I wish there was a way that I could whisk you away from all of this and keep you out of harms way and let the cops do their thing."

I reached out and took his hands.

"Andy, it's very kind, and touching that you want to do that for me. Honestly, no one has ever done that for me before. But you have to remember, that I am the cops. This case was on my desk before I met you.

"But, I too must confess I have deep feelings for you right now. To the point that they scare me more than a little. I thought that when we ended things, that my life was about over. It took months of walking around like a zombie before I felt that I was able to function normally again. It was shortly after that that I joined the academy. Personally, I think this timing plain stinks. If we'd met up again at any other point in time, I wouldn't hesitate to follow up on my feelings. However, with these unsolved murders, and the two of us in the middle, I'm not sure that this is the right time to follow emotions."

He nodded his head. "I mentioned that to my aunt last night, well, early this morning."

I looked at him. "You were talking with your aunt this morning?" I searched my memory and had a vague recollection. "Isn't her husband stationed over in Germany, or something?"

"He was. Aunt Marge and Uncle Bill spent quite a bit of time over in Europe. He was in Germany, Turkey, England and a few others." He bit his bottom lip, as if he was debating the best way to say something.

"Wouldn't your uncle have been out of the service by now?" I asked doing the math quickly in my head.

"Yeah. He died a few years ago."

I reached out and took his hand. "I'm sorry, Andy. I didn't know."

He kissed my hand and continued. "Anyway, I talked with Aunt Marge around three this morning on Skype. She lives over in Spain, so when I couldn't sleep, I tried her line. She was awake and had some time."

So, I thought, that explained the voices when I came back to bed. But why had he sounded so distraught?

Before I could ask, he ran his finger along my cheekbone and explained further.

"Monica, you need to understand, I've never felt like this before. And all of my emotions are so much stronger because of the whole blasted mess." He rubbed his hand on my arm, and looked like he was searching for something.

Finally, he spoke again. "When I couldn't sleep, I called my Aunt. She'd lived in Spain while my uncle was stationed there with the Air Force. When he was killed in a crash, she came home for a while, but discovered that she really liked it better over there. So now she works with an organization that assists battered women and children, and is quite content.

"Marge has a way of listening to someone's problems and finding the right words to say. Last night, she was listening to me. She listened while I explained the dilemma that I'm in right now. Not the part where some group of sadists are trying to whack me, but the part of me that has fallen helplessly in love with a woman who has steel for a backbone, and the tenacity of a mule when she sets her mind on something. But she has a heart that is soft and fragile, and eyes that light up when you say something unexpected. I needed to find out how to tell you that. And, I suppose, how to deal with the fear that I'm facing knowing that you're going to be going after those sadists."

When he finished speaking, he slowly leaned down and let his lips touch mine.

Heat sprang up from my body anywhere that his skin touched mine. I felt hotter than the morning sun, passion blooming in my heart. My mind was too caught up in the feeling to even try to think rationally.

"Monica?" a female voice called.

"What was that?" I whispered to Andy.

His eyes were glazed over, not ready to have this session called. "I'd like to pretend that I didn't hear anything."

The sound of someone tripping echoed out from around the bend. "From the crash, I don't think that we're going to be alone for much longer," I moaned.

Sam stood, facing the direction the noise came form and let out a deep "woof."

Andy sighed. "I think you're right," he said before he lightly kissed my forehead, took my hand and led me back towards the house, and whoever was thrashing around in the brush.

"There you are," Jackie said picking herself up off of the ground.

"What happened to you?" I asked.

"The commander sent me out here to find you two, and I didn't watch where I was going. Got caught up in the scenery, and tripped over something." She eyed me carefully, probably noticing my smirk. "Don't laugh at me. It could happen to anyone," she retorted.

"I didn't say a word," Andy chimed in, and extended a hand to help her up.

"So, the commander wants to see us, huh? Wonder what's up?" I mused.

Jackie looked at me as if I'd just stepped off of a flying saucer. "You're kidding right? That information that we all risked our necks over yesterday? Well it ties into the excitement that we had at the bookstore as well. My guess is that he'd like us to get back to work on solving that pesky little murder that dropped in our laps a few days ago."

She inhaled sharply, closed her eyes and slowly exhaled. "Besides, I overheard him say something about the F.B.I. coming in for a talk today, so you need to get your ducks in a row."

I nodded. Taking the walk with Andy had been necessary to clear things up between us. But the reality was, right now I was supposed to be on the clock, not handling personal matters.

"Let's get you in," Andy stated as he tugged on my hand again. When I glanced over, he shrugged, "I'm the reason that you're not in there working right now. Let me go apologize to the commander, and see what I can do to help make it up."

As we entered the house, I noticed that the guards that I'd talked to last night were no longer there, but had been replaced by a couple that reminded me of Laurel and Hardy.

Commander Willoby sat at the small table sipping a cup of coffee. "There you are," he said looking up when we walked in. "I was wondering if you two had decided to run away."

"Sorry, Sir," I mumbled, standing with my back as straight as I could make it.

Jackie came through the other door carrying a laptop computer. "Here's the file you asked for, Commander."

She looked around the small kitchen briefly. "Um, maybe I should—"

"Sit down," the commander said pointing to a chair. He looked to Andy and me, "You two as well."

Andy rubbed his hand on my back as I settled into a chair.

"We've had a bit of excitement in the past twenty-four hours," Commander Willoby began. "The culmination was our endeavor at the bookstore. As you all know, we have video tapes that show our suspect, but that's not the first time that we've seen him."

I nodded. "Yes, Sir. Andy and I saw him one night shortly after the shootings. We were at Donetello's."

"Actually, Dietz, it goes back even further than that." He opened a manila envelope and withdrew a picture. "This is from one of the cameras that was operating from across the street on the day of the shooting at Cathy's Collectibles. Notice anyone?"

I stared at the photo, and then looked unbelieving to the other faces around the room. "This one," I said pointing to the dark haired man, "is our friend from last night, and this is the one that Sam took care of during the break-in at my house."

"Monica! What are you going to do?" Jackie blurted out.

"What do you mean, what am I going to do? I'm going to track this bum and nail his hide to a door."

"All in due time, detective. Now to sweeten this pot, I got word from the F.B.I. just a little while ago. It seems that they have identified our mutual friend as one Alexander J. Browning."

"Do they have any information on this Browning?" Andy asked.

"They were gathering what they have, and will be briefing us here in about an hour. Since we have the time, I thought it might be a good time for us to come up with a game plan of our own, so we can ask the right questions and give ourselves the best opportunity to make progress here."

"Sir?" I asked timidly. "If this Browning character is the one responsible for things, do you think that the Feds are going to try to take the case away from us?"

Willoby looked at me over the rim of his cup. "That, detective, is yet to be seen. I think the answer to that is going to depend on what they have on him, and how well we play our parts."

Andy looked around the table, "Then let's get started. This guy's given me enough sleepless nights. I want to be in on the team that takes him out."

The commander thought for a moment, and shook his head. "Son, you became a member of this team the moment that they tried to take you and Monica out.

"Now, why don't we go through the info one more time and see if we can put together a time line that we can give to the Feds?"

"Well I'll be. Did you turn in your lab coat, Andy?"

Everyone turned to look to the source. The three federal agents that we had met with at the beginning of this case now stood staggered in the doorway.

Andy stood, extended his hand, "Howya doing, Tom?" he asked as he pulled his old friend in for a one arm hug.

Pleasantries were briefly exchanged, before we got down to business.

Director Shuman began. "When Commander Willoby contacted me and explained what had happened over the past seventy-two hours, I was dumbfounded. This group, and yes, we are fairly sure that this is a group, is escalating. At least, we can share the background on your suspect. Hector?"

Agent Immentz opened up his brief case and extracted several envelopes. Opening the first, he laid a picture of Browning on the table. "This is your suspect, identified as Alexander James Browning. He's used the aliases of A.J. Brown, Alex James and Jimmy Brown that we're sure of over the past three years. Our sources indicate that he is making a move to take over part of the Irish syndicate in the greater Boston area.

"To the best of our knowledge, Browning is unmarried and not in any kind of permanent, or even serious, relationship. His parents died in a boating accident five years ago, and his only remaining family is his brother, Stephen Ralph Browning."

Another file was opened, this one showed the photo from a Massachusetts driver's license. "As far as we can tell, Stephen Browning has no criminal record, is self employed as a freelance computer programmer and lives within his means."

"A computer programmer?" Andy asked and looked to me with a raised eyebrow.

Agent Weine leaned in, "What did I miss, Andy?"

"You haven't really missed anything, Tom. It's just that somebody had to program the chips in the smart coat. If Alexander is involved with the manufacturing of the coat, perhaps he tapped his brother for the programming skills."

"Have you made any progress on the kidnapping?" Jackie asked.

"Not much. Now that we have an ID on Alex Browning, we're going to focus on finding him," Director Shuman said. "It's been weird, though. Normally if someone is kidnapped, there is a ransom that is demanded. So far, there's been no contact at all."

We went over the data that we'd collected as well. When we were done, the only thing that we were sure of was that we needed to find Alex and Stephen Browning, and do it fast.

"Commander, Director," I said acknowledging both men, "I think that it's time that Jackie and I got back on the street. Us sitting here isn't being terribly productive."

A heated discussion ensued, but in the end it was decided that Andy would join Jackie and I and we could get back to work. It was probably the best chance of drawing the Brownings out.

To ensure our safety, the FBI would have people tailing us to act as security for us. I didn't really like the idea of the tail, but it sure beat sitting here twiddling my thumbs while I waited for information.

By the time the FBI agents left, I was starving. Commander Willoby had requested food to be brought in, but it hadn't yet arrived, so I was poking through the cupboards in hopes of finding something to tide me over.

"What did you think of their presentation about Browning?" Jackie asked.

I hadn't heard her come in, so I spun around with a guilty look on my face. "Oh, I don't know. We seemed to have almost all of the same information once we had his name. Nobody seems to know who he's working for, and it seems to me, that that is the important link right now."

Jackie nodded, "Yeah. If we had some idea of who employed him, we'd have a place to start looking."

"I think we already do. We start by following up on the brother."

CHAPTER 16

"Hmm, that's interesting I said." We were all sitting around the table working on laptops that the commander had procured for us.

"What's that?" Jackie asked.

"I'm looking at Stephen Browning's financials. Most of his income appears to come in either at the beginning or the middle of the month, and it's coming in from several sources. None of them look too big; in fact I'd estimate that he's making less than a hundred-K a year. Every three months, he gets a bigger payday, but again going back over the past year, that has been pretty consistent."

"Might be royalties," Andy said.

I hadn't noticed that he'd been paying attention to our conversation, and assumed that he'd been absorbed in going over the details of his reports.

"Pardon?"

"Didn't you say he was a freelance computer programmer? Freelancer's get paid in two main ways. They either get a flat fee for the contracted work, or they get royalties if they develop something and then license it to another company. It's entirely possible that he's developed some program that a specific industry uses and then he licenses them to use it for a monthly fee."

I looked back to my computer screen. "It's certainly plausible. From what I can see here his income and expenses have been fairly stable over these last two years. However, it looks like he started making some credit card purchases about six months ago. That was a big change in his pattern. In fact, those are the only uses of credit cards I'm finding."

"What were they for?" Jackie asked.

I scrolled through the data once more. "I've got weekly purchases at Simon's, there's several restaurants on the list. Even has a motel room last month."

"Maybe he's got a girl?" Jackie noted.

I opened the file that the FBI had left. "There's nothing in here about him being in any kind of relationship."

Andy looked perplexed. "When do they start doing research on a person?"

"How do you mean?" Jackie asked.

"Well, I'm wondering what causes the feds to create a dossier on someone? I'm fairly sure that they don't have the time, money or manpower to keep tabs on everyone, so there must be a key that gets triggered before they start to put the package together."

"I see where you're going, Doc," I said. "From what we've gathered, brother Alex is involved with some dastardly deeds, and has been for the past ten years. The feds, do a quick search on brother Stephen, just to be sure that little brother isn't following in the step of big brother. When Stephen comes out clean, they basically leave the file. Perhaps do a cursory check every so many months or years just to keep it close to up-to-date."

Jackie nodded, "Yeah, that would fit right in." She shuffled some papers that she'd been working on. "From what I've got here, they did a quick check within the last week, but the last notation prior to that in Stephen's file was from almost a year ago. If he started dating someone, they didn't catch it."

"Looks like our first job tomorrow is to go visit Stephen."

Stephen Browning lived in a small condominium complex in Osterville. I pulled up in front of 312-B, and parked on the street.

"I see our friends found a parking place," Jackie noted with a nod of her chin.

Andy and I looked down the street to where a beige Chevy sedan had pulled to the curb four houses down.

"Nothing against the law enforcement profession," Andy said. "But don't you think it would be wise to come up with a surveillance vehicle that didn't look like an unmarked police cruiser? It is so obvious to anyone who looks out, that the cops are right there."

I sighed, "You're right, Doc. They do stand out, don't they?"

With shake of my head, I led the group to the door and knocked loudly.

No answer.

I knocked again, louder.

The door on the next unit opened up. An elderly woman dressed in polyester slacks and a sweater appeared. She leaned on an elaborate wooden cane, "He's not there."

Turning to the woman, I pulled out my badge. "Hi, Ma'am. I'm Detective Deitz, this is my partner, Detective Jackie Gannon. We're with the Blackberry Creek PD. And this is Dr. Andrew Carson with the crime lab. Could we ask you a few questions about your neighbor?"

She looked shocked that the police were at the door. "Well, I guess that I could answer a few questions. I'm Ethel Houseman. Why don't you all come on in and I'll have Sissy get some ice tea for us."

"Thank you, Ms. Houseman," Jackie responded.

We followed her into the house and sat.

"It just don't seem right that Steve would be in trouble. He's always been such a nice man," she said as she led us into a very tidy sitting room.

A young blonde woman appeared in the door between the sitting room and the kitchen.

"My great-granddaughter, Sissy. Sissy, these are the police. They've got some questions about Steve. Would you bring in the pitcher of tea please?"

She left without a word while we sat on the plastic covered furniture.

"How long have you known Mr. Browning. Ms. Houseman?" I started.

"Oh, let me think. He bought the place next door about six years ago, I guess it is now. He seems so nice. You know, normal. I can't imagine him being in trouble. What'd he do?"

"Right now, we don't know that he's done anything. His name came up in a search for a person of interest, and we were hoping to speak with Mr. Browning to see if he knew where this person might be."

"Oh. Well, I haven't seen Steve around in the last week or so. It's kind a of strange, now that I think about it. Usually, we'd see each other at least once a day, and he's always told me before when he was going out of town." She paused, pressed a finger to her lip, "I just realized he never told me that he was going, or when he'd be back."

"Ms. Houseman, did Mr. Browning keep regular hours?" Jackie asked.

"You mean did he go to work and come home at a regular times? No. Not that I could ever see. Steve was a smart boy with those computers. He'd set himself up so he worked from home.

"The condo management doesn't allow people to run businesses from here, but they allow workers to, what's that term?" she paused, stared at the ceiling. "Oh yes, telekinesis, or something like that."

"You mean tele-commute?" I asked.

"Yep. That's what it is! I'm too old to remember all of these fancy new technologies."

Sissy came back in carrying a tray full of glasses, ice and a pitcher of tea. After she poured glasses for everyone, she took a seat in a large wing-back chair.

"Ms. Houseman, when did you last see Mr. Browning?"

"I'm not really sure. It was sometime last week, but I don't remember the day. Is that going to get Steve in trouble?"

I nodded, "No, your not remembering is okay. We're just trying to set up a time line."

I turned at the gasp. Sissy was leaned back in her chair, but her eyes were wide.

"Are you alright, honey?" Ms. Houseman asked her great-granddaughter.

The response came back a weak "Yeah."

Had we just found the woman in Stephen Browning's life? I decided to shift my focus for a moment.

"Sissy," I asked, "when was the last time that you saw Mr. Browning?"

She sat erect in her chair. "The last time I remember seeing him was the morning of the fifth. I didn't talk to him, we just waved he was getting in his car."

"Do you remember what time it was?"

"It would have been around ten-thirty or so. I'd just brought Granny back from her doctor's appointment. I got Granny in and I'd run back out to the car to get a bag of groceries I'd set in the trunk."

"Do you remember if he was carrying anything?"

She thought for a minute. "Nope. He just waved to me as he was getting into his car."

"Sissy, there really is no subtle way for me to ask this, but were you involved with Mr. Browning in any way?"

"You mean like dating him?" she gasped in disbelief. "He's probably fifteen years older than me. We'd talk once in a while, but we didn't really have anything in common."

"I don't think he dated much," Ms. Houseman said. "He didn't go out of the house very often."

"I think he may have been seeing someone," Sissy offered quietly. When we all looked to her, she shrugged. "The last time I actually talked to him was probably two weeks ago. I'm taking a couple of classes at Bedford Community College. I was just coming in from my late class when I saw him. He was headed out and was spiffed up, ya know? I made some comment on how nice he looked, and he blushed a bit. It was kinda cute. Anyway, he said he was taking someone very special to dinner.

"I didn't think anything of it at the time. Just hoped that they had a great evening."

We talked for a few more minutes, but it was quickly evident that they didn't have anything else that was going to help our investigation along.

We stood, "Thank you both for your time today." I fished one of my cards out of my pocket and handed it Ms. Houseman. "If you think of anything else that might help, please call me at this number here."

Back at the car, Andy turned and mumbled, "If he didn't have anything with him doesn't that indicate that he wasn't trying to run?"

"Hold on, Doc," I managed. "Just because the neighbor didn't see him loading up bags doesn't mean that he didn't already have them in the car. We don't know what happened. He may be running or he may have fallen into bad things. Either way, I think we need to take another step."

Jackie looked up from the laptop, "According to the data that we were just sent by our pals behind us, Stephen Browning owns a three year old blue Toyota Rav-4. I've already put a BOLO out on it. You want me to call in about getting a warrant to search the property?"

"We need to know what's going on."

It took less than an hour for the ADA to arrive, warrant in hand. The condo's manager was there as well to unlock the door.

"You're staying out here," I said turning to Andy. "We'll clear the area and secure it. Once that's done, I'll bring you in."

He didn't look happy about the prospect of not going through the door with us, but he nodded.

Jackie and I walked to the front door, while our "babysitters" went to the back. I guess this was one good point of having the feds tail us— instant back up.

Rapping on the door again I called out, "Mr. Browning, this BCPD. We have a warrant to search your premises."

As I expected, there was no response. I keyed the mic on my radio, "We're going in." I nodded to the manager who unlocked the door and stepped out of the way.

Holding my gun in my right hand, flashlight in my left I pushed the door open with my shoulder and went in.

The beam of light illuminated a living space that in shape and size mirrored Mrs. Houseman's. Living room right off of the entryway with a low set of bookshelves that separated it from the open kitchen and dining area. A single hallway led towards the back of the unit.

As my light scanned the overturned furniture and broken electronics I carefully made my way to the hall. The chaos that was evident in the front of the condo continued down the hall.

"Be careful, Gannon," I said quietly as I turned side to side.

"What happened?" she whispered.

"Dunno. Living room is clear."

Jackie headed towards the dining area. "We've got books scattered all over the place," she commented using her light to point to the mess on the floor. "Somebody was looking for something, and they didn't care if they trashed the place."

I made my way to the single doorway and entered the kitchen. The carnage continued here as well. I shone my light into the first doorway on the left, and noted that the utility room had been rifled through. The next door was the bathroom where it appeared that the medicine cabinet had been emptied onto the floor.

To my right, Jackie was stepping over broken plates and glasses as she made her way through the kitchen. "Wonder what they were looking for?"

"Who says they were looking? Maybe they just wanted to make a mess to get everyone to think that they'd taken something," I countered.

"You think so?" she asked.

I shook my head and smiled wryly. "That's the thing with this job, Gannon. You never know what happened until you've solved the case."

I continued back into the last room on the left. In the original plan, this would have been the second bedroom. But it seemed that Stephen

Browning had converted it into a work space. A large 3-sided wrap around desk sat in the corner. The hutch section had probably been filled with the numerous books on programing that were now strewn across the floor. A smashed iMac sat on the shorter work desk, its screen spider-webbed. Papers littered the last work area.

I heard Jackie's voice through my ear-bud, "All clear here."

I keyed my mic again, "This is Dietz, unit is clear. No sign of Browning. Send in the crime scene unit."

Jackie and I were poking around the office area when Andy came in. "Looks like they had a grand old time here," he said, eyes wide looking at the carnage.

"Let's just say that they weren't very orderly. However, I would guess that they were looking for something very particular."

Jackie stopped sifting through the books on the floor and looked over. "Why do you think that?"

I held out the box that I'd just picked up. "There has to be close to three grand in here. All in cash."

"That's interesting. They ransack the place, trying to make it look like a robbery, but leave the valuables? That doesn't make a lot of sense to me," Andy lamented.

I shook the box lightly while I tried to organize my thoughts. "Maybe they were after something more valuable than money," I offered. "What haven't we found here?"

"Jimmy Hoffa?" Jackie sassed.

"Wrong guy, right track. We haven't found Browning."

"Wait," Andy commanded. "You think that all of this is from them chasing after one guy, Monica?"

"I don't know. It's possible that he put up a huge fight and this is the result. It's just as likely that someone wanted to throw us off the trail, grabbed him and then messed the place up to keep us mired here. Your guys are going to be crucial in making that determination, Doc."

"Great. We've already loaded up five boxes worth of evidence, and I'm not going to be in the lab to work with it. It's kind of depressing knowing that you all are depending on us so much, and I'm not really a part of it."

I walked over to him, rubbed his arm. "Andy, you are a part of this. A big part. You may be right about not being able to be in the lab, but your input and insight can be a huge asset to our investigation right now.

"It's not often that we get to have a lab guy on scene. You may see something that you recognize as being important immediately that would take us a couple of days to have found the relationship."

He looked at me, "You want to run that by me again? Perhaps this time as a coherent thought."

Jackie piped up, as she walked over. "I know what Monica means. I remember a few detectives talking about a case last year. They spent two days sifting through the remnants of a burned house looking for how the fire started. One of the crime lab guys happened to come to the station to pick up some evidence for a different case, and was talking to one of the investigators. He saw the photos sitting on the guy's desk and casually remarked something like 'oh gee I haven't seen one of those in years'. Because of his experience, he recognized the source just from the photos.

"That's what Monica is saying about you in this investigation. Your expertise may speed things up considerably."

He looked lighter when she finished. "I think I'll go back out and do a thorough walk through."

I watched him walk back down the hall. "Nice job, Jackie."

"Thanks. I didn't want to tell him that the odds are it won't happen like that, but you never know."

"That you don't. Besides, now that he's thinking about it, he'll be looking for it and he may find something."

I went back to the search. I grabbed a pile of papers from the desk and began fanning through them when something fell and cracked at my foot.

"Blasted all," I muttered. "I thought this was all paper." Bending down to see what I'd inadvertently broken, I found a picture frame.

Turning the frame over, the face of Stephen Browning smiled back at me. He was at the beach with his arm draped over the shoulder of a woman. Her face was currently obscured by the cracks that now spread over the glass.

I pulled the picture out of the frame. A willowy blonde smiled towards the camera, her right arm wrapped tightly around the Stephen's waist.

"Jackie! I know who he was seeing."

"You do? Did you find a love letter or something?"

"We'll call it something," I said passing the picture over to her.

She looked at it, then back to me. "I don't recognize her. Is she one of your friends?"

I shook my head. "No. It's Catherine Evans. The missing woman from Cathy's Collectibles."

CHAPTER 17

"You're sure? You mean that Alex Browning kidnapped the woman his brother was dating?" Jackie asked.

I held the picture out to her. "That's her, no question."

She wasn't convinced. "Monica, I know that it looks like her. But she looks different here than she did in her driver's license shot. You've never actually seen her have you?"

"No, Jackie, but do you remember me saying that I had some kind of innate talent, a really good memory? It's not quite eidetic, but I see something, and it remains with me for a long, long time. I'm sure this is her."

We both turned at the knock from the door. Andy was there with a puzzled look on his face.

"I think I'm missing something here," he said.

"We've got proof that Stephen was dating the woman who was kidnapped," I relayed

"That really makes things interesting, doesn't it?" He paused, seeming to be trying to organize the data in his head. "Why would Alex kidnap his brother's girlfriend?"

"He needs the leverage," Jackie said flatly. "He wants the brother to do something, Stephen is refusing, so he needs something that will get Stephen to do what he wants."

"I think you may be right, Jackie. Let's see if we can figure out what Stephen was working on last."

"I'll leave you two to that," Andy quipped. "I came back to tell you that we've managed to find some trace of the woman here. I was thinking that we'd need to run what we could for DNA, but it seems that you've already identified her."

Jackie jumped in first, "Monica may have identified her from the picture, but, I think we're going to need that positive ID from your lab."

Andy nodded. "I'll put a rush on it. In fact, I think I'm going to get one of the agents to ride with me, and I'll go back and run it myself."

He crossed to where I was standing. "Take care of yourself, okay? I'll meet you back at the house tonight." He leaned down and kissed my forehead.

I watched him walk out while I was simply frozen in place. Two other officers looked on with raised eyebrows.

Jackie tugged on my arm. "Monica? You okay?"

"Yeah," I huffed out. "I feel like I'm running behind in this relationship thing between him and me. I've never had to worry about public displays of affection at a scene before. With him, now I'm off balance, and I don't think I like it. The off balance thing."

I sighed, "Okay, let's get to work."

"What's next?"

"Right at this moment, I see that we have two pressing questions that we need answers to. What was Stephen Browning working on last? Did he leave here under his own free will, or was he removed from here?"

"Wouldn't the state of the living area, with everything strewn, indicate that he was forcibly removed?" Jackie queried.

"Not necessarily. If Stephen left on his own, let's say he had a warning that something was going to happen and he split before it did, and somebody came for him later and couldn't get what they wanted? It's possible that they made the mess in their search.

"What we're going to need to do is look at all of the pieces. It'll be like doing a big jigsaw puzzle."

"I hate jigsaws," Jackie lamented.

I simply shrugged my shoulders, thinking to myself that if you didn't like puzzles, being a detective was definitely the wrong occupation. "Why don't we try to get the answer to the first question now, and give the CSI team a little more time out in the rest of the house?"

"Okay. Where do you want me to start?"

I looked over at the computer. "Why don't you start there? I'll go into the bedroom, maybe we can find a journal or something."

Jackie nodded and went to the computer table. I stood there for a brief moment and took a final look around the room before I headed for the master bedroom.

I stood just inside the door and slowly turned in almost a complete circle.

A writing desk sat against the shared bedroom wall next to the open louvered doors for the walk-in-closet. Most of the back wall was glass providing a nice view of the little pond that had been landscaped into the condo park. I could see that a small, but private, patio was accessible through the large glass doors that were centered on the wall. Against the wall that separated Browning's condo from Ms. Houseman's, was the headboard of the king-sized bed. On the wall to my right, I noticed another doorway, presumably to the master bath.

Clothing was strewn across every surface in the bedroom.

"Were you in a hurry to pack, Steve, or was somebody pawing through everything?" I quietly asked the empty space.

I started in the bath, checking the medicine cabinet and the drawers. When my flashlight swept across the little zippered bag on the shelf I thought that I had the answer to question number two.

"You in here, Monica?" Jackie called from the main room.

I stepped to the door, holding the black bag. "What does this tell you?"

Jackie looked at it, baffled. "I'm…not really sure," she admitted.

"Let's try this. If you were going on a trip, what's the first thing that you're going to pack besides your wardrobe?"

She stared at me and her eyes lit up. "It's his toiletries!"

I nodded. "Looks like he ended up leaving his shaving kit, toothbrush and a whole bunch of other personal odds and ends behind."

Jackie looked around the room. "He must have put up one heck of a fight, if they made this much of a mess getting him out of here."

"I don't think they'd have made this mess when they took him. There would have been too much noise.

"When we just knocked on the door, Houseman came to investigate. If there'd been a struggle, she'd have heard it."

Jackie absorbed this. "Yeah that makes sense. So, you're thinking that he left on his own? Why would he leave his kit?"

I shook my head. "I think we have two separate incidences. My guess is that Stephen was drugged and then removed. His place was torn apart later."

"How are we going to prove that?"

"We'll have to look at that rest of house carefully." I scanned the view out the back again. "Did you find anything?"

Jackie pulled out a notebook, "It seems he's been working on a project for the past few months. We were able to get a list of the files that he's been accessing, and if I'm guessing right, he's making a game of some sort."

"A game? Why do you think that?"

"Well, he's got folders that were labeled worlds, characters, vehicles, prizes. Sounds like a game of some sort. I was thinking that we could have the lab guys take it in and get their take on it. They'd probably have an idea on what language it was in at least."

I nodded, "That makes sense. Let's get them on it now, and then we can finish going over this room."

Jackie headed back to the office, and I went back to the bath.

I paused, "Hey, Jackie" I called out after her. When her head reappeared in the doorway, I continued. "After you get them going on the computer, why don't you check the kitchen?"

"What am I looking for?"

"Glasses that were left on the counter or in the dishwasher, for that matter. See if there are any water bottles. Something that would confirm if Stephen had been drugged."

"Okay," she acknowledged before leaving again.

I went back to searching the master bedroom. My attention kept going to the writing desk. "Okay, Steve," I asked the empty room, "why do you have the desk here if you've got your office next door?"

Taking a seat, I began sorting through the neatly stacked piles, I found bills for his credit cards and the payment book for his car. The drawers held nothing of major interest aside from his address book and some writing paper. I started flipping through the address book, hoping that perhaps he'd have a different address than what had turned up for his brother.

"Blast it all," I muttered. The entry here was the same as what had turned up in the official records.

Pushing back from the desk, the roller of the chair got stuck in something. As I tried to move, I heard the faint sound of wood knocking.

"Why would you keep your writing desk so the chair would continually get stuck?" I wondered. Standing, I went to move the chair when a thought occurred.

I pushed the chair out of the small dip in the floor, removed the plastic protective covering then pulled out my flashlight and crouched down.

There, hidden in the cut pile a small line was barely visible. I pushed a fingernail underneath and gave a little tug. The sound of Velcro being pulled apart filled the room.

"Whatcha got there?" Jackie asked.

I turned to see her standing in the doorway. "Not sure. I was searching the desk and the chair stuck. It didn't make sense why he'd leave the chair there if it was constantly sinking down. When I looked, I found that part of the rug had been cut through. Haven't gotten any farther than that."

Jackie walked in and peered over my shoulder. "The floor looks to be made of tongue and groove boards, probably pine."

"Yeah," I said. "But look here. It looks like that board's had the tongue cut off. And see how it's been cut into a new length?" I pointed to the two crooked end cuts.

"It was cut in place," Jackie added pointing to where the saw had chewed into the adjoining board a little.

"Makes me wonder what Stephen was hiding in here."

I pulled out my Swiss army knife, and carefully pried up the edge of the questionable board. "Would you look at that?"

"It just looks like a plain wooden box," Jackie noted.

Pulling the box free, I tried to lift the lid. The top moved slightly but a metallic clink sounded after only an eighth inch of movement. "Must be something important. He's got the thing locked."

I turned the box around so the lock was facing me. "Guess we'll have to hope that we can find a key or else we'll have to wait until we're back at the station and get a locksmith over to do it."

"Lemme see it," Jackie sighed.

She took the box, studied the lock and grabbed a few paper clips from the desk.

"Jackie, what do you think—"

There was an audible click and she smiled and lifted the lid. "There you go."

I stared at my partner in disbelief. "Okay. First let me say thanks for getting it opened, but I'm going to have some serious questions about where you learned that particular skill."

Her face blushed. "No problem getting it opened for you. The, ah, skills in question came from a past part of my life. Part that I'd like to leave behind me, but it keeps catching up with me."

She looked up now. It wasn't embarrassment that I saw in her eyes. It was fear.

"Jackie, what's going on? Is it something that I need to be aware of?"

Her shoulders shrugged. "The fact of it is, Monica, that if our paths had crossed ten years ago, we'd have been on opposite sides." She paused, "This isn't the time or place right now, but as my partner, I think you need to know. So tonight, after shift why don't we go out and I'll fill you in. Okay?"

I nodded, my mind going a million miles an hour. It took everything that I had to put this aside and look at the box's contents.

"Anything of significance in there?" Jackie asked.

Her voice was even, but I could see how much effort she was putting into making it that way.

"All there is a small notebook and some micro cassettes."

I flipped through the book. Most of the pages were covered in a series of numbers with the occasional letter thrown in. "I'm taking a real stab in the dark, but I'm guessing that it's pretty important, but I've got no idea what it is or what it means."

I passed the book over to her. She looked at the notations, then back to me. "I think you need to get Andy on this pretty quick."

I called Andy as we headed out the front door. Our FBI baby-sitters were standing guard and looked confused as we exited the house with our few bags of evidence.

When the nearest one raised an eyebrow, I commented "We're taking these to Dr. Andrew Carson at the crime lab."

He didn't say anything. He just nodded, and with a quick hand motion to his partner, they headed back to their car.

As we pulled away from the curb, I glanced in the mirror. Our two friends were right where they were supposed to be.

Everything was normal, or as normal as they can be when a group of crazies is trying to kill you. That was until I looked over at Jackie.

She sat with her head turned slightly staring out the window, lost in her own thoughts with tears running down her face.

"Is there anything I can do to help?" I queried.

She shrugged as she wiped the tears with the back of her hand.

"I'm willing to listen. Anytime you want to talk through whatever it is."

She turned to look back out the window, and sighed. "I was going to tell you later, but just the anxiety of waiting is crushing me right now." She took a steadying breath and launched into her story. "Everyone of us has a past, but for some of us, that past isn't a pretty picture. For that matter, mine is downright ugly, Monica."

"The world is seldom what it seems. Each of us colors our memories with our own experiences. Two people doing the same thing will have different experiences because of that."

Jackie let out a little laugh. "Ain't that the truth? I guess you could say that my" she paused, looking for the right word. "I guess you'd call it my dilemma, is directly related to what you just said. But," she warned me, "probably not in the way that you think."

I pulled out of the residential area back onto the highway for the short drive back to the lab. "Okay. Now you've got me confused, Jackie."

"I'm not going to play the 'My Daddy left me when I was young card'. The fact is he did, and my Mama and I made it the best that we could. She was working two jobs, trying to just keep a roof over our heads and food on the table. This meant that I was home alone quite a bit.

"I've always been a bit of an extrovert, I needed people around me. During those long hours of being alone, I found myself going down and sitting on the stoop of the apartment building that we lived in. Didn't take long and I met some other kids and I started hanging with them.

"What I didn't know then, or maybe I did and I just didn't care, was that they were all members of the gang that ran the neighborhood. You could say that my time with them was an interesting and diverse education. By the time I was twelve I was pretty adept at picking pockets, and was known to have a steady hand. Joco, he was one of the leaders, took me under his care, and taught me the finer workings of picking locks.

"It didn't take long before I'd graduated from pinching a wallet from an unsuspecting mark to what would become my specialty: Breaking and entering. I hardly ever went to school, I was too busy with the rest of the group helping myself to things that I wanted."

I glanced over at my partner. Her eyes were closed, fists clenched as she inhaled deeply and then blew it out. I wasn't sure if I should say anything or not, but she went on before I had made up my mind.

"I was fourteen when it happened. I'd taken care of the lock on a third floor window. Sasha ran into the building to take care of the alarm system. For us, this was business as usual. The part that we hadn't counted on was that an undercover cop was watching the building for part of his drug case. He called it in.

"Two minutes later, we heard the sirens and the pounding on the door. Sasha, Little Mic, Joco and I all headed for the window and the fire escape.

"To be honest, I don't remember the next part at all. The officers who responded said that in the confusion on the fire escape I either slipped or was knocked off. All that anyone is sure of is that I fell from the third floor. I ended up breaking nearly thirty bones and was in a coma for more than a month. When I came to, I found myself handcuffed to the bed, and my Mama sitting in a chair crying.

"To finish the saga, I'll just say that all four of us were arrested that day. Little Mic, made a deal. He was just sixteen, and scared of going to prison. He copped out to several other robberies, and testified against the rest of us.

"Sasha and Joco are still in prison. One of their priors included a double homicide. Little Mic was sentenced to four years somewhere. That was part of the deal he got, he'd turn the evidence, but then do his time somewhere undisclosed for his own safety. Because of my age, I got sent to Juvie. I spent two years inside, Monica."

"But something changed for you, didn't it? Otherwise, why would you have become a cop?"

For the first time since she opened the locked box, her smile reached her eyes. "Yeah. His name was Officer Timothy Keegan. He'd been working undercover and saw me open the window that day. He saved my life that day, in more ways than one. After I fell, he was the first one there, and his quick thinking and care literally kept me alive until the paramedics arrived. Even after that, it was day-to-day for several weeks. But after I came out of it, he came to see me one day.

"It turns out that his daughter had gotten into a rough patch when she was about my age. By the time he'd clued in it was too late. She'd OD'ed. I think he looked at this as a way to make up for his mistakes as a parent.

He talked with Mama and me, and let me know that things were bad, and I was going to have to make a serious choice, but that if I'd let him, he'd be there to help me. He came to the detention center where I was held, and continued to talk to me and helped steer me in the right direction.

"By the time I got out, Tim had helped me get caught up academically and was there to make sure I stayed on the straight and narrow. Along the way, he became a surrogate dad to me. He's why I became a cop. He cried when he presented me with my badge after the academy.

"He's got a right to be proud of you, and you of him. You're a better cop because of that. You understand what might push someone to step over that line."

"Thanks," she smiled weakly. "I was worried that once you knew my past, you'd, you know, want a different partner."

"What we've survived makes us stronger, and hopefully more intelligent. Your experiences are a unique tool that you can pull out someday and use to make a life affirming change in someone else's life."

"You mean, like, pay it forward?"

"Exactly," I said as I eased the car into a parking space. "Now, let's go see if we can decode Stephen's little black book."

Chapter 18

I strode through the now familiar halls of the crime lab like I knew where I was going. Only this time, Jackie and I had our own security detail.

We exited the stairwell, turned and I noticed that Andy's personal guard was standing just outside the door.

He nodded as we approached and opened the door.

"How's it going, Doc?" I asked as I walked into Andy's office.

Andy looked up from his notes and smiled. "Things are going okay, I guess. I'm not used to having someone right there every time I turn around. We're working on the DNA angle. Right now, though, there isn't much that I can do other than wait."

It was my turn to smile. "Well, we may have something for you to play with while you're waiting for the computer to finish chewing on things." His eyes brightened when I pulled the evidence bag out of my bag. "We found this in a hidey hole under his floor."

Andy took the sealed bag donned a pair of gloves and carefully slit the bag open.

He flipped through the book quickly. "Let me guess. You want me to decipher what ever is written here, right?"

I nodded. "If he's got it hidden, there has to be a reason that he didn't want anyone else to find it. And, whoever was there before us tore the place apart, looking for something."

Andy's face was grim. "This is definitely something. I'll get on this right away." He started to turn towards the door to his lab and then hesitated. "Monica, by any chance are they sending his computers in?"

"Yeah. They would have gone to the station to be taken apart by one of the techs there. Why?"

"Can you have them sent here? I'm thinking that perhaps the book corresponds to information on the computer. In order to solve one, you'll need the other.

"I'll do what I can to have it to you by the end of the day."

"Thanks." He let out a long sigh, "I'm going to be so happy when this is all over."

I crossed over to him, held both of his hands, "We're going to get through all of this. Then we're going to take some time to relax. Just you, me and the two fur-balls. Okay?"

He nodded, leaned his head down and softly kissed my forehead. "Go catch these guys, would you?"

"I'm on it, Doc. See you tonight."

As we walked out of the lab, Jackie was glancing at me. Finally I needed to know, "What's up?"

Her smile widened. "I was just wondering how you're doing it."

"Doing what?" Now I was concerned.

"How you're compartmentalizing your involvement with Andy. Over the last week, everything has been upended, including you getting tossed into a relationship. I was wondering how you're doing it?"

I opened the car door, "To be honest, it's taking a bit. I'd much rather take off right now on that week or two of relaxing and not worry about the murders and the missing Cathy Evans. But right now, the most direct route to getting to that time off is by nailing these guys. So that's what I'm doing."

We headed out of the lot and turned towards the downtown area. Each of us was in our own thoughts as the streets passed by.

I pulled into the department lot. "Hard to believe that this is the first time I've been here in almost a week," I muttered as I reached for the handle.

"I see our two friends are coming in with us," Jackie stated.

I glanced in the mirror, the two agents who had been assigned to us were making their way across the lot towards the door. I let out a sigh. "It's going to get interesting going in there with these two. Oh well, might as well get it done with."

Pushing through the doors in the main area, we made our way over to the reception area and waited for Tammy Lichen, who essentially ran the department from here.

Tammy was a tall brunette who seemed challenged to find clothes that were sized appropriately. Her skirts were often just north of her knees and her necklines usually plunged into the deep south. Both offenses were constantly overlooked by her supervisors due to her undeniable knack of running things.

As we waited, she was joking with a deliveryman from one of the local couriers. I recognized the company as one that we often used for transporting documents and evidence between in town agencies.

Tammy's eyes grew big as she saw us and waved.

"Todd," she said to the deliveryman. "I'll call you later once I finalize my schedule." She turned to us, "Monica! My God I couldn't believe what I heard. You've had about the worst week possible. Are you okay?"

I noticed that the recently dismissed Todd was looking at Jackie and I as if we had just risen up through the floor. Tammy however didn't miss a beat. "Todd, this is the detective that I was telling you about. Her house was blown up, then she was attacked. It's been unreal."

Todd's demeanor changed. "Glad to hear that you made it out of those events unscathed." He turned back to Tammy, "I've got to run. Call me as soon as you can, okay?" He gave her a wink and headed out the door pushing his handcart .

"We just started dating a week ago," Tammy volunteered as she watched him exit. Her eyes remained glassy for another moment before she turned to me. "So, what can I do for you today?"

I shrugged, gestured to the two agents, "After our last little encounter, Gannon and I have been assigned federal baby sitters. We need to have them checked through."

Tammy looked at the two agents, checked their badges against the documentation that was in a file on her desk. "Okay, you guys are all set. Enjoy your visit."

I was muttering to myself as we turned towards the detective's area. Several of our colleagues were smiling at us as we walked in.

"Good to see you back, Deitz," Jenkins commented as we walked by his desk.

I stopped a few feet short of my desk and stared. I sensed Jackie as she shifted to the side to a get a look at what had stopped me.

"What'd they do, find every scrap of paper that wasn't stapled down and toss 'em on our desks?" Jackie asked incredulously.

I just shook my head. "Not sure, Jackie. But let me assure you, when I find out who did this," I turned to look at my associates, many of whom were struggling to keep from laughing out loud. "When I find out who decided to play this little prank, I won't get mad. I'm not even going to hold a grudge. However, I believe that the word I'm looking for is reciprocity."

A few of the heads shook vigorously and the squad room quickly went back to work. I noticed Jenkins and Westly sneak glances towards us as they feigned work. "Let's see what all this is," I motioned to Jackie as I slipped into my chair.

Thirty minutes later, we were back in the car heading back out. A cardboard box full of files that might be pertinent to our case and a bunch of miscellaneous papers that had landed on our desks over the past week was now secured in the trunk. Pulling back onto the main street, I watched as the FBI sedan followed only a few car lengths behind.

"That went well, don't you think?" Jackie said breaking the silence.

"I guess so. There was something off though, did you notice?"

Jackie thought for a moment. "You mean in the squad room? I don't know the guys there too well, so I'm not sure I'd have noticed."

"No, it wasn't just the squad room," I countered. "It's that one nagging whisper that is telling me something's about a half-bubble off of plum,. I just can't put my finger on it."

"Let me know if you do, okay?" Jackie asked. "So, it seems that the admin that took care of us was pretty impressed with you."

"Tammy?" I asked surprised. "There are days that I think she likes to live vicariously through the rest of us. She's a bubbly personality, wrapped in good looks. The guys seem to always notice her, and she runs through them fairly fast. It's just her way of…" my voice trailed off.

Jackie turned to face me. "What's up?"

"His face. Todd's face."

"Yeah, Todd has a face. It even appeared to be fairly nice one. Maybe if Tammy'll be done with him soon, I'll take it upon myself to do a more intimate study of his face."

No, no, no. I'm not making myself clear, Jackie," I said as pulled into a parking lot near the edge of town. "I've seen Todd around the building so many times, that I never think about it. But when I watched the videos from the days of the explosion and the threats, it wasn't his face that was there."

"Well, that's good to know that the admin isn't making noises with a bomber. And, I guess that it's equally important that we can say that he wasn't involved. It's one less suspect that we'll need to work through."

"I never said that he wasn't involved. He just wasn't the one that walked into the building on those days!"

Jackie looked over at me like I had three heads. "What? What do you mean that he wasn't the one that walked in, but that he still may be involved? I'm confused."

I didn't have it in me just yet to be calm and compassionate with her about this. I grabbed my cell phone and punched in the numbers for the delivery service.

"Thanks for calling Cape Crusader deliveries. How may I direct your call?"

"This is Detective Monica Dietz, and I need to speak to who ever is in charge. Now."

"Uh-uh, sure. One moment."

Soft music came out of the speaker for ten seconds before a gruff voice burst on. "This is Jonathan Brinks, who is this?"

"Mr. Brinks, I'm Detective Monica Dietz with the Blackberry Creek police department. I need some information."

"Has one of my guys been involved with a accident, detective?"

"Not that I'm aware of, Sir. I'm investigating an incident that occurred downtown last week, and I'm just trying to verify some details about one of your drivers who may have been in the vicinity."

"You think he did something? Do I need a lawyer?"

I took a deep breath to calm myself. "Mr. Brinks, I am wondering about the driver who normally does the route that stops by the police station and the crime lab? I just would like to talk to him, to see if he has any information that might help us."

The sound of papers being shuffled came through. "As long as he's not in trouble, I guess I can give you his name. That'd be Todd Thomas. Good kid. Been with us about nine months now. Anything else, detective?"

"Just one last question. Was Mr. Thomas at work last Thursday? I mean if he wasn't working on the day of the incident, there's no need to bother him."

"Yep. He's been on every weekday since he got hired. Aint' missed one yet."

"Thank you for your time, Mr. Brinks."

"What was that all about?" Jackie asked as she stared at me.

"I'm trusting that my memory didn't choose now to begin failing me, so that means that Todd Thomas wasn't the delivery guy who came by those scenes on Thursday. But if he didn't take any time off, that means that someone convinced him that not making that stop would be in his best interest."

Jackie's expression indicated that she was catching up. "So, you're saying that either he was accosted and held prisoner while someone borrowed his uniform and made that delivery, or he was complicit about the entire thing."

"Now you've got it," I said to Jackie. "Let's do a run on Mr. Thomas, and we'll go find a quiet spot to do a little work."

We found a small coffee shop about a mile down the road, pulled in and went to the back table. Our two friends found seats near the entrance.

"Probably not going to help their business," Jackie nodded at the two agents who had loosened up enough to unbutton their suit coats.

"As bad as it sounds, I'm not going to worry right now about that. As long as nobody puts us together with them we're relatively safe."

I pulled out my cell, and called Andy.

"Hey, Doc. I've got a favor to ask."

"Okay, Detective, lay it on me," he sighed.

"I need you to break down the video of the delivery guy coming into the crime lab on the day of the bombing. I've got a face that I don't think is going to match, but I need to verify."

There was silence on the phone for what seemed like a very long time. When Andy's voice come back on, he sounded confused. "Let me get this right. You want me to compare the face of the delivery guy that dropped things off at the crime lab on Thursday to a face that you're going to send me. You don't think that they're going to match."

"Bingo," was all I said.

"Monica, do you think you're pushing too hard? I mean, this doesn't seem to make much sense to me."

"Andy, I'm fine. What I've got here is at least one crime being committed that ties in with the bombing and all. I'm just not sure of what crime I need to talk to this guy about."

"I'll grab the stuff and bring it with me. Maybe what you've got will make more sense when I'm there and can see, you know and it just doesn't sound like," he let out a long sigh. "And I'm babbling. I'll get the stuff and bring it with me. Are we meeting back at the house?"

I looked around at the little shop, noting their menu and the ambiance. "I'll tell you what, why don't you meet us at Maven's." I gave Andy the address, hung up and turned back to Jackie.

"I feel sorry for him," she said.

"You want to explain that, Jackie?"

She chuckled lightly. "He's so head-over-heels in love with you, that he's doing something that he doesn't fully understand for you blindly."

There was something to what she just said and I sat still for a few seconds letting it soak in.

"What did I say, Monica?" she nearly pleaded.

"Two things actually. The first being that you think he's in serious love with me. That's new and exciting for me, as I've never had that before and the power that it gives me is terrifying.

"But, perhaps more importantly, maybe we've been looking at this all wrong. We made the assumption that Steve was doing this for his brother. Maybe he's doing it for somebody else."

"Cathy? Do you think Cathy was involved with the whole mess? Shooting up her storefront, being kidnapped? I don't know, that seems a bit far fetched."

I nodded. "It does, and we at least need to look at the possibility. But what I was thinking was more along the lines of a ransom. The Kidnappers haven't sent anyone a ransom note. Maybe they're not after money, per se. Maybe they want a particular service instead."

Jackie stared at me open mouthed for a brief moment. "That's scary. Scary, but entirely plausible. Since you came up with the idea, I'll call it in," she said as she grabbed her phone and headed to the door.

I'd finished my chi tea latte when Andy stepped through the door. He spotted us, and made his way back to the table while his guard settled into an extra chair with the other two agents.

"Hi, Monica. Jackie." He sat next to me and opened his brief case and pulled out a laptop. "I brought what you asked. From what I can see, the guy you asked me to scan isn't the one who made the delivery."

"I'd figured that," I said. "Let's try one more for the giggles of it. Run the facial recognition again, but this time lets compare the delivery guy with Alex Browning."

Andy started typing, Jackie looked over with wide eyes. "You don't think he'd do that too?"

"Why not?" I answered. "He's been involved in every other step of this fiasco. What's one more piece."

"Sorry to interrupt," Andy blurted out. "But I've got a match." He looked from Jackie to me. "You're right. It was Browning."

"Can you pull up the picture of the package?" Jackie wanted to know. When I gave her a quizzical look, she shrugged. "Maybe we can decipher the tracking code on it?"

I gave myself a mental head-slap. Seconds later, Andy had it on screen.

"I'll get a search started on that right away," Jackie said triumphantly.

"What does this get us?" I asked aloud.

"I'd say you're starting to break through the layers that Browning has hid in for so long. You're going to unwrap him before too long. And then," he looked at me with prideful eyes. "Then, you're going to nail his sorry rear end to the wall."

A waitress came and took our order.

Jackie's phone rang as the waitress walked away. "They've started a track on the tracking number, trying to reverse where it originated. It's going to take a little bit. So what's next?"

"Let's see if by some chance our friend Mr. Thomas has at some point been associated with either of the Brownings.

By the time our food came out, we had three laptops running checking facts.

"It looks like our deliveryman has a bit of a checkered past," I said between mouthfuls of the BLT. "He's got a sealed juvie record. We're going to need something solid for us to find a way to get into that record."

"Right now, I'm not coming up with much," Jackie added. "The best I can do is that he grew up in the same neighborhood as the Browning brothers. Looks like he was probably a year behind Alex at the school."

"Gives us circumstantial, but nothing concrete. You get anything, Doc?"

Andy turned his screen. "Not sure. It appears that your Mr. Thomas ran with a group of kids that called themselves the West End Boys. Looks like he may have used the alias of T-Square."

"The West End Boys?" I asked excitedly. When both Andy and Jackie looked at me, I smiled. "That was the same gang that Alex Browning ran when he was a juvenile delinquent."

"Oh my God," Andy said quietly.

I looked at him, and his face was losing color fast.

"Andy! What is it?" I grabbed his hand, which was now almost as cold as ice.

Andy turned his head. "I'm sorry, Monica. But it seems that Todd Thomas wasn't the only one who was a known associate of that group." He spun his laptop around so I could see the list.

Three from the bottom was the name that had caused the reaction. John "Jack" Steele.

CHAPTER 19

I held Andy's hand as I looked at the name on the screen. "Any chance it's a different Jack Steele?"

"I don't, I don't think so," Andy mumbled. He let out a long sigh. "When I saw the name I thought that it had to be a different person. But the image that pops up when you hoover over his name is definitely him."

"Listen, Doc. We all do things when we are younger that we hope won't hurt us when we're older. Many times we try things once and then forget about them. And, even if Steele was involved in the gang, something might have happened along the way that caused him to change his ways." I looked over at my partner with a slight smile as I finished saying this. "All that we know for sure right now, is that at some point in the past, your lab assistant was involved with a group that Alexander Browning was also in."

"We'll need to interview him," Andy stated. "I can't be a part of that, but I'd like for you two to do it. I need to know what his motives are and whether or not I can trust him."

Jackie spoke for the first time in ten minutes, her voice was thick as if she was trying to keep her composure. "I'll make a few calls. Maybe Ted and Matt have something on that group, and can give us a more up-to-date picture."

She dropped her napkin on the table had hurried for the door. I saw her wipe at her eye as she stepped out the door. I could only imagine what was going through her mind right now, but to have this conversation only hours after she'd told me of her past, I knew that she was sure to be shaken. I made a mental note that I would need to talk to her privately as soon as possible.

Turning my attention back to Andy, I wrapped my arm around him and just held him hoping that the gesture would be comforting to him.

His head leaned to the side until it rested on mine.

Each of us were lost in our own thoughts while we sat there. I kept wondering what the connections were. We already had a link from Alex to Steve to Cathy. But where was the connection between Cathy and Toby Williams?

"You okay?" Andy's voice seemed to echo in my head.

"Huh?" I asked startled and moved so I could see his face.

"You started mumbling something unintelligible. It almost sounded like connections and names, but I couldn't make anything out."

I shrugged and then filled him in on my thoughts.

"I think you're right, Monica. There have been too many connections along this whole thing. We just haven't dug down far enough to uncover the important ones yet." He'd started rubbing his hand in small circles on the small of my back while he was speaking, and I felt myself curling like a cat into the hand that was petting it.

A named flashed in my mind, and I spoke it before I realized what it meant. "Juliet Lewis."

Jackie had just come back to the table when I blurted out the name. "How'd she come up again?"

I looked from Andy to Jackie. "I think she's the missing link."

"Want to explain that for those of us who didn't quite catch everything?"

"I was thinking about the connections that are involved in this case. There are far too many for this to be strictly coincidental. These connections are the link to what's been going on, and more to the point, probably the link to solving it. Juliet is the missing link between all of the connections."

By the blank stares, I knew that I had their attention, but they hadn't followed my train of thought.

"Okay, let me try it this way," I offered. "We know that Alex Browning was intimately responsible for the attack on Cathy's Collectibles. We've deduced that Browning was one of the men who was sent to kill me at my home when we didn't drop the case like we had been told by the unnamed caller. There is video evidence that he delivered something to the crime lab on the day of the fire.

"However, right now, it's all circumstantial. So, we need to take it one step further. We need to find the connection between the victims and Alex. Juliet Lewis is that connection.

"She was the one who went into the hospital and killed Jenkins. Her name came up on the rent rolls from one of the other homicides, and she was the one who bought the wire that was found in the jacket that Williams was wearing."

Andy held up his index finger. "Her print was also found on that was on that wire."

"Point taken. So what is the connection between them?" I asked.

By this time, we had finished our dinners, and were now finishing our drinks. The three of us remained silent as we contemplated what it was we were trying to establish. Jackie was the first to break the silence.

"If we make the assumption that Lewis was in with Williams on the suit, then do we also make the leap that she was involved with his businesses in some way?"

I looked over the rim of my teacup. "It's a good a place to start as any."

"Perhaps she was a silent partner in one of them and she decided to double cross him," Jackie suggested.

Andy surprised me by answering before I had a chance. "I don't think she was trying to double cross him. I think it might be the other way around. Williams was trying to cut her out of the process."

"Okay, Doc. I'm leaning in the same way, but why do you think that?"

He blushed when I asked him to justify his thinking, but he forged on. "If she was trying to cut him out of the deal, wouldn't it have made sense for her to be the one who ended up with the jacket? He had the jacket, and now we've got it. She's got no recourse to get it back. She's lost that particular asset.

"If however, we look at it as he was trying to cut her out, it makes more sense. She's the woman scorned and she'll stop at nothing to ensure that he can't have what he's taken from her."

Jackie looked between Andy and I. I simply nodded.

"I tend to agree with you, Andy, that he was the one that was trying to make the break from her. But," I said as my eyes focused on Jackie. "I think we need to take another look at Williams' financials. We need to look deeper into each of the businesses that he claimed on his taxes, and track down any loose ends there."

I closed my eyes for a second, aligning my thoughts. "I think we may also want to do a search of employees for all of his companies as well as for Brewster Industries."

"What are we looking for?" Jackie wondered aloud.

"Not sure, but I'm guessing that when we see it we'll understand that it's important."

"Then let's get cracking," Jackie agreed.

We stood and dropped cash on the table for the tip, and headed for the door. Our three friends from the FBI sandwiched us. Two heading out ahead of us, and the last following us.

I couldn't help but think that our three-car procession looked like a caricature of a parade as we made our way back to the compound that we had now taken over as our headquarters.

I parked the car at towards the rear of the little house. Light from the kitchen window spilled out and illuminated the small stoop. None of us moved, we sat in silence each collecting our own thoughts. I jumped at the knock on the window.

"Everything all right, Detective?"

I shook my head, "Everything's fine, Matt. We're all trying to think about what we might have missed, and…" my voice trailed off.

"I know how that goes. Why don't you all come in? Coffee's fresh, and it's a bit warmer inside."

As we got out of the car, he waved to the other two cars before he answered the unasked question.

"Agents Fredrickson and Stevens called in on the radio to update your arrival, so I was watching out the window. When you didn't get out right away, well, we were kinda worried that something had happened and we'd missed it."

Walking into the kitchen the sounds of other cops in the next room carried through. They were arguing about some sporting event that was going to be coming on shortly. Matt shook his head.

"Gets to be late mid-November, and everybody's worried about how the Celtics are doing. Me? I'm more interested in watching the Bruins," Matt said with a smile. He looked over to Andy, "You interested in catching part of the game tonight?"

Andy looked up from a sheet of paper that he'd been staring at since shortly after we started our drive back. "What? I'm sorry, I really wasn't paying attention."

Matt laughed, "Just wondering if you were interested in catching the game tonight? From the sounds of the other two, I'm going to be outnumbered, and forced to watch basketball. I'm looking for someone who might be able to even things up for me a bit."

Andy passed on the invitation, and continued walking and climbed the stairs all without taking his eyes off of the paper he held.

"That is one serious dude," Matt said. "Great personality when he's not knee deep in some scientific problem."

He smiled at us, and headed off to join his partners in the other room.

Jackie frowned. "He never asked me if I'd like to watch anything. I happen to love hockey."

"Didn't ask me either," I pointed out as I grabbed a mug from the cupboard. "Wonder what Andy's working on that has him so caught up right now."

"I don't know. Must be awful interesting, though. He didn't even grab you or give you a kiss before he went upstairs."

I threw the dishtowel at her before we both started laughing.

"Where do you want to set up?" she asked after getting a cup of coffee.

"I'm thinking right here for now. Plenty of room on the table for the laptops, and we're a bit away from the commotion of the other room."

Ten minutes later, we were sitting across from each other, Sam had come in and taken his position next to me and was contentedly chewing on his rope toy. Motion in the hall caught my attention, and I looked up.

Andy stood in the door, still clutching the paper, but his eyes were bright and a smile stretched from ear to ear.

"Andy? What's up?" I asked warily, wondering if he was going to play some kind of trick.

"Just a clarification before I begin. The missing woman, the one we believe to be romantically involved with Steve Browning? Is her middle name by some chance Elaine?"

I looked over at Jackie who shrugged. "I-I don't know. Why?"

"Before I explain, is it possible that we confirm that? Everything that I think I have hinges on being certain of that."

Jackie was already tapping the keys on her computer.

"According to the DMV, middle name is Elaine. You win the prize for this round, Andy."

He visibly sighed, and if it was possible, his smile widened. "Gotcha you dirty dog." He tossed the paper onto the table.

It was a photocopy of one of the pages from Steve Browning's book.

I stared at the random numbers and letters, and then back up to the still grinning man.

"You broke his code?"

Andy nodded. "He's a clever guy. The lab boys started running this through using one of the computers. Only problem is, that most of the codes that we break are based on letters. The only time that numbers seem to appear is when you're using binary or hexadecimal. After you had his computers sent in, I started working on them while Tess Edwards, one of the computer geniuses we have, oversaw the running of the program. When it came back as unknown, Tess brought it up to me. I told her I'd take a look at it personally.

"I'd found a few files on his computers that I thought might help so I spent most of the afternoon pouring over those, but didn't really find anything that earth shattering. I did however find a file, a letter actually, where he wrote to Cathy. I probably would have forgotten about it, except that I noticed dots under a few of the individual characters.

"I took the time to go through and follow the clues, and found several nonsense words. Words that just happened to match three of the files on a hidden sector of the drive. When I opened the first, all I found was a matrix consisting of twenty-six rows and twenty-six columns. My first instinct was that we were looking at a sophisticated Vigenere cipher. The numbers really threw me.

"When I looked at this," he said pointing to the paper, "it was like the matrix jumped out at me. I went back and looked into the other files that were there. One had a single word, Elaine, and the other had a relatively basic equation that I immediately recognized. It's one that's used in what's called a Caesar's Cipher.

"You've lost me, Doc," I managed.

He stopped open mouthed and looked at Jackie and I. She was sitting with her mouth wide open and staring at him, and I had a feeling that I wasn't much better off.

He sighed, "I forget that not everyone loves solving puzzles as much as I do." He grabbed a cup of coffee and then sat at the table with us.

Picking up the paper he looked at it for a moment, and then began. "Okay, you understand the basics of using a cipher, right?"

Jackie still wasn't responding, so I guessed it was up to me.

"I think so. You're using one letter to represent another letter in the same alphabet, right?"

"Close enough. What you so elegantly described is what is commonly known as a Caesar cipher, and can be expressed mathematically using a clock or mod system where the system is equal to the number of possibilities. For example, in the English alphabet, we have twenty-six letters, therefore we'd use a mod of twenty-six. Once we reach the end, we start over. So far so good?"

"Yeah," I said trying to sound confident.

"Now what Mr. Browning did so eloquently, was to set up one of these ciphers, but it was based on another form of cipher, called a Vegenere cipher. This type uses a matrix that has each letter across the top and the side. But because each row begins with the letter in the first column, the letters move one column to the left for each row down. The way that it works is if you know that key word, you spell it on the side, and it tells you the letter to put in place.

"What we've got here," he said fingering the paper, "Is an interesting twist on this cipher. He used numbers instead of letters, and didn't begin at one. He picked an arbitrary number."

"Let me see if I'm getting this. You solved not one, but two, codes to be able to decipher what he wrote in his journal?"

"Ah, actually it was three. I had to notice how the numbers he used changed so I could configure the basic sequence."

Jackie had come out of her stupor finally. "So, why were you so concerned about Cathy's middle name being Elaine?"

"Because, after finding that name in the one file, I was guessing that that was the key that he'd used to encrypt his notes."

I let out a long breath, and spun the pencil I was holding in my fingers as I tried to organize my thoughts.

"So, if we take it that you are correct, and that these ciphers use this code or whatever, does that mean that you can now translate his book for us?"

Andy threw his head back and laughed so loud that he woke Sam up who joined in the gleefulness with his bellowing barks and howls.

When he finally was able to control himself, Andy gave me the answer that I was looking for. "The simple version is yes. To be honest, once I thought that I was getting somewhere with things I tried my solution on a few of his pages. When everything came out looking readable, I knew that I had to verify her middle name."

"How long would it take to decode the entire book?" Jackie asked.

"Depends on what resources I've got. If I can use a computer here, and," he checked the wall clock. "Let's see, Clarice comes on in just about an hour. So if I get things set up, and can have her scan and send me the images it'll take probably two or three hours tops to have the entire book decoded. Then it'll be up to you two to figure out what it means and how it applies."

I looked over to Jackie, "Let's get a space set up and get a computer ready." "Thanks, Andy," I said and leaned over and gave him a kiss on the cheek.

It was cute how he blushed when I did that.

"Ah, shucks. Twern't nothing, Ma'am" he said in a pretty good drawl.

We were all laughing about it when Captain Willoby walked in.

"Must be nice to be able to sit around laughing all day. We need to get this case solved, and I mean now!"

Taking my safety in my own hands I interrupted his tirade. "Ah, Captain?"

His look would have wounded others, but I've worked with him for over ten years. "Captain, I think you should grab a cup of coffee, pull up a chair and take a look at what Dr. Carson just gave us."

Chapter 20

Walking Sam early the next morning I let my mind wander.

From the data that Andy had turned up last night, and granted it was still preliminary and needed to be verified, it appeared as though Stephen Browning had nothing to do with his brother's criminal activity. However, he may have been aware of something that was happening.

In one of the later pages of the journal, the translation stated, "A.J. wants me to break coat code. Big money. I'm talking with Cathy about how to get this to the police."

We had circled around to the far side of the pond, and I looked back at the innocuous house. In all aspects, it appeared intensely routine and ordinary. But at this very moment, I knew that there were five armed officers inside and plans were being devised on how to best bring Alex Browning in.

How was it that Alex Browning kept moving without being seen? I had wondered about that earlier, but now as we were getting more desperate to figure out what the real motives were maybe it was time to revisit that thought.

Whistling for Sam, I continued to walk around the pond, heading back to the house.

I had to figure out the pattern that Browning was using. More importantly, I needed to find the link that tied everything together.

Pushing the door open, I stepped to the side as Sam trotted past me into the kitchen and to the stand that held his bowls.

"Have a nice walk?" Andy shoved a steaming cup of tea into my hands, spun me around so my back was against the counter, and kissed me.

"The walk was good," I cooed, "but the reception upon return was even better." I smiled, kissed him again, and then leaned into him and just held on.

Somehow, and I don't know how, this wonderful man had crashed back into my life, and without a doubt, it was better now. I still couldn't admit to myself, let alone anyone else, that I was falling deeply in love with him.

So I held onto him for all I was worth, and savored the moment.

"Sheesh! Maybe you two should just go up those stairs and use one of the rooms there. That way those of us lonely souls who are here too wouldn't screw up their breakfast by walking in on you."

"Good morning to you too, Jackie," I replied.

She glared at me over the rim of her coffee cup. "It's way too early to be that happy. Give me an hour and a few of these," she raised her cup. "And then we can talk about what kind of morning it is."

She took a long pull, closed her eyes and sighed. "Nothing better than a hot cup of caffeine to get the body moving."

Opening her eyes, she looked to me. "I know that we officially don't go on duty for another fifty-three minutes, but wondering if you've determined what our game plan is going to be?"

I sighed and raised my head off Andy's shoulders, but his arms never left my waist and his hands kept rubbing small circles on my back.

Thinking like this was hard. Thankfully, I'd always been good at multi-tasking.

"Right now, I think we follow our plan from last night. We track the money and the employees and try to find the link. We'll talk with Todd Thomas. We need to start looking for Alex Browning and see if we can get him in a box for interview. I'm hoping that he can lead us to Juliet Lewis and she'll hopefully be able to take us to the next level."

Andy's hands stopped. "What do you mean the next level?"

"From her past record, Lewis doesn't have the knowledge nor the managerial skills to run a major operation like this. That means that there is someone higher up that is calling the shots."

"Managerial? You make them sound like they are running a major corporation here. Why does it matter if the crooks have MBA's or not?"

I took a long sip of my tea, wrapped my arms around Andy's neck and looked him right in the eye. "The only real difference between the organized crime boss and the CEO's of most large corporations is which side of the legal line they fall on. These guys run multiple businesses, with probably fifty percent being totally legit. The others may be a front for some kind of illegal activity, but they still need to be run properly. It takes someone who has that skill to be able to delegate the orders and keep the worker bees in line. That's a skill level that she just doesn't have."

"From her dossier, it looks like she'd like to learn," Jackie added coming over to lean on the counter. "She's becoming more aggressive and doing more than has been indicated in the past."

"Is it possible that she's interning with someone?" Andy asked.

The question caught me totally off guard. "I don't know. Honestly, I'd never thought about that. Maybe somehow she's gotten in with one of the bosses, and is trying to learn the ropes, but that doesn't seem logical. They're not apt to bring in anybody who is not a member of the family. But, if she is interning with someone, they'd be the next level." I started to sip my tea, then stopped. "Interesting thought. What if we bend the idea a bit—"

"She's dating one of the bosses!" Jackie said suddenly.

I nodded my head. "I think we just added a new thread into our search. We need to find a boss who'd be willing to look her way. That may speed up our attack."

Andy leaned in, kissed my forehead. "I'd love to stay and watch you two work this out, but I need to go into the lab and work on those ciphers. I want to be able to verify without a doubt that they are correct."

He started to back away then stopped. "Are you going to be able to talk to Jack today? And what do I do with him until he's, you know, cleared or whatever?"

I didn't waste anytime thinking here. "We'll plan to be at your office around nine, okay? We'll talk to him then. Can you keep him on a task that isn't a security issue until then?"

Andy thought for a moment. "Yeah, that shouldn't be too hard. I'll find him something to keep him busy but not in the thick of things. Thanks." He kissed me once again and headed up the stairs.

Jackie laughed and shook her head.

"What?" I demanded.

"You guys are just too cute."

"Keep it up, Gannon, and I'll get a new partner!" I teased as I headed for my own room.

Andy had met us in his office just before nine, and had located a workroom that we could use to talk to Jack. We had no sooner sat down, when the door opened and Jack walked in.

"Um, hi detectives. Dr. Carson said I needed to come talk to you."

I could see the sweat beading on his forehead. "Thanks for coming in, Jack. Why don't you pull up a chair? Would you like a cup of coffee or a soda?"

"Um, yeah. A Coke would be good. Thanks."

"I'll be right back," Jackie said as she headed for the vending machine in the hall.

"Okay, Jack," I said softly trying to put him at ease. "At this time, you're not in trouble, you're not suspected of anything and you're not being arrested." I paused as Jackie reentered and placed the can on the table. "Detective Gannon is going to read you your rights, and we're going to record this interview just to be sure that we are all protected."

Jack's eyes darted from my face, over to Jackie's, around the room and settled looking longingly at the door.

"Do you understand your rights, Jack?" Jackie asked.

He swallowed hard, nodded, "Yeah. Yeah, I understand them. But what I don't get is why are you talking to me?"

"Relax, Jack," I tried again. "We're talking right now like a couple of friends about things that happened when we were all younger. We're looking for a man by the name of Alexander James Browning. According to our files, you were at one time a known associate of Mr. Browning, and we're hoping that you may have some information that we can use to find him."

"I haven't seen A.J. in years. You gotta believe me." He screwed his eyes closed, while his hands pulled at his hair.

"Okay, Jack, do you admit to knowing Alex?"

"Yeah. We grew up in the same neighborhood. I knew him, and his brother Stevie. Everybody called Alex A.J.. I really didn't have much to do with him. He was ahead of me at school. He ran with a different crowd."

"The West End Boys?" I tried.

"Yeah, them," Jack spat out.

Interesting, I thought. He didn't seem to have any fond memories of them, yet he was listed as a known associate. "Jack, did you ever run with them? With the West End Boys?"

Jack's eyes sprang open and his jaw fell. "Is that, is that what this is all about? Oh good grief, my mother was right. She always said that if I ever went near that group of hoodlums, I'd pay for it forever. And apparently I am."

His fist slammed into the worktable. "I didn't exactly 'run' with them. I was trying to gain the affection of one of the girls who followed them on the fringes. Her name was Angela Woodsbury, but everyone just called her Angel. In an effort to get her to notice me, I tailed along with a large group one night. A couple of the older guys, including A.J. swiped some beer from one of the local quickie-marts and started causing a ruckus.

"All I remember is that there was a loud bang, and the group scattered. In hindsight, they scattered like the rats that they were. As they were running off, somebody knocked me down and dropped a bag next to me. The cops arrived seconds later, found me dazed and sitting on the ground with a bag next to me. The bag contained a small caliber handgun. What I didn't realize was that the bang I'd heard was somebody shooting at a shop owner during a robbery.

"I got hauled downtown, they called my folks and then they started to grill me. As it turned out, they weren't able to find any GSR on my clothes or me. They brought the shop owner in for a line up. He looked at the group the cops had assembled and got irate, started screaming at about them needing to get with it."

Jackie looked up from her notepad. "Any idea why he was so upset?"

"From what I gathered, the owner had told the first cops that the guy who had shot at him was white, blond and over six feet tall. I hadn't hit my growth spurt yet, and was still around five-five, or so."

I looked over at Jackie. The description that Jack said had been given matched hundreds of men. It was probably only coincidental that it happened to match Alex Browning.

I turned back to Jack. "So what happened after the line up?"

He shrugged. "I'm not really sure. They held me in a holding area for a while, finally they released me to my parents who grounded me for the next six months. After that, I stayed as far away as I could from those guys."

"Did you keep in contact with any of the members?"

"Absolutely not. My parents would have skinned me alive if I'd even tried to contact one of them after what happened to me. By the time my

Mom freed me, most of the group had moved along. The whole appeal had lost its shine."

Jackie scowled, and I could only guess that she was debating about asking something. "What about the girl?"

Jack sighed. "Never saw her again. When I got paroled from my parents, I heard that Angel had gotten busted with a bag of dope."

A thought flashed, "Jack, had you ever seen Angel with drugs before?"

"No. She swore she'd never touch the stuff. It's one of the things I never understood. She never liked the stuff, yet she had a bunch of it."

"Do you think she was trying to sell them?"

"No."

Jackie looked over, "What are you thinking, Monica?"

"I'm seeing a pattern here. They seem to dump off the evidence when the heat is too hot. Nice guys."

Jack snorted, "Yeah they're a bunch of charmers all right."

"Thanks for your time, Jack."

Jack shuffled out of the room. When the door closed, I looked to Jackie, "Impressions?"

She looked tense, and when she spoke, I could her the edge in her voice. "I think he was in the wrong place at the wrong time. He doesn't come off as an ex-gang member. I-I don't see him as a security threat, Monica. In fact, I really feel for him. He was the patsy. They played him like a fiddle, hoping that he'd end up taking the rap for what they did. I know what it's like—that life and they way things happen to those around you. One night he disobeyed his mother's wishes, and he's right. It's going to haunt him for the rest of his life. He doesn't deserve that."

I sat quietly watching my partner's face, wondering what thoughts she still harbored secretly. "I agree. Everyone does things as kids we wished later we hadn't. Luckily, most of us get a second chance."

I stood and collected my notebook. "We'll have to see if there is some way that we can amend the file so that anyone else who looks at it, sees that he's been cleared and is not an associate."

"That'd be nice," Jackie said quietly.

I started for the door, stopped and turned back to her. "Jackie, what you said there. About knowing the life and the consequences, your insight on this is what's going to make the difference for him. You know what's what there. Maybe you'd like to be more involved in getting his name off of that list?"

"I'll think about it."

Turning out of the doorway, I saw Jack sitting on a chair down the hall, rocking. Though I couldn't hear it, the body language said that he was crying. "I need to stop in and see Andy for a minute. Be right back."

As I knocked on the open door to Andy's office, I caught Jackie making her way down the hall.

"Gotta minute, Doc?"

"For you, I'll free up as many minutes as I can."

I shook my head as I dropped into the visitor's chair in front of his desk. "We're both on duty here. And since the tax-payers aren't interested in paying for us to explore our feelings for each other, I think it would be most prudent to keep this professional, Doc."

"You're a spoilsport Detective," he said with a smile. "Now what can I do for you?"

It took me about five minutes to give him a rundown on what we had learned from Jack, what our conclusion was at that point, and for Andy to update me on the progress of the translations.

"We've started at the beginning of the journal and the first quarter or so of the entries have been translated. We should have the entire book finished sometime this afternoon. Thus far, it seems that Stephen Browning was not involved with the smart suit. He did however note that his brother had requested some information about where to acquire certain types of computer chips.

"From the next few entries after that, it appears that he gave Alex some addresses, but nothing more."

I let those thoughts percolate through my mind. "If Stephen gave Alex the information, wouldn't he have had to have some idea what was going on?"

Andy shook his head. "Not necessarily. Several of the IC chips that were used, are common in many electrical devices. It's only when they were compiled in that specific manner that they function to make the suit active."

I thanked Andy for his time, and stood to leave.

Andy had come around from his desk, and shadowed me to the door. As I turned to open the door, I noticed his slight smile. "What are you grinning at, Doc?"

He grabbed my waist, spun me and pushed my back into the wall. His hands caressed my cheeks, and lifted my chin. His lips crushed mine.

Resistance was futile.

Heat built in my stomach, and my mind stopped worrying about the pieces of this puzzle that didn't fit. My only thought right now was him.

My arms snaked around his neck, my hands clasped to hold him where I wanted him. And for the first time in my life, I let myself go.

Nothing else mattered right this minute. It was primal. It was hot. It was just the two of us.

The phone on his desk rang out a long warbling tone.

It broke through our consciousness, and we pulled back slightly.

His eyes were still dancing with excitement but his expression was one of shock.

His hands left my waist only to push at my arms. "Monica, I'm sorry. I never should have…not here. I'm sorry—"

I stood on my tiptoes to lightly kiss him again. "Shh, Andy. I was right there with you. No need to apologize."

"But here? In my office?"

I smiled at him. "It looks like we're going to have a lot to talk about later. And as far as it being here at the office, we've spent the last week working round the clock. Let's just chalk this up to our sub-conscious feelings overtaking the tired rational ones, and giving us a preview of events to come."

His face broke into a smile that stretched from ear to ear. "The best preview that I've seen in some time. Take care of yourself, Detective, and know that I'm looking forward to the full feature."

CHAPTER 21

I came out of Andy's office with a slight stagger, and quickly wondered if Jackie was going to clue in to what had actually happened behind the closed door.

Turning, I noticed that she and Jack were sitting on the bench together, her arm wrapped around his shoulder.

I spared myself a glance into one of the windows that lined the hall. Other than my hair looking like I'd just been through a category-2 hurricane, nothing seemed immediately out of place. As I walked down the hall, I did what I could to tidy up my hair.

Jackie's voice carried as a whisper down the hall, and I stopped twenty feet from where she and Jack sat, not wanting to overhear private information.

Jackie's head came up, her eyes went wide and her lips curved into a smirk.

"You about ready to go?" I asked.

"Yeah." She turned back to Jake, pressed a card into his hand, "Call me if you want to talk."

We walked in silence down the corridor, our escorts followed us constantly searching for the threat that we all hoped wasn't coming.

Cars were backed up on the highway as we crept along on our way to the Milford Detention center. Jackie had done a quick search and found that Angel had been incarcerated there nearly nine years ago, and had only a few months to go before she would be eligible for parole, so we had decided to pay a visit to her today.

Jackie glanced up from the laptop she'd been working on. "Wonder what's causing the tie up."

I shrugged. "I haven't heard anything over the radio about any accidents or other problem. Then again, this wouldn't be the department's area. The State guys would be in charge here."

Now she turned to look at me. "So, you and Dr. Cutie were in his office for a bit," she noted with a sly smile. "Anything fun happen?"

I glared at her, but I couldn't keep a straight face. Good thing I don't play poker. "We, um, talked. About how things are going with Stephen Browning's book."

"Huh. The last time I checked, Monica, when you just talked, your hair doesn't get all messed up."

"Keep it up, Gannon. Glad I was of entertainment value. Now, can we perhaps focus on our impending interview?"

Jackie smiled and spun the computer. "I've got a list of questions right here based on what Jack told us."

Milford sat in the middle of what used to be farm fields. Gray stone rose up, surrounded by the glittering razor wire. Working farms still surrounded the center, ensuring that any prisoner who tried to escape had no cover for better than a mile in any direction.

"Nice place," Jackie commented dryly as we pulled into the lot.

I surveyed the scene. "Makes sense. If you're insistent on breaking the rules, they're going to bore you death with the scenery here."

"Don't forget the sure to be stimulating paint job, too."

A woman who looked to be in her early thirties escorted us into the welcome room.

Our weapons were secured, and we were led into a visitation room. "Prisoner Woodsbury will be escorted in shortly," our guide stated calmly before she left.

"You okay, Jackie? You look a little peaked."

Jackie was pacing back and forth, rubbing her hands on her upper arms. "It doesn't matter how long it's been, or for what reason I'm in a place like this, I start to get anxious."

I walked over to her, draped my arm over her shoulder. "I'm sorry. I never thought about how being in a place like this might affect you. If you need to bail, I'll understand."

She forced a smile. "It's not your fault. And I know that it's unreasonable right now, but I still have a hard time shaking it."

I looked around the room. It was depressing. Gray paint on the walls, with a lighter gray on the ceiling. Only the furniture had any color to it—dark blues and blacks on the cushions. The only bright object in the room was the Coke machine that was against the wall in the corner.

A buzzer sounded, and the large steel door opposite us slid open.

Dressed in oversized brown workpants and a ragged coat a tiny blonde woman shuffled in. Her head bowed, looking at the floor as opposed to the people in the room.

"Sit" the male guard said in a gruff voice, and she obeyed without word. He secured her to the chair before he made his way to the corner.

Another buzzer sounded, and this time a tall thin man with skin the color of cocoa entered, dressed in a pinstripe suit and carrying a briefcase.

"Sorry I'm late. I'm Sampson B. Howell, the third. I've been assigned by the courts to be Ms. Woodsbury's legal representation. I'd like to know what this is about."

I looked again at the small woman, whose head still had not looked above the tabletop. "We believe that Ms. Woodsbury may have information regarding a person of interest in a current case. We're hoping that she will be willing, and able, to help us."

"What's in it for her?" Howell asked. "With luck, she'll be out on parole in a bit over a month. Why should she help you now?"

I bit back my response about doing what's right for society. I had a bad feeling that this woman had spent too many years paying for a debt that wasn't hers. "Evidence that has come to light in the last day, indicates that the person we are looking for was also involved in landing Ms. Woodsbury here. I think she was likely framed. I'd like the chance to put the slime responsible behind bars." As an afterthought I added, "I'd also like to see her get a fair shot when she's on the outside."

The lawyer's eyes narrowed a bit, but he leaned over and whispered to his client.

For the first time since she entered the room, her eyes came up.

They were a brilliant blue, and anywhere else but these surroundings, and I'm sure she would have been a showstopper.

It was as Jackie and I had said earlier. They had taken the life out of her.

"I don't know what I can tell you that I haven't already told the others," she stated in a fragile voice. "But I'll help if I can."

I pulled out the seat across from her and was trying to get my thoughts in order when Jackie spoke first. "Angela? Would you like a Coke?"

The first spark of life hit her eyes. "Yes, please. Regular, if you don't mind."

I watched my partner go the machine in the corner. "Angela, my name is Detective Dietz. The woman getting your Coke is Detective Gannon. We are currently investigating a shooting that has resulted in four homicides that occurred about a week ago. The main suspect is Alexander Browning."

"There's a name from the past." She shook her head. "I'd really like to help you, Detective, but I haven't had any contact with A.J. since before I got locked up."

There was something in her eyes that told me that while this was technically true, she knew something more.

Jackie was back with the Coke. "Looking at his past track records, it seems to me that he doesn't think anything about throwing somebody else under the bus, so to speak, to save his own hide."

Angel's face hardened. "He's the one that's responsible for this. I never touched the stuff. My cousin OD'ed on drugs, so I never wanted anything to do with them. But that night, A.J. came over to where I was hanging out. He and I almost never talked, but that night, he was quite talkative.

"Five minutes after I left, couple of cops hauled me over. They claimed that they'd gotten an anonymous tip that I was selling dope. 'Soon as they opened my bag, there it was. A brown paper bag filled with clear little baggies. I immediately knew that I'd been set up, and tried to run. Nobody ever listened to my pleas. I got sent here for possession, selling and resisting arrest. I've lost nearly ten years of my life. My parents won't even talk to me. The only family member who'll even admit that I still exist is my brother, Jason. They tell me that I'm most likely getting out in five weeks, and then what? I've got no family, no home, nothing! All because A.J. Browning thought that the heat was too much, and made me his scapegoat."

"Angela," I said softly. "This is exactly what we suspected. We need to find him and get him off of the streets. Will you help us?"

"What can I tell you?"

"How about telling us about the West End Boys. Who was involved, who ran things?"

She nodded her head, "I can do that."

"I appreciate your help," I said. "Let's record this so we can use it for evidence"

As soon as I had the recorder set up, Jackie recited the Miranda rights, and we motioned for her start.

Angela sipped her Coke, closed her eyes and began.

"The West End Boys didn't really have a leader, in the normal sense of things. It was kind of like, you know, everybody respecting their elders or something. The older kids gave the younger ones directives, and they were followed. But as I recall, it seemed to me that a lot, and I would guess that it would be most, of the older kids took their lead from A.J."

"When you say A.J., are you referring to Alexander James Browning?"

"Yeah, that's him. He was charismatic, and smart. He made people laugh. Until you got on his bad side, you understand?"

I nodded, so she continued.

"What A.J. wanted, seemed everybody else soon wanted it too. When he wanted some extra cash, it wasn't long before the gang began shaking down shops for protection money. Or selling drugs, for that matter. If somebody crossed A.J., they were brought in line right quick." She hesitated for a minute. "Something else that just crossed my mind. It didn't always make sense as to why A.J. would do some things. We had other gangs in the area, but the Boys never went after them. To my knowledge there was never any kind of turf fight, even when all groups were pushing. There must have been something else."

"Did you ever see A.J. meet with an outsider?" Jackie tried.

Angel thought, "Not exactly. I seem to recall, about a week before I was framed, that I saw A.J. climbing out of a car. Not one that I recognized."

My mind came up with a dozen possibilities, and even though the odds weren't in my favor, I had to ask. "Was there anything distinct about the car?"

"It was one of those long white Cadillacs, with all of the windows tinted real dark. Nothing really jumped out, other than," again her voice trailed off.

I thought Jackie was going to jump out of her seat. "What are you remembering?" I prompted.

"I'm not sure. The license plate. It was one of those custom ones, you know? I remember it because I thought it was kind of funny."

"What was it?" I tried.

"It was the number two, the word 'BAD', number four and the letter U."

I scribbled '2BAD4U' on my note pad and spun it around. "Like this?"

Angela looked at the note, "Yeah, that was it."

Jackie looked at the notation, chuckled then her eyes went hard. "Angela, how did you end up involved with the West End Boys?"

Angela shrugged. "Hard to really say. Some of the kids from school hung with some other kids. Somewhere along the line, one of them was in the gang. It quickly became the 'in' thing to do in the neighborhood, you know. There were always people there that were in the same predicament that you had. It was like instant friends and family.

"Jason knew a few of the kids, and as little sisters tend to do, I tagged along. I never really got into the mix of things, always staying on the edge. But I knew everyone, and most of them treated me as if I belonged.

"I never got in trouble, at least not until A.J. came to visit me," she sighed in disgust.

"Angela, thank you for your help," I said closing my notebook. "You've given us some insight as to where we might take this investigation from here." Jackie and I stood, and Angela's eyes looked wistfully at us. I took two cards out of my purse, and gave them to her. "The first card is my contact info. If you think of anything else that might be helpful, please call. The second one is for my cousin, Marc. He runs a small store in Boston. He had some bruises growing up, and since he's tried to help others who got caught in bad situations. I think he'll be able to help you with living arrangements and employment opportunities as well, so give him a call."

Her eyes filled with tears as she mouthed the words "Thank you" and clutched the card in her hand.

Turning back onto the highway heading back, we were both silent lost in our own thoughts.

"You didn't have to do that. Giving her those cards," Jackie finally stated.

"No I didn't. But I remember how things were for Marc. He was never arrested or formally charged, but the rumors went nuts. He struggled and finally he made something of himself. Now he tries to make it easier for others. Just the kind of guy he is."

"I-I can really appreciate that," she stammered, her voice thick with emotion. "I had several breaks that went my way, but it still is always an uphill battle. It's nice to know that there are people out there that really care."

She wiped her eyes with the sleeve of her jacket, and started typing on the laptop.

"The plate she gave us traces back to an Albert G. Richards. A quick look of previous data, and it appears that he did own a white Caddy ten years ago."

"Hmmm, Albert Griffin Richards. Things just got a little more interesting, I said.

"You've heard of him?"

I nodded, "Yep, as have you. His legal name is Albert Richard Griffin, the owner of Brewster Industries. And a few people in our department know him even better. Get on the horn and see if Bill and Sylvia can meet with us. We may even want our friends behind us to bring in a few more for the party."

Jackie turned to look at me. "Who is this guy?"

"If I remember correctly, he started playing in narcotics trafficking before he was out of high school. Last I'd heard, he'd graduated into the big leagues and was now trying to build his own organized crime syndicate."

"Sounds like a sweet-heart. I'll make the calls."

"Locating Griffin isn't going to be a walk in the park," Sylvia said. "When we were trying to nail him for running drugs, he either knew, or learned about, every nook and cranny."

Jackie was perplexed. "How'd he end up staying on the streets, if everyone was looking for him?"

Bill shook his head, "Jackie, I wish I could give you an honest answer. The guy plays by his own set of rules. I mean, you looked up his license plate right?"

Jackie nodded before Bill continued. "What address came up for that plate's registration?"

"Twenty West Bay Road," she answered confidently.

Bill punched keys on his computer. "Let's see. Ah, here we go, two-one-one-seven West Bay Road is…" he spun the computer screen so we could all see the image from Google Earth. "Looks like it's the public library to me," he said with a grin. "Like Sylvia said, he had all the moves ten years ago. If he's still around, I'd be willing to bet that he still has 'em and has picked up a few new ones."

"That's not making me feel any better, Bill," I countered. "There has to be a way that we can pinpoint him." My mind wandered for a moment, trying to look at other options. "What kind of car does he currently have?"

Jackie went back to her printout. "According to this he's got a 2013 Avalanche. What are you thinking?"

I grabbed the phone and punched in the numbers. Maybe OnStar could be of service. I paced the small conference room while I waited for them to try and locate Griffin's car.

"Well, that's going to make things tough," I finally said walking back to the main group. "According to OnStar, right now he's located in Kansas."

"Do you think he moved there?" Jackie offered.

"No. I'm thinking that this is another of his ruses." Going to the computer, I typed in the coordinates that the GPS had reported. "Well, unless this picture is really old, it appears that he's sitting in the middle of wheat field."

"There has to be something. When are we supposed to be meeting with the agents from the F.B.I.?"

Bill checked his watch. "You've still got time for a deli run, if that's what you're thinking, Sylvia."

My cell rang, and I looked at the readout. Andy. "Ahhh, what's up, Doc?"

"Nice Bugs impersonation," he responded. "Actually, I may have something that will help us. I found a phone number in Stephen's log that I think will connect us to Alex."

I could hear the hesitation in his voice. "What are you concerned about?"

"There are a couple of factors that we don't know. For instance, what if he only gave that number to Stephen? If we call from one of our numbers, it would show on his caller I.D., and he may not keep the phone long enough for us to track him with it. I'm also concerned that he may be using a cloaking device that would scramble the signal, and give us erroneous data."

"Yeah," I conceded. "Either of those would be bad right now. We need something, though."

"Well, I may have something. It's a very little something however."

"How little is little, and what is it?"

"I got the results back from the soil samples we sent out. Now, we knew that they were left from the last glacial front, but their mineral composition was still unknown. Based on what I just got, it appears that the soil that we found came from somewhere near the Nantucket Sound."

"That's more like it," I sighed. "I think it's time to get hold of the aerial division and have them do a little recon."

CHAPTER 22

Leaning against the counter that night I closed my eyes, wishing that the burning sensation would dissipate. Of course, after spending the last six hours on the computer, I didn't hold much hope of that happening. The fact that I'd found out that Todd Thomas had recently taken off for a vacation in Mexico didn't help my mood. So, I stood in the kitchen, waiting for the next pot of coffee and my mug of tea to finish brewing going through several breathing exercises in an attempt to relax.

"Did we get anything useful from the boys and girls in aerial?" I heard Bill ask the group in the other room.

Since Agent Immentez had better resources that I did, I'd turned that job over to him. So now as I waited, I craned my head to hear his report.

"We sent a pair of choppers over to the general locale. They were using video and infrared cameras, so we could get a pretty good picture of anything that was there. They couldn't loiter very long without attracting attention, so they did a series of sweeps. Luckily, there is a series of power lines that run almost the entire length of the target. Hopefully we were able to disguise our mission by pretending to inspect the lines.

"Between the two, we surveyed the entire target region, and now the footage is being analyzed by the bureau. If we find any vehicle matches, we'll be sure to let everyone know."

"What about looking for people?" Jackie inquired.

"People show up as well. It may not help us other than tell us where security is located if we need to go in."

"I was thinking," she countered, "that it might show us two people being held hostage."

There was a general sound of agreement that came from the other room. My thoughts were interrupted by the shrill whistle of the kettle.

I'd just finished filling my mug when two arms came around my waist.

"Hey, Monica," Andy whispered startling me since I hadn't heard him come in.

"Hey back." I turned so I could face him. "You okay?"

"Yeah. I think so. It's just been one of those days. After we talked, I kept plugging away at Browning's phone info. Not sure what we can do with it."

"Well, we're, and that's the department and the bureau, currently collecting data on the target zones that the soil information gave us. Little by little it'll come together. It'd sure be nice if we could…"

"If we could what?"

I motioned to him to follow me out to the other room.

"Quick question," I blurted. "I know that we can turn a cell phone on by remote, and once we've done that, we can use it's GPS signal to locate it. Could we try locating Stephen Browning's phone?"

"Don't you think who ever took him, would have tossed it somewhere?" Agent Weine asked. "I mean, if you're going to go through the trouble of kidnapping somebody, it'd be pretty stupid to keep their phone."

"Perhaps," I allowed, sitting on the couch. "But, if we assume that Alex was behind his being taken, and that Cathy was taken to force him to do what Alex wanted, will Alex kill him? If they need him that badly, they can't afford to get rid of him."

The two agents looked at each other, and then shrugged. "It's possible, but not probable," Weine consented.

"Then let's add a search for Stephen Browning's phone to our to do list as well." Sylvia added.

"Try tracking his car as well," Andy added from his position in the doorway. "They may have reconfigured their own vehicles GPS units, but would they have done it to his?"

"Looks like we're going to be busy tonight," Bill sighed.

"Monica!" Andy yelled from the kitchen three hours later. "I found it! I found it!"

Every head in the living room turned to the doorway as he rushed in.

I was encouraged by the smile on his face. "What'd you find, Doc?"

"I was going through the stuff that we downloaded from Stephen's book. There were a few codes that were embedded into the log entries that we had no idea what they were for, so while you were all setting up you searches, I decided to play around with trying to crack them.

"What I found is an encryption code. One that is designed to work on GPS units and will cause a false reading to show up."

"Andy, let me see if I've got this right," Weine interrupted. "You've got the code that would cloak a GPS unit? How is that going to help us?"

Andy nodded, held his hand up like he was directing traffic. "Okay, Tom, let me try it this way. You've all tried to locate Alex Browning's vehicle and cell phone right? Did either of them show up in a locale that was anywhere close?"

I didn't have to look around the room to know that every head was shaking right now.

Andy continued, "So what that means is that they've encrypted their GPS units to give the false data. That's not exactly news. Now with me finding this encryption code, I've got the method that they used to do that. All I need to do—"

"Of course!" Agent Immentz said surging to his feet. His face now matched Andy's. "He's right. With the codes, we simply reverse engineer the coding and then we can build a way that will pierce their shield, so to speak. They've cloaked themselves, and we'll have the way to remove it."

"Brilliant!" "Perfect" "About time" echoed around the room.

I simply stood, made my way over to Andy, and proceeded to kiss us both senseless.

Sam and I paced around the small bedroom that we were staying in. I needed a way to get rid of my nervous energy, but I'd exhausted all of my usual methods. Sam followed me around, always my protector. I paused and stared out the window, trying to pick out the small pond in the dark. Unconsciously, I scratched Sam's big head, and welcomed his weight as he leaned into me, giving me the equivalent of a hug.

"What am I missing, Sam?"

Andy was downstairs working with three others on how they would be able to reverse the GPS cloaking. Jackie had spent the evening searching financials trying to finish tying Alex Browning to Albert Griffin until her headache was visible to anyone who looked. It had taken a directive from the commander before she'd opted for a trio of aspirin and a few hours of down time.

I'd spent the evening going over the reports that we had, looking at topographical maps and trying to figure out where we went next.

A light knock sounded on the door.

"Monica?" Andy whispered. "Are you awake?"

Sam rushed to the door to greet his new friend. I followed a few steps behind.

Opening it, I saw Andy silhouetted by the light from the hall. "What's up?"

"We did it. We've got a version running right now, trying to locate their phones and vehicles. Thought you might want to come down."

The kitchen was crowded as the three techs worked on the terminals that had been brought in, while the commander and the agents watched from behind.

"How confident are you with the returns?" Commander Willoby asked the nearest tech who looked to be almost too young to be in the FBI.

"This is the first run, sir. I believe that it will give us the location to within about a quarter mile. Not perfect just yet. But as we tweak the coding, we'll be able to refine that down to only a few feet."

I watched as the computer screen showed a series of blips then changed perspective.

"Okay, we're getting the best results here," the tech pointed to his screen which displayed a faint outline of the Massachusetts with five small circles. "Changing the resolution, we can bring you into this area here."

I slipped out to the living room and grabbed the maps that I'd been working with earlier.

"I still can't confirm which of these is the actual point and which is the echo," the tech was saying as I came back in.

I compared the areas that he was showing on the screen with my map. "I think we can eliminate three of them. The soil profile indicates that it would be most likely one of these two," I said pointing at the one nearest the coast and one a few miles north.

"How long do you anticipate it will take to tweak your system, son?" the commander asked of the tech.

"Well, Sir, it depends on—hold on." He turned back to his screen and began tapping furiously. "Carl, run the data on who he's calling."

One of the blips on his screen, the one nearest the coast, changed from amber to green. "Detective," the tech nodded to me. "It seems you were right on the money."

I stared unsure of what he was saying. It was Andy who broke the silence. "You caught him making a call?"

"Yeah. Now we just need to figure out who he called. But we got him. Your boy is right here, right now. And the nice thing that he didn't know, we were able to get a unique identifier on him because of that. It'll be no problem tracking him now."

From the other side of the room, Carl spoke up. "I've got a number, and part of the voice recording. He spoke to a woman for about two minutes."

We listened as he played it.

"Listen, Alex, Griff wants this taken care of immediately," the woman's voice said.

"I'm pushing him. He's being stubborn about this, just like he's been his whole life. He says he wants proof that his little friend is okay. Maybe we should bring him part of a finger or something."

"That may just push him over the edge. Why don't you tell your brother that if he's real good, and does what he's supposed to, I'll arrange a visit for him over the weekend? And to sweeten the pot, I'll call tomorrow night, and the two love birds can chat for a few minutes."

"Sounds like a plan to me. Later then."

The line went dead.

"The male has been identified through voice print as Alex Browning," Agent Immentz said looking up from his own phone. "Not sure who the woman is."

"Can you run a voice comparison to Juliet Lewis?" I asked. "She's involved here somehow."

Immentz nodded. "We can do that. And we can monitor the whereabouts of that phone until we gain confirmation that it is her. Once that happens, we'll have the warrants for tapping in place."

"And hopefully, we can toss her in a cell for a very long time," I added.

Watching the sunrise over the Nantucket sound, I looked around. I knew where the other fifteen officers and agents were, but most were totally invisible to my eye. I could only hope that they would remain so to the eye of the career criminal.

I was sitting in a van that was parked about a quarter mile from the compound where we had isolated Alex's cell phone. Jackie, Mark and Adam had been assigned with me as well. "What do we have on the compound so far, Adam?"

He checked his computer screen. "Seems like a fairly reasonable layout. It's a single floor building with three separate entrances. Front door leads into a foyer that leads into the study, the dining room and the main hall. Kitchen is to the right, behind the dining room, and has a second door that leads to the garden out back. To the left is another hallway that leads to the three bedrooms and the great room. Sliding glass doors in the great room lead out to the deck behind the house. There are three bathrooms. One in the master bedroom, one by the first bedroom and the last off of the study.

"Right now, it seems that our suspect is in the study. That is, if he's carrying the phone on his person."

I nodded. "Most likely he is. Any idea on where they might have his brother stashed?"

Adam shrugged. "The chopper's infrared is picking up four people. Two in the study, so presumably, Alex has company. Then we have one in the kitchen area and one in bedroom number one."

"If we follow the idea that Stephen was taken against his will, he's most likely the one in the bedroom."

"Makes sense," Mark chimed in. "If they're holding him there, they're probably not going to let him wander around on his own."

The radio crackled. "All units, thirty seconds to go."

Mark tightened his seat belt and started the van.

The plan was fairly straight forward. An F.B.I. hostage team was heading in and we were going to block the driveway and provide support. Another two teams had circled behind the house and were preparing a simultaneous entrance through the garden. There were teams stationed on each exit. Our lookout and communications van was under the guise of a telephone repair truck that was just at the edge of the property.

If everything went according to plan, the Feds would bring everybody out, and then we'd get our chance to go through the house.

I didn't exactly like sharing the collar this way, but that's the way things happen.

Everyone tensed when we heard the "go" command. The van lurched from its place and turned in behind the F.B.I. van.

I watched, one hand on the door, the other on my gun, as the agents headed in. The staccato bursts told me that gunfire was being exchanged, and I could feel the odd combination of adrenaline and apprehension.

A chair crashed through the window to my right, and I watched as a lone figure bounded out running for the trees to the north.

"It's Alex!" I shouted as I hurled myself out the door.

I could hear the footsteps of at least one person following me, but I never turned to see who it was.

Browning apparently had heard them too. His head swiveled just before he reached the tree line. The gun came up and he loosed five rounds.

Diving out of the line of fire, I tucked and rolled to my right and sprung back up. The defensive maneuver had cost me a few seconds, and he'd used those seconds to get a few more feet ahead of me and reach the trees.

I pushed myself harder than I ever had before. He was only twenty feet in front of me now, and running wildly.

I realized two things as I entered the woods. No one was behind me and I was going to need help to catch him.

A bullet dug into the soft ground just left of my foot. I ducked behind a large maple and felt the impact of another round hitting the trunk. I could hear that he was no longer running, and now I was pinned down. Where the heck was the rest of the team?

More impacts hit the ground and the trees.

I needed a diversion, and quickly.

Looking down at my feet, I saw a rock about the size of a baseball sticking out from ground. Kicking it with the heel of my boot, I broke it free of the sod.

Shifting my Glock to my right hand I picked up the rock. I really only had one chance, so I needed to make it good. I knew about where he was, so I cautiously looked to the side away from where we had come from. There was a large tree about fifty feet away.

I tossed the rock towards the tree and dropped down. When I heard it hit its mark, I swiveled out, gun level and instinct took over.

He spun towards the noise that was behind him.

I pulled the trigger. Twice.

My ears were ringing from the sound of the shots, but I'd watched him go down. Two blooms of red; one on his upper left, one in the abdomen. Still crouched, gun ready, I quickly made my way over to him.

I stepped on his hand "That's far enough, Browning."

He looked up at me with distain. "Why didn't you shoot better, cop?"

I answered him honestly. "I wouldn't want to let you take the easy way out, Alex. I'd much rather get to see you spend the next thirty years or so in a small box. Besides, I still haven't had a chance to have a real heart-to-heart with you. So many questions."

Wrenching his arms behind his back, I cuffed him. "Suspect is down, north woods about twenty yards in. Requesting assistance," I said into the radio.

My call was answered a moment later when the Lieutenant and Kerri came running in.

"Dietz, you'd better get out there," the Lieutenant said grimly. "Jackie is asking for you."

"Jackie? What happened? She was right—" The awful truth hit me. Jackie had been right behind me when Alex had taken the first shots at me. The ones that I'd dodged. "Is she…" I couldn't finish the question.

Kerri laid her hand on my shoulder. "She's tough. She'll pull through this."

I headed back towards the house. Behind me I could hear Kerri reading Alex his rights, ahead I could see flashing lights.

Jackie was tough. She'd get through this, Kerri had said. But could I? What would happen to me if she didn't?

I raced out of the woods, breaking into the lawn of the estate. EMTs were working on someone lying on the ground, surrounded by grim faced Adam and Mark.

"Jackie!" I ran over.

Her eyes fluttered when she heard me call. "Sorry, Monica. I wasn't fast enough." The words came out weak. Her eyes closed and her head rolled to the side.

"No," I choked out. "Don't you dare die on me, Gannon! You hear?"

CHAPTER 23

Staring at the pages of the novel currently clutched in my hands, I tried to make myself relax. It was useless. The past two days since the shooting had been among the most stressful that I'd ever endured.

The act of arresting Alex Browning had required a high price. Both of Browning's associates had been killed when they'd tried to draw on the F.B.I., but of greater immediacy to me was that one trooper had been killed and my partner critically injured.

Jackie had been rushed to Central, where it took fourteen long hours of surgery for the doctors to feel that she had a fighting chance. She was still in ICU, and under a drug induced coma. The captain and the Lieutenant had both told me I needed to go get rest, but I'd refused to leave. Andy, who'd been there holding my hand the entire time, was the one who finally broke through and convinced me to go.

Alex Browning, on the other hand, had been awake and was being questioned by the feds. I was going to get my chance to go at him in the morning and needed the rest.

So, here I was, under orders, essentially locked in my room at the house trying to fall asleep. But I knew I didn't want to sleep. Every time I closed my eyes I saw Jackie lying there. Bleeding. Gasping for breath.

I tried to concentrate on the soft snores that came from Sam. Wishing that there were some way that I could drift off to a dreamless sleep.

Giving up, I climbed out of bed and walked to the window.

Stars were peeking out from behind the clouds. I rubbed my hands on my arms, trying to erase the coldness that I felt. My head turned at the tap on the door.

"Yes?" I called softly.

The door cracked open and Andy's head poked in, "I heard you moving around in here. Why aren't you asleep?"

" I can't. The dream comes back." I moved over to the door, if nothing else right now I felt I needed to be physically closer to him. "Every time I close my eyes, I relive that moment. I see him turning and firing. I hear the sound of the impact, but I keep running. Chasing him."

Andy pulled me into his arms and led me to the bed. Cuddling on the edge, he stroked my hair and tightened his grip on me. "You did your job, Monica. You got him. And, Jackie did hers. I," he hesitated. "I can't say that I understand. I don't. But I can empathize with you about this. You feel responsible for her getting hurt. But you're not. You're not the one who pulled that trigger. The only one that is responsible for that is Alex Browning, and you know that."

"I know that intellectually, but it's hard to get it out of my mind."

"I forget. You don't forget easily, if ever. That memory of yours, which is an advantage in your line of work, can also be a hindrance, especially with personal traumas like this one."

I could only nod.

"Do you think it would help if I held you while you slept?"

I shrugged.

He laid me down on the bed, spooning in behind me and started murmuring a song in a language that I didn't recognize.

Knowing that I had my knight and my dog to protect me, my mind finally shut down and I drifted off to sleep.

Sun poured in through the window causing me to squint when I first opened my eyes. I could feel the pressure of Andy's arm, still wrapped around my waist, and was thankful that I had someone that I could count on to be what I needed right now.

I slid out from under his arm and took my yoga outfit with me to the bathroom.

"Interesting pose," he said forty minutes later with a wink. "How much more do you have to do?"

"I've finished most of my routine. I should be done in about ten minutes. You want to join me?"

"I think, I'm going to pass for now and just watch and see if I learn anything."

"Thanks for being there last night," I said as I leaned into the next stretch.

He'd propped himself up to lean on one arm while petting Sam with the other. "Monica, you're too important to me to let anything happen to you. I've told you that before. I'm going to do whatever it takes to keep you safe and sane. Well, as best as I can given your profession," he amended before I could protest about the safety issue.

"So, what's the plan for today?" he asked while I was rolling up my mat.

"Alex Browning. The feds have spent two days questioning him about the whereabouts of Cathy Evans. Today, it's my turn to talk to him."

"Do you think he knows where she is?"

I stared at him. "Yeah. He hasn't told anybody anything useful yet, but I think he knows what's going on. I just need to figure out how to get it out of him."

"Any idea on what approach you're going to take with him?"

"Not really. I was kind of hoping that it would just, you know, come to me. Why?"

"I may have something that you can use."

"Really? What?"

"I'll show you. When we have breakfast."

I stood in observation, looking through the one-way glass. "Slimy little grub, isn't he?" I mumbled to no one.

"He is," Captain Willoby said. "Sorry to startle you, but I wanted to come down and see how things go with him."

"I'm anxious to get in there and get him going. But, I need to remember to keep my perspective as well. From what we know about him, he's always been the one calling the shots. I need to knock him off balance and keep him there until he says something that we can use."

"You'll get him, Dietz. I have confidence in you."

We both looked up at the sound of a door closing. A tall thin man with silver hair strode into the interview room, smiled at Alex and shook his hand heartily.

"Speaking of low life," Willoby said. "Should have figured Browning would get Simon Morales. Defense attorneys are a shady bunch, but this guy makes most of them look like white knights. Be careful in there."

I peered through the glass, watching the interaction between the two men. It was time.

I strode into interview, clutching my notes.

"Detective, I'm Simon Morales, and I demand that you release my client. You have him here on trumped up charges, and I won't allow that."

"Sit down, Mr. Morales. Alex Browning is under arrest for kidnapping, murder, conspiracy to commit murder, attempted murder, assault with a deadly, aggravated assault, arson, use of an explosive device and fraud. Now, it's not my job to grant clemency. It's my job to get scum like him off the street. Some of those charges are federal, and he'll answer to them in federal court. But right now, we're going to talk about the ones that I'm involved with. We'll get to the assaults, and attempted murder and murder in a few minutes.

"So, Mr. Browning, can you tell me why you blew up my house and destroyed the fourth floor of the crime lab?"

"I didn't do nothing. Why would I want to waste my time worrying about some cop?"

I nodded my head. This was about what I'd expected. He'd deny everything and then try to blame somebody else. "Do you have any idea who might have done it then?"

"If I did, I'd want to buy them a beer. If that's what it takes to keep you cops from sticking your noses into everyone else's business, then hey, it works for me."

"Mr. Browning, why were you keeping your brother prisoner at the residence on Klein Street?"

Alex grinned. "I wasn't holding my brother prisoner. He was a guest in my house."

"And you always keep guests in a room that is secured by three deadbolt locks and has riot bars on the window?"

"Steve was working on some very, um, secretive stuff. He needed the security."

"Funny. When we talked to him, he had a little different name for it. He said that you were blackmailing him into creating a special computer code."

"He's my brother. Why would I blackmail him? Besides, he knows almost all of my secrets. It wouldn't work, if you know what I mean."

"Oh, I agree whole heartedly. I mean, why should two brothers try to outdo each other. I just figured that since he already gave us his side of the story, maybe you'd like to give yours."

"My client will be doing that and more." Morales sneered when he spoke.

I quickly came to the realization that I didn't like him as a human.

"That's okay, Mr. Morales. We've got everything that we need." It was time to play a trump card. "You see, when we talked to Stephen Browning, he gave us the codes. He explained how his girl friend, Catherine Evans had been abducted from her place of business and was being held by his brother's group.

"The crime lab was able to decipher the scrambler codes, so we were able to listen to phone conversations between the group. The intel that we've gotten from the phone taps has Juliet Lewis telling one of her friends that she'd orchestrated everything, but had Alex running around doing all of her dirty work.

"So, since we've got the evidence, this is really a formality. I'm sure that the prosecutors will be going for the death penalty, since his list of crimes include murder. We know that he was responsible for five deaths, including one police officer.

"If you don't have anything to say, anything that might sway me from working to make this better, I'll just write up my report based on what we have and see you in court."

I pulled my papers together, and prepared to stand. Hoping that they would cave.

"What? Who the heck is Juliet Lewis? And, what do you mean that I'm being left to hang? And, what do you mean, five murders?" Alex snapped. "I didn't kill no cop!"

I glared at him. "Let me see. There was Toby Williams and Todd Jenkins from Cathy's Collectibles, Leo Spiro, Derek Hanson and trooper Stanley Roberts."

Browning gasped. "I didn't have anything to do with Derek. He died when—"

He stopped at the glare from his lawyer.

"Oh, don't stop," I encouraged.

"Don't say anything, Alex," Morales warned.

"But I'm not going down for things I didn't do. I never touched Leo or that Jenkins guy! It was Jewels. She was bragging about it when we met with Griffin. I'm not gonna let her make me her patsy."

"But Toby Williams had played you all. You helped him get that fabulous coat, designed to steal credit information, and then he tried to cut you all out. He found his own programmer and was going to leave you all with nothing, right?"

"Yeah, the lousy double crosser. I'm glad—"

"Alex!" Morales hissed, placing a hand over Browning's arm.

"Yeah, I'm sure you're glad that he's out of the picture. I mean, you had to teach him, and everyone else who follows, a lesson. It probably felt righteous when you shot him, right?"

"Sure did. I loved watching him twitch—"

His face froze as he realized what he'd just said.

I smiled coyly at him. "Gottcha. Now, since you've just admitted that you did shoot Toby Williams, why don't we talk about the others?"

"Can you give me a few minutes with my client?" Morales asked frustrated.

I used my cell phone when I stepped back into the observation room and called the prosecutor assigned to the case. I figured that perhaps the best way to close everything here was to offer a deal.

Through the window, I could see the two men arguing, and couldn't help but smile. When it looked like they were done, neither looked happy.

I made my way back into the room. "All set now?"

When neither objected, I resumed my seat. "Okay, Alex, you've already implicated yourself in the murder of Toby Williams. Tell me about the others."

"Hold on, detective," Morales jumped in. "How about this? My client will plead guilty to manslaughter on the Williams case, he'll give you information about the other murders that were committed by another party, and we can drop the kidnapping charges?"

"The DA isn't going to go all the way down to manslaughter. Murder 2, and if he gives information about the other murders, this office will not pursue the kidnapping."

The two men shared a look. Alex grimaced before he gave a slight nod.

"Okay, we'll take the deal," Morales said.

"Good. Let me call the DA, as I'm sure they'll be happy about this as well, and then you can tell me about everything else."

It took about fifteen minutes for me to get everything in order before I returned to the interview room. Alex was not looking very happy at the moment, and I really didn't feel sorry for him at all. He'd spent most of his life to this point, bullying and blaming others. Now it was time to face the music.

"Okay, Alex," I began. "We've set up everything for the deal. Now, tell me about what happened to Toby first."

Morales nodded, so Alex began his tale.

"Griff was looking for some new ideas, you know. Anyway, Toby come up to him and tells him about this one, for making a suit that can collect data. Now, Toby'd worked for Griff for several years, and had earned Griff's trust. So after a little bargaining, Griff said he'd underwrite the project for Toby.

"Once Toby had the design drawn up, he told Griff that he had the program already set. Griff decided that he wanted his own version of the program, and sent me to see my brother and to, um, convince him, yeah that's it, convince him that it would be in his best interest for him to help with the design of the computer chip that would be the brain of the system. Stephen, well, let's just say that he didn't like the idea and refused.

"While this was all going on, Griff kept playing Toby. He had his girlfriend go up to Boston and pick up the special wire that Toby said we needed. Toby got everything together about six weeks ago.

"As I was trying to work on getting Steve to, um, reconsider our job offer, we heard a rumor that Toby was going to sell the product to some out of town dude. I think it's safe to say that Griff wasn't happy about this. When Toby ignored Griff's request to meet, I was told to take care of things anyway that I saw fit. Griff only wanted two things: sole access to the suit and the technology that would run it.

"So, that's when you decided to hit Cathy's Collectibles?" I asked.

Alex shook his head. "Not exactly. I'd been trying to think of ways to get Steve to do what we wanted, and the more I pushed the more he resisted. I found out about his relationship with Cathy, and we decided that we'd use her to put the necessary pressure on my brother to get him to do what we wanted. I'd planned to persuade her through other means.

"We'd been following Toby trying to find an opportune time to relieve him of the coat. That's when we found him with Jenkins. Jenkins worked for Manny Thompson, who has been Griff's biggest competitor for nearly twenty years. I couldn't let him get that coat. It was purely by chance that they walked into Cathy's store. As things unfolded, I realized that I had a way to take care of several things at once. I got rid of Williams, and I grabbed Cathy.

"After I dropped Cathy off at Griff's for safekeeping, I went over to Steve's. It was a fairly easy matter of drugging him. We did a quick search to ensure that he hadn't left anything that could be traced to us."

I referred to my notes. "A couple of questions before we move on. When you talk about Griff, do you mean Albert Griffin?"

Alex nodded. "Yeah. I've been working for him for nearly twenty years."

"Do you happen to know Mr. Griffin's girlfriend?"

"Not really. He just calls her Jewels."

I flipped over a picture of Juliet Lewis. "Is this Jewels?"

"Bingo. That'd be her."

I decided to push him further. "Jenkins survived the shooting at the store. What happened next?"

"Well, Griff, he decided that we should finish Jenkins off. But he was in the hospital, right, so I told him, I said 'Griff, there ain't no way we're gonna be able to get at him there.' But Griff, he just smiled and said 'where there's a will, there's a way.'

"Jewels was there, and she said she knew just how to do it. Griff looked at her hard, but then for some reason told her to give it a try if she wanted to. I think, looking back at it, I think she was trying to get made in Griff's organization.

"Anyway, she took off, said she'd be back in a while. I didn't think anything more about it that night. Next morning, I hear that Jenkins was dead."

"How did Leo Spiro fit in?" I prompted.

"Ah, Leo. All he wanted was a good time. I recruited him with the promise of some prime weed. When Jewels found out about that, she pushed Griff to get rid of him. I think he gave her the go-ahead on that. Griff started putting the pressure on me about then as well. He had Toby's design for the coat and Steve was in the house and was beginning to work on the programing for us. We just needed to be sure that the coat didn't fall into the wrong hands, and that the cops would just let everything go."

"But we didn't, did we? You called me, threatened me about that coat, didn't you? Did you also torch the crime lab, Alex? What about my house?"

He hung his head down, not even looking to his lawyer. "Yeah. That was me. I figured that if I could get you to back off, it would keep the heat off of us, and then I could figure out how to get by the security to either destroy the coat that you'd collected or steal it back. I coerced the delivery guy, Todd Something-or-other, to give me his uniform so I could be sure you got the messages. When you refused to give up the investigation, I got, desperate, I'd guess. Coming at you at your house wasn't the smartest thing I could have done. It ended up getting Derek killed. I still don't know what happened to him."

I knew. I thought of my gentle giant, and the memory that he'd killed to protect me that night.

"You've done okay, Alex. Now tell me where I'm going to find Cathy," I said.

He rattled off an address over on the Cape.

I looked him directly in the eye as I stood. "When we stormed the house on the sound, you attempted to evade us, Alex. During the firefight, you killed a state trooper and critically injured my partner. As these aren't part of the deal, you will be charged with Murder 1 on Roberts, and the attempted murder of a police officer, resisting arrest and assault with a deadly. Other counts may be added later. I'm sure the Fed's will be in touch regarding the kidnapping."

Alex's eyes bulged. "You said you'd drop that charge!"

"No," I countered. "If you review the recording, you'd find that I said that this office wouldn't pursue that charge. Kidnapping is a federal offense. I don't have any say on that one."

Exiting the room, I immediately made two calls. The first was to the hospital to check on Jackie. The second was to the commander. It was time to go to the Cape.

CHAPTER 24

"How's Jackie doing?" Kerri asked as she climbed into the passenger's seat.

"They've upgraded her from critical to serious. She's still in ICU and sedated, but they're optimistic about things." I answered.

Spinning the car onto the expressway, I pointed us towards the Cape.

"I did a bit of checking while you were securing the warrants. It seems that the address that Browning gave you is owned by Richards Properties, which is owned by A.G. Richards."

"A.G. Richards," I mused. "Bet that stands for Albert Griffin. If I remember correctly, he used his maternal grandmother's maiden name for some of his aliases. So that would fit."

"Do you think he'll be there?" Kerri wondered aloud.

I thought about it. If what Browning had told me during the interview was straight, then Juliet Lewis was involved romantically with Griffin. If she was in charge of keeping Cathy at the Cape house, then there was a possibility that Griffin himself would be there. But, there was something else that Browning had said. Something that had made more sense to me.

"I don't think so," I stated. "Browning made a comment that Lewis seemed like she was trying to be "made" in the organization. I don't think Griffin is going to be sleeping with one of the foot soldiers of the group. So, if she is there, the odds aren't going to be good that we're going to get him at the same time."

We pulled up in front of the address, and I shook my head.

"Did Browning actually call this a house?" Kerri asked.

"Yeah. If I had to take a guess, this place is at least 12,000 square feet. The garage is bigger than my whole house…" I paused, remembering that my house was now a pile of splinters.

"Maybe after we bust these bozos, you can buy this one from the city," Kerri said. A hint of humor eked through in her voice.

I just closed my eyes, trying to put the thoughts of my house out of my mind.

Kerri broke the silence after a minute. "How do you want to do this?"

"I have a feeling that if we walk up to the door and ring the bell, they're likely to answer with gunfire. For that matter, I think we're going to have a problem getting to the door to begin with."

Kerri looked at the house again. "You're probably right. A six-foot tall wrought iron fence is liable to keep people out. What's next?"

"Let's head up the road a bit, and we'll call in some reinforcements," I said as I pulled back into traffic.

"Are your straps secure, detective?" the pilot, Tim Larriat, asked.

I looked over at the young man who was going to "crash" his helicopter on the front lawn of the estate. "I'm ready," I lied. "You ever done anything like this before, Tim?"

Tim shrugged. "Did it once or twice when I was in the Marines. It was an effective way to get into hostile territory quickly and relatively quietly. By the time the goons inside realize what they've heard, police will be entering all entry ways."

It was hard to relax as the five blades of the rotor carried the Enstrom through the cool air. The plan appeared simple enough. There were five of us in the helicopter. Once we were close to the estate, Tim was going to cut the engine, and we'd simulate an emergency landing onto the estate. The hope was that if anyone was paying attention to us, they'd assume that we were in trouble, and less likely to cause a fuss.

At least until we made the entry.

Of course, the plan was deceptively simple. We had to trust that the helicopter would autorotate down in a controllable manner, and that Tim could drop us mere feet from where we would need to be.

Tim's voice sounded calm as it came through my headset. "Autorotation beginning in five…four…three…two…one…engine off."

Once the engine shut down, things were eerily quiet. Just the rushing wind as it swept over the blades of the now free-wheeling rotor.

I snugged my seatbelt one more time, as I watched the ground coming up faster than I'd like through the windscreen.

"You may want to unlatch the doors," Tim said. If he had any concerns about this, his voice didn't betray him.

The two officers who were seated next to the doors, released the mechanisms, and left their hands on the handles, ready to throw them open as soon as we touched down.

The helicopter slowed and flared before it gently set down on the front lawn. "Go! Go! Go!" the team leader called through the headset.

I leapt from the copter, and headed for the front door. Kerri joined up with me on my left side. "That was exciting," she muttered as we climbed the steps, guns drawn.

I simply grunted in consent before I banged on the door three times, "This is a joint police task force. We have a warrant to search the premises."

I could hear shouts coming from inside the house followed by the sound of breaking glass.

"Take the door, Harris," Agent Immetnz said as he nodded to an agent who carried a small battering ram.

With a quick practiced motion, the agent hurled the ram through the door and immediately sidestepped out of the way.

I followed Immentz through the door going low, while Kerri and Harris secured the entrance and provided cover.

It took less than a minute before we had four suspects in custody.

"Well, let's see who we've got here," Immentz said as he walked along the line of cuffed individuals. "Kirby Thomas, I haven't seen you in almost two years. When did you get out on parole?" he asked the tall, gaunt man.

When Thomas gave no answer he continued on. "These two," he said pointing at two young men, neither of whom looked to be more than eighteen, "I don't believe that I've had the pleasure of meeting you before."

Harris pulled the wallets from the men, "Gomer here is Sean Lacoby, and his accomplice is Geoffrey Scott."

Immentz nodded before he turned to face the woman, "Juliet Lewis. I suppose I'm glad to see you here. At least now we can stop the manhunt and arrest you for murder."

"I want my lawyer," she snarled. "I want to know why you broke into Griff's house in the first place? We ain't done nothing."

"Excuse me, Sir?" a young agent said coming into the room. "We, ah, found a door that was hidden behind a bookcase. When we knocked and called, there was a muted cry from inside. We just can't figure out how to open the door."

Immentz shook his head. "Didn't they teach you guys how to get through a door at Quantico?"

The young agent blushed slightly. "Yes, Sir, they did. However, the training didn't include getting through this kind of door."

I watched the interaction from across the room, keeping most of my attention on Lewis. When the agent admitted defeat with the door, her bad-tempered snarl changed into a smug grin.

"She knows something," Kerri muttered to me.

"Yeah. But since she's already requested a lawyer, we can't do much in the way of questioning her." I paused to think for a minute. There was a probably a very scared woman being held in that room. How could I get the information out of Lewis without technically infringing on her rights?

I didn't have a good answer. My attention went back to the two F.B.I. agents.

"It's got some kind of electronic lock on it, according to Walters. We're not sure how big the room is, so that takes out the possibility of using torches to cut through. We're stuck, Sir."

Immetnz wasn't looking happy. He had his hands stuffed into his pockets, and a scowl was etched on his face. "Any way to use a computer to bypass?"

"Probably, but the closest agent we've got with that kind of skill is located in Boston. It'd take him minimum of two hours to get here."

"Agent Immentz?" I interrupted. "What about Dr. Carson? He's the one who broke their cloaking device. He'd only be a few minutes away," I suggested.

Immentz thought briefly. "He's good people. Give him a call, and let's call the guy in Boston. We get everyone we can on this." He turned to head out of the room and stopped. "Let's take these four, and cuff and shackle 'em in the wagon. We're going to hold off transporting until we get through that door."

I'd noticed Lewis' eyes go wide when I mentioned that Andy had broken their cloaking device. They were even wider at Immentz's plan of holding them on site in the van. I followed a hunch and trailed behind the agents leading our suspects to the waiting vehicle.

Lewis started to struggle as she was led near the van.

"I don't wanna go in there and sit and wait!" she bellowed. "Let me sit out here, please."

"What's the matter? Afraid of the dark?" the agent nearest to her asked.

As they were getting ready to hoist her into the back of the van, I decided to try a slightly different approach. "Hold on a sec," I said jogging the last few feet. "Let me talk to her for a minute before you toss her in."

"You want us to stand guard with you?" the agent asked.

"No. Just cuff her to the handle out here. I'll call you when I'm done."

"You got it," he said.

Thirty seconds later, Juliet was cuffed to the back of the truck and the two agents were standing about twenty feet away.

"Okay, Juliet, seems to me we've both got some choices to make here. It appears that you have issues with small dark places, and you heard the lead agent. You're going to be sitting there until we get through that door. Dr. Carson is good, but it took him nearly four hours to break the coding that you were using to disguise where your cars were. Now I know that you've requested a lawyer, and you have the right to refuse to talk until he's present. But, you're not going to be making that call until you've been processed. And that's not going to happen until we've gotten into that room."

I could see that she was trying to figure out how to get out of this safely. Finally she looked over her shoulder into the dark enclosure, and shuddered. "I'm not saying a word to you, but maybe F. Scott Fitzgerald was right and the best thing a girl can be in this world, is a beautiful little fool."

I watched as she delivered these words. Her eyes were wide. Was it fear of going into the van? Or, was she trying to make sure I got a message?

I waved the two agents back over. "I need to check something out in the house, but I may need to talk to her again. Why don't you watch her here for a few minutes."

I turned and strolled back into the house, and followed the sounds of the investigators to where they were looking at the door they'd found. I walked over to the bookcase and began looking through the titles.

"The Great Gatsby," I murmured, pulling the book off the shelf.

"Planning on doing a little reading, Detective?" Immentz commented.

A quick look at the book revealed a bookmark that was mid-way through the novel. Opening it, I lifted a small typed sheet from the pages.

"Would you care for the instructions on how to open that door?" I asked, turning the paper towards him.

"How did you know that they would be in there?" he demanded.

"Lewis's file says that she suffers from claustrophobia. When you said to throw them in the truck until we got through the door, I figured her fear might help. I gave her a chance to stay outside for a few extra minutes. She took the ring, as I expected. She never directly said it was here, but she gave me the veiled clue."

Even with the directions, it took nearly five minutes for us to unlock the door.

As it creaked open, a faint whimper emerged. I grabbed my flashlight, and shone it into the small space. The beam swept over the dirty face of a woman.

"Cathy? It's all right. I'm Detective Monica Dietz. You're safe now."

I leaned back in the chair while waiting in Commander Willoby's office and stared out the window. It'd been two days since we arrested Lewis.

"How's your partner doing?" the commander asked when he walked in.

Straightening up, I replied, "She's getting stronger. When I went by to see her last night, she was still sedated, but they're planning to bring her around over the next day or so. It looks like the worst of things are over for her."

Willoby nodded as he took his seat and opened one of the files on his desk. "It seems as though Ms. Lewis became a bit of a canary, and sang you a pretty nice song. She was even nice enough to tell us about the two custodians that she bribed to get information from within our department and the crime lab."

"Yeah," I conceded. "I have to admit I was a little shocked to hear about Lenny Mox. Seemed like a nice old guy when I'd run into him after hours. As for Lewis, she admits her part in the creation of the suit coat, claims she had knowledge of, but disavows any personal involvement with, anything else."

"What's your next step going to be?"

"Theoretically, we could end it here. We've got Browning cold on the Williams' murder, and conspiracy to kidnap. We've linked him to bombing my house, and the fire at the lab. He'll be going away for a long time.

"Lewis would do time for the intent to fraud. We've got enough circumstantial to charge her with at least conspiracy on the kidnapping. The thing is," I paused and stared out the window again. "The thing is, I think she's directly responsible for at least two deaths. We have her on video at the hospital, and Spiro was killed in an apartment that she rented. But in both cases, we don't have actual physical evidence. Plus, from what I'm seeing with the way this organization has been set up, Lewis and Browning are nothing more than foot soldiers. If we stop now, they're just going to be replaced in short order."

Willoby rubbed his eyes. "I'm guessing you'd like to go after the boss?"

"Yes, Sir. Albert Griffin has been on the fringe of things for a long time. Right now, we have some circumstantial evidence that we could bring him in on."

"Is that your recommendation? Bring him in?"

I shook my head. "Not at this time, Sir. If we make a play for him now, it gives him the advantage of knowing that we're coming for him. He'll get his fancy team of lawyers to file motion after motion and delay upon delay until he has a way to flee. No, I think the better way right now is to continue working on tracking the money and phone records.

"If we can show that he told one of his underlings to kidnap Cathy Evans, or to get rid of Toby Williams, and then paid them to do so, we sew him into a few conspiracy charges. Makes it much harder for his lawyers to get him out."

The commander got up and paced. I was used to this behavior. He always thought better when he walked around.

He stopped by the window and peered out over the downtown view. "Have either of our guests said anything that might help us nail him?" he asked.

"Yes, Sir. Browning implicated him as giving the directions for the hit on Williams, Jenkins and Spiro, as well as ordering that Alex convince his brother to encode the coat. The residence is owned indirectly by Albert Griffin under a known alias, so that helps."

Willoby turned towards me. "I've often thought about that old phrase, a bird in the hand is worth two in the bush. We've got two birds in our hands right now safely in a cage, but I think we'd best work until we get the one that's still out there hiding in the bush." He sneered, "I think we've danced to Griffin's tune long enough. Get on the computer, call in favors,

I don't care what it takes, but get something that's going to stick. I want you to nail his butt to the barn door, Detective."

"I'm on it, Sir," I answered before I left.

CHAPTER 25

"Blasted computer," I muttered as the screen froze. Again.

"Arguing with inanimate objects, Detective?"

I turned to find Andy sitting on the corner of my desk. "I'm not so sure these things aren't alive. It never seems to fail that the more pressing the task, the more they do their own thing. The only constant is I'm constantly frustrated with them."

"Would I be correct that since the desk is littered with candy wrappers, you didn't take a lunch break?"

I glared at him. "I'm an adult, and I can eat what I darn well want, when I want it."

My stomach growled, and I grimaced.

"Come on, Monica. Let's go get something that resembles real food. It'll help you think better."

"Listen, Doc. It's a well known fact that chocolate is one of the main food groups."

"Among women, sure, but according to the AMA, it's junk food." He looked at me with a tight grin. "I'll make you a deal, let's go eat, and afterwards, I'll run the computer for you."

"Are you trying to bribe a public official, Doc?"

"No. I'm just trying to prevent the early death of an innocent electrical device."

I gave him a quick poke in the side as I pushed by him to grab my jacket. "I'm driving and you're buying."

I could feel the pressure of his hand, as well as every eye in the room, on my back as we walked out.

"You look like something my cat dragged in," Andy said as he carried our tray to an empty table.

"Thanks," I grumbled, unwrapping my burrito.

He set his food down, reached across the table and took my hand. "Monica, I've told you before that I love you. You've come to mean too much to me to let you abuse yourself like this." He shook his head, "What we're going through, all these experiences are too new to me. I can't say that I've ever been shot at, or had a house blown up around me. But they don't have a fraction of the impact of you being here with me does. And, I can honestly say, I've never had those kinds of feelings before either. That's why I feel obligated to take care of you."

Meat dropped out of my burrito, as I sat there frozen. A myriad of thoughts ran through my mind. Nobody outside of my immediate family had ever wanted to try to take care of me. How was I to respond?

"Andy, I'm flattered. I don't know what I did to deserve those kinds of feelings. But right now," my voice hitched trying to hold back the tears. "Right I'm so tied up in this—"

He slid next to me as I lost my internal battle and sobbed, offering me what I needed right then—a shoulder to cry on.

"Knock, knock. How're you feeling, Jackie?" I asked as we walked through the door.

Jackie looked up from the magazine that she was reading and scowled. "They've got me locked down in here. I can't even get up to use the bathroom. It's a little humiliating, ya know?"

I carefully leaned between the wires and the I.V. to give her a hug. "You scared the bejesus out of me. I thought," I fought back the tears again. "I thought that I'd lost another partner. You can't do that to me. I'm just getting you broken in."

Andy set the vase of flowers on the table and rubbed my arm in solidarity. "Good to see you awake, Jackie."

"Hey, Andy. I guess, from what the docs told me, that I'm lucky to be able to be seen. Sounds as though it was pretty close."

I laughed weakly. "Pretty close? You coded twice on the way in, and then they had you on the table for fourteen hours. You were at least lucky enough to be unconscious for the next two days. The rest of us were keeping a vigil at your bedside."

"Yeah, that's what my mom said." When my eyes furled in question, she answered. "She came down from Boston. You just missed her, actually."

"I can't wait to meet her and let her know what a hero her daughter is," I said.

Jackie looked up with pained eyes. "Did we get him?" she whispered.

I nodded. "Yeah, we got him. I ended up putting a few slugs in him, but they were only flesh wounds. When we laid everything out for him, he caved and turned evidence against Lewis and Griffin. He's currently in a cage waiting for sentencing. We found Stephen on site, and he's responding well. Lewis was holding Cathy Evans at a different location. So, thus far we're doing okay. We've rounded up a total of eight of Griffin's goons. And we're working on piling up enough evidence to put Griffin out of business for the next three lifetimes or so."

"And you stopped in here, to visit with me? Why aren't you working?" she demanded.

"Monica's been working almost around the clock," Andy answered before I could. "The only way that I've been able to see her over the past few days is if I stop in the station. Today, I found her at almost four-thirty hunched over at her desk surrounded by Milky Way wrappers, and looking like an extra from one of those zombie movies. I dragged her out and forced her to eat a real meal."

"I wanted, no, I needed to see you, and be sure that you were doing okay. Since Doc lured me out with the promise that he'd help with the computer work, I figured we'd stop on our way back into the station."

"I'm glad you did. Monica? I'm sorry that I wasn't faster."

"Shut it," I said. "Listen, Gannon, if I'd been faster on my feet, I might have been able to subdue Browning before he started shooting at everyone."

"No one's blaming you," Jackie said.

"I am," I stated. "It may not be rational, but it's how I'm feeling. I was the first in line, yet I didn't get hit. You and Trooper Roberts weren't as lucky, and I'll have to live with the fact that on a mission that I was lead on, two officers were hit."

Jackie grabbed my hand. "Monica, you know that we were just doing our jobs. You didn't shoot us, it was Browning who fired those shots. It was a result of his choices that caused the injuries. You're the one who put him in a cage. Remember that."

"Did you find anything?" I asked Andy several hours later.

"I've started a few runs. Nothing concrete yet, but there are a few things that look pretty promising." He turned the computer screen so I could see. "We've got a payment from AGR Clothing going into JTL Systems. Upfront, it may not seem like much, but when we go down a few layers, the picture changes. AGR is an offshoot of Brewster Industries, which is owned—"

"That's one of Griffin's," I noted.

"Want to take a guess about JTL?"

"I'm hoping that you're going to tell me that it's somehow tied to either Alex Browning or Juliet Lewis. So, based on the initials, I'm going to go with Lewis."

Andy nodded. "Bulls-eye."

I frowned. "But just because they've dealt with each other in business doesn't exactly implicate Griffin in the kidnappings or murders."

"That's true," he said, leaning back in his chair. "However, the next step is to look at the amounts and the invoices. AGR paid out twenty grand to JTL over the last ten days. Now, on the surface that arguably could be legit. But, I tend to be cynical."

"Me too," I said reaching for the phone.

"Carla?" I asked when a sleepy voice came on. "It's Monica Dietz."

"Do you have any idea what time it is, Detective? It's nearly two A.M.."

I grinned sheepishly. Oops.

"I'm sorry, but we just got a lead on a case that involves two kidnappings, and five murders," I explained. "I need two warrants ASAP, for all financial records, invoices and stock for AGR Clothing and JTL Systems."

"Are you planning to pull an all nighter?" Carla demanded.

"I think so," I admitted. "We're starting to get some momentum going here, and these warrants will give us the way to confirm a larger plot than we originally thought."

I hoped I wasn't going too far out on the proverbial limb here, but I needed those warrants.

Carla sighed. "Okay, I'll have them faxed to you in about fifteen minutes."

"Thanks," I said just before the line clicked off.

Andy was looking at me. "Let me guess. That was the judge, who didn't relish the idea of being woken in the middle of the night, right?"

"You trying for a detective shield, Doc?"

"No, can't say that I'd want one. I prefer working in the lab. Normally, you're less likely to be assaulted there."

"We've got about fifteen minutes before we'll be able to do anything else. Why don't we take a break, grab some food, and recharge before we take the next round?"

"That works. Where do you want to go?" he asked rising.

"We can head over to Shirley's. They're open all night," I said taking his hand as we strolled through the mostly empty station.

"Temperature's really dropped tonight. At this rate, we might have snow by Thanksgiving," Andy said as we stepped outside.

I glanced around. Something wasn't right, but I couldn't put my finger on it.

I started to scan, left-to-right.

"What is it, Monica? You've tensed up," Andy whispered.

"Not sure. I feel as though somebody's watching us right now."

"Should be safe enough with our escorts over there," he said pointing to the car where our federal baby-sitters were.

"Um, Andy? Look at the car carefully. Is there anybody in there?" I said. Every nerve in my body was on alert now.

"The two agents who've…wait, now that you mention it, it does look empty."

"Back inside now," I ordered.

The glass in the door shattered as the bark of the gunshot echoed across the lot. I pushed Andy down behind a concrete bench to the side of the door, sprawling across him.

"Where the heck are they?" I asked as the next shot rang out.

The concrete seat fractured inches away from my face. Instinctively, I put my head down lower. From the direction of the shrapnel, I had a rough idea on which direction our attacker was. Peering under the bench, I could make out the first two rows of windows on the building across the street.

There it was! Four windows in, on the second floor, a window stood wide open.

I managed to get my Glock out, and had it pointing at the window, but training kept me from pulling the trigger.

"Damn!" I cursed.

"What?" Andy's muffled voice came from underneath me.

"I cant' be sure what's in there. I won't take the shot unless I'm sure of my target."

I tried to shift myself so I could get a better view.

Three more shots rang out in quick succession, forcing me to take cover again.

When my head came up, I saw the figure running out the side door.

With my gun still in hand, I was off the starting block like an Olympic sprinter. I didn't waste my breath trying to convince this guy to stop.

Air hissed through my teeth, but I kept pushing my body to go faster. My sides burned through the effort. I sized up my quarry as I pursued him. Looked to be about five-three, judging the relative height against the doors of the shops that lined the deserted street. Whoever it was, they were spry and very agile.

We crossed the next intersection, and were coming up on East Main, when they veered off and around the corner.

I had to focus harder now. Couldn't let them get a chance to duck into a door way to either ambush me or escape. I dove and ended up behind a mailbox. Peering around the edge, I could see the suspect still running, but he'd angled toward a waiting vehicle.

A white Avalanche. I knew this vehicle. Well, not so much it, but I knew whose it was.

Springing from my hiding place I again ran in pursuit. The suspect was only a few yards from the waiting car.

I passed under a street lamp, and everything changed.

The Avalanche surged from the roadside, striking the suspect with the left front fender. I watched in horror as the figure flew into the air, doing three complete flips, arms flailing helplessly and landed head first with a sickening crunch.

I didn't waste my time worrying about the now injured suspect. I had a bigger concern. The Avalanche was accelerating straight at me.

I dove to the right, and just missed getting creamed. The driver slammed on the brakes, skidding and finally careening off a lamppost.

I rolled up on one knee, preparing to take a shot, when the white lights flashed on, and the Avalanche reversed towards me again.

I bolted into the street, crossing towards the only refuge that I could see; a small alley that appeared too small for the Avalanche to follow.

I'd taken two steps into the alley when I realized I was in trouble.

"Well, well, Detective," a calm voice said. "I figured that you'd come to me if I waited here long enough."

I searched the shadows, but I couldn't see anything or anyone. Glancing back over my shoulder, I saw that the Avalanche was now parked tight against the entryway to the alley.

The driver hadn't been chasing me. He'd been herding me. Driving me towards whoever was waiting, unseen in this alley.

"Griffin, it's over for you. We've tied you into several felony charges. So, even if you kill me, you're going away," I said, amazed at how calm my voice sounded.

"I don't think so, Detective. You see, in order for that to happen, you need to have evidence against me. After I kill you, it will be a simple matter of having Lonnie walk into the station and destroy what you've dug up. And as for your so-called witnesses? They might as well already be dead. Before noon tomorrow, those canaries are going to come down with a permanent case of laryngitis. Once all that is done, I'll be free to go my own way. So, no, Detective, it's not over. It's just beginning."

I heard him cock the hammer of a revolver. I kept searching for some clue as to where he was, but saw nothing.

Light erupted from the muzzle only ten feet away. Instinctively, I twisted and squeezed the trigger of the Glock in the general direction. I hated not being sure of my target, but this was a matter of life and death.

Pain ripped through my left shoulder, and I felt myself spinning away from the source of the shot.

I heard the sound of garbage cans toppling as someone thrashed at them. Griffin must have dived behind some to get out of my line of fire. I needed to get out of this alley before he could take another shot.

The Avalanche stood between me and any hope of escape, so I did the only thing I could think of. I shot the car.

Steam poured out of the ruined radiator, and I hoped that it'd be enough to confuse the driver and Griffin. Gritting my teeth against the stabbing pain in my shoulder, I sprang onto the hood of the car, and used it to vault myself over.

"Get her!" I heard Griffin yell from behind me.

So, I hadn't killed him. It'd been too much to hope for. But right now, I had more pressing matters. I needed to get away from him and get somewhere where I'd at least have a chance at being found before I bled out.

"She's over there," a new voice shouted moments before the sidewalk erupted from the assault of automatic weapon fire.

Ignoring my shoulder, I dove behind a large brick planter.

"Bloody hell," I murmured as I took a quick survey of my surroundings.

"Got her now," the driver said as the planter took multiple impacts.

"You'd better, Lonnie. We can't let her get out of here. I'm too invested in this to lose now."

Cautiously, I slid to my right so I could see around the planter. Two figures were stalking me. Lonnie must be the one on the left who was carrying some kind of rifle. That meant that the other figure would be Griffin.

I lined up my sights, and squeezed the trigger. Lonnie sprawled backwards, firing a salvo of shots as he fell. He didn't appear to be moving after he went down. Griffin dove for cover behind the truck.

"It's just you and me, Detective," Griffin yelled.

"And the cavalry," I muttered to myself as I pulled out my phone to dial 9-1-1.

The ground beside me exploded. "Blasted it all!" I shrieked, pulling my legs up.

Where was he? If he could see me, then I had to be able to see him.

Of course, he had the advantage. He'd seen me dive behind the planter. But, hadn't he taken cover?

I pushed myself to the left side of the planter. Stretching my neck, I could make out the tail end of the Avalanche. He wasn't visible over the top, but as I looked at the road, I could make out his foot.

Carefully, I pulled myself to the point where I could get my gun up. I had one shot at this.

Focusing on his foot, nothing else mattered now; I squeezed off the first round.

"What the heck?" Griffin yelled as he reacted from impulse, and stood up.

My second round caught him in the chest, causing him to drop his gun and crumple to the ground.

Lights suddenly flashed everywhere.

"Over here," someone yelled.

I felt myself being rolled over, and something being pressed on my shoulder as the world around me went black.

"Come on, Monica," Andy's voice broke into my consciousness.

I struggled to open my eyes, and winced at the bright light. "What? Where am I?" I moaned.

I could feel Andy's hand gripping mine. "You're okay now. The docs here say you'll be fine in a few days."

My brain started waking up. I recognized the smell of the sanitizer, and I could hear the beeps of the monitors. "Doctors? Why am I in the hospital?"

His laugh was rough. "You got shot. Scared ten years off of my life in the process. Don't you remember?"

I strained, searching for the memory that would make this all clear. "It's coming back," I said softly. I tried to move my left arm, but it wouldn't respond.

Andy must have seen the panic in my eyes. "Your shoulder's busted up pretty good, but they put it back together for you."

"What about Griffin, and his driver?"

"I'll handle this, Dr. Carson," Commander Willoby said. "Griffin got hit twice. Once in the foot, once in the chest. He lost two toes in the process, but is recovering nicely and is currently under guard. He'll be transferred to a federal facility once it's cleared. His driver, whom we identified as Lonnie Theringer, was dead at the scene. One shot, right through the heart. The body of Amy Rider, a known associate of Griffin's, was also recovered from the street. Upon hearing Dr. Carson's testimony, she was checked for GSR. It seems that she was the shooter who drew you out after she killed the two agents who were assigned to you. As far as the department is concerned you're on medical leave for a few months."

"I can't be out a few months!" I yelled. "I need to work, I need to testify and—"

Andy's hand tightened on mine. "Monica, you need time to recover. Besides, I thought that maybe taking a week or so, and heading to the south-west for a few days might be beneficial to your healing process."

"The south-west?"

"I saw your parents last night when they came in. We had a nice long talk. I'd like to take you to Arizona to see my mom."

Nerves coursed through me. "You want me to meet your family?" I asked in disbelief.

"Yes, very much. And, I'm sure that they'll remember you, I'd like to introduce you as my fiancée. That is, if you'll marry me," he said pulling out a small box.

Flipping it open, he held it out to me. A flash of color emanated from the solitaire. "What do you say?"

I threw my arm around his neck. "Yes! I never realized how much this would mean to me, until right now."

He slipped the ring onto my finger carefully. "We're going to have an intriguing future together, Detective Carson."

"You'd better believe it, Doc." As far as I was concerned, everything was right in the world right now. And I was going to hold on to that feeling for as long as I could.

CONTINUE READING FOR A PREVIEW OF

MISAPPROPRIATED
MEANS

"Hey, Sunshine, let's go. You got yourself a visitor today."

Bridgette Mahoney looked around at the empty rec room and at the solitary guard who stood in the door. "But I never get visitors," she stammered. "Who is it?"

The guard shrugged his shoulders, "Dunno. Some guy came in asked for you."

Fear curled in her stomach. Was it someone sent by Angelo Rodriguez, *el rey de los bandidos*, the king of the Bandits? Were they here to kill her she wondered. Well, she was going to find out regardless. What ever was waiting for her in the visitation room had to beat sitting alone.

Keeping her thoughts to herself, she followed the directions of the guard to the visiting area since she'd never been in this room before. Never had a visitor, so why would she?

The door clanked open, and she was escorted in.

Blue tile lined the floor, and gray paint covered the walls and small tables sat scattered about the center of the room. In fact, if it weren't for the bars on the small high windows and the guards at the doors, Bridgette thought, this could almost pass as a cafeteria in a government building.

Her eyes spied the Coke machine that was positioned near the visitor's entrance. She longed for a diet Coke, but they weren't allowed to have money in here. And since this was her first visitor ever, she didn't hold the odds high that she'd be having one today.

She sighed.

"Don't cross the yellow line," the guard said as he turned her towards a small table to the right.

She saw the dark haired figure there and scowled instinctively. How dare he? she thought.

She nearly turned back to the guard to request to be taken back. But he raised his eyes to look at her.

He looked nearly as miserable as she did.

His dark hair was cropped short, almost like a military cut. Dressed in a gray tee-shirt and blue jeans, he slouched at the table disguising his six-two frame. She knew that his ice blue eyes held secrets, and that his mind would be trying to ferret her secrets out.

He'd looked up at the sound of the heavy door. There she stood. Tall, only a few inches shorter than himself he recalled, moss green eyes and topped with unruly fire red hair.

A thin smile tried to form on his mouth. He reached down beside him and lifted a can of diet Coke and with a beckoning motion set it on the table.

She walked slowly towards him. Wary. This was the man who was responsible for her being here right now.

No. She stopped herself. She was the one who had committed the crime. He was only doing his job when he arrested her.

"Agent Franchini," she said gently as she slid into the bench that was mounted to the floor. "I'm not sure I'm supposed to talk to you without my lawyer. But, what brings you here today?"

"Hi, Bridgette. I need to talk to you about..." his voice trailed off.

"I gathered that. But don't we normally have to go to the other room for that? Agent—"

"Dom. Let's start with this, please call me Dom today."

Bridgette sat back startled. This was so unlike the stiff formal agent who had badgered her over the first two weeks of her incarceration. She looked at him again, and he truly looked perplexed, almost as if he were weighing options. "Okay, then, Dom. What's going on?"

"I think," he stammered again, "that I need to begin by telling you a story." When she shifted and gave him a strange look, he tried to smile. "I think it will help both of us."

Popping the top to his own Coke, he took a quick swallow and then began. "I was the middle child. I had two sisters, Elaine was older than me by three years, and Cindy is younger by two." He looked up into Bridgette's moss green eyes. There was confusion, hurt and strength there. He'd pushed open this door, now he had to follow through.

"When I was fourteen, Elaine was dating a guy by the name of Todd Kinyon. Todd seemed to be an okay guy, but unbeknown to us he had a drug problem. His problem was that he was selling the stuff, but had stiffed his supplier.

"He and Elaine were stopped at red light in Cincinnati, when gang members opened fire on the car. Elaine was pronounced dead at the scene, and my life was thrown into chaos. I vowed at that moment that I would do whatever I could to protect others from what my family and I suffered. And I would make it my life's work to get the gangs and the drugs off of the streets."

There was sorrow in his eyes Bridgette noted. But a good actor could do that too she knew. "Why are you telling me this?"

"Bridgette, I know that you don't trust me. And I can't condone what you did. But I can understand the reason that you hacked that system. I also know that you've been trying to tell Shawn Daniels something important, and that he keeps shutting you down. I also know that the D.A. wants to nail you to the wall so that he can ride the wave all the way to the governor's mansion.

"Right now, I'd like to get your side of things."

Tears began to form in her eyes. "Why? Why do you care?" she asked fighting back the sobs that were so close.

"Because I know how I felt when I lost Elaine. You? You've dealt with losing your entire family to them. I guess you could say, I empathize with you."

"Why now? Why not come in during the day with your partner?"

"Fair question," he admitted. "I've been ordered to officially let this go. I can't do any of this on company time. But, when I found out about your history, and knowing that you kept trying to tell the attorneys things, it just didn't add up. So, I came on personal time. To try to be a friend."

Bridgette gnawed on her lip. This was it. This was the guy who'd slapped the cuffs on her and dragged her out of her apartment. This was the only person who'd paid attention when she was trying to share information that might get her a little leniency. She was doomed anyway, at least if she told him the truth someone would know.

Maybe she'd actually have one friend.

She sipped her prized diet coke and began the tale

Dom leaned back in the wing chair in his living room and thought about what Bridgette had told him. If things checked out, he'd have no option other than to take matters into his own hands.

But how? That was the real sticking point.

Officially, he wasn't supposed to be involved with her case any longer. But if he didn't do something, she was going to be spending the next twenty years behind bars.

Oh, there was no doubt that she'd done what they were accusing her of, but now that he had the rest of the story, he could see that there were definitely extenuating circumstances.

If her story checked out.

He jolted back to reality when the phone rang.

"Hello?"

"Hey, Dom! Missed you today at the golf course."

"Hi, Brian. Something came up. Sorry."

There was a pause on the other side, "You okay, Dom? This is the first time in five years that you've missed a league game."

Dom weighed his options. The safe course was to keep everything to himself. But, if he let Brian in on what was going on, the Mahoney woman would have two people in her corner.

"Bri, listen, I've got myself into a real mess here. I'm stuck and I don't know where to take it."

"I'll grab Deke, a pizza and a six-pack and we'll be over in about thirty."

Before he could say anything else, the line went dead.

For the next twenty-eight minutes, he paced the room wondering how he was going to tell his two best work-buddies about his activities today.

They didn't knock; they just entered like they owned the place. Like the brothers he'd never had, Dom mused.

They'd met each other at Quantico several years before as they were going through one of their training rounds and had hit it off immediately.

"Okay, the cavalry is here," the blond headed Brian, joked as he walked in balancing the pizza box on one hand.

Deke followed carrying a six-pack of guiness. "I sure hope you blew off this dweeb today for someone who has long legs and a toned body."

Dom dropped papper plates onto the table. "You'll be happy to know that yes, a woman was involved today."

Deke smiled, "Involved or the star attraction?"

"You ditch a golf match for a woman? You could have at least brought her along. You know moral support, and all that stuff."

Dom stopped, a slice of pizza dripping cheese in his hand. "There's no way I could have," he mumbled.

"What's that, Dom? You know that girls play golf too. What's holding you back? Afraid that I'll steal her out from under you?" Brian asked with a wag of his eyebrow.

The pizza dropped from Dom's hand, and he leaned his head forward covered his eyes with his palms.

"Dude, I was just joking about the girl, and," he paused. "Man, she's really got you tied up. Listen, why don't you call her now and—"

"I can't call her! She's in prision!"

"Dom," Deke said silencing Brian with a look. "Can you tell us about what's going on?"

Closing his eyes, Dom leaned back in the chair and took a deep breath. "You guys remember that case about a month ago? The sting that we were trying to put on the Bandits and the money that we'd arranged to use to buy the weapons and that whole fiasco?"

Brian nodded, Deke answered verbally. "Yeah. That Moloney woman screwed everything up. Now the agency is breathing down our necks wanting the money back, the D.A. got a confession out of her and she's cooling her heels in the slammer. Good riddance, I say."

Dom's eyes flashed open. "I thought that you were supposed to be the romantic one." He let out a long sigh. "Her name's Mahoney, but anyway, that's the case."

"Dom, you know Mayers' took you off of that case. Said that your mind was getting conflicted over the memories of your sister. Jacobs got his confession, so all that's left is for them to tell her how long she's a guest of the state."

"Do you know anything about her past?" Dom asked. "Before you condemn her, I just want to ask you a question."

Both men looked at him.

"How far would you go if it was your family that's been killed by the gangs?"

"Dom, look, Deke and I agree that what happened to you with Elaine was rough. But you made your choice. She made a different one. You choose to work within the law, she broke it. She stole a million dollars from the taxpayers. She's got to pay. Why are you getting all worked up about this?"

"I went to see her today."

Deke's mouth hung open for a second. "You went to see her? At the prison? On your day off? What the heck are you trying to do, get yourself fired?"

Brian surged to his feet, and went over to the window. Standing with his hands on his hips, looking out over the small lake that cut through the valley. "Okay, tell us why you're disobeying the captain's orders and visiting jailbirds on your days off."

Before Dom could say anything, Deke blurted out, "Did she happen to tell you where she hid the money?"

"I went to see her today, because the last time I was in interview with her, she kept trying to say something to both of the attorneys and neither would listen.

"She admits to hacking the computers and siphoning the million, but there was something else there. And Daniels wouldn't let her say a word."

"Listen, pal-of-mine, you're right. There is more there. Under that red hair and green eyes is the mind of a manipulator," Brian snapped. Turning back towards the table he continued, "I understand that she's had a crappy hand dealt to her. How does that really concern you?"

Dom shifted in the chair, sipped his beer. "I guess I need to know that justice was done."

"It was. She's in a cell now. How much more justice do you want?" Deke asked, now perturbed. "Look, if she wanted to get back at the group who killed her family, or whatever, why not help law enforcement agencies instead of working to undermine us?"

"She tried." Dom stated simply. "That's why I went today. To listen to what she had to say, and try to connect a few dots that I've uncovered."

Brian hissed, "Great! You're working on this off the books, and you've dragged us into it."

"Brian, I didn't want to get you guys involved with this. Really. But her story just tears at me."

Deke sighed, "We're already in this far, Brian. Let's sit down and hear him out." Turning to Dom he said, "Tell us everything."

Dom took another swig from his beer and began. "After her family was gone, she put herself through school, worked and created a life for herself, eventually moving up into a position with Jokam and Hyde, the defense attorneys. While she was there, she uncovered and fed information to various agencies, State police, county sheriff and when it was prudent even the F.B.I. hoping to bring down the gang that she sees as responsible for killing her family. For some reason, nothing was ever done with anything that she delivered, and I don't know why.

"She found out about the weapons buy a few days before it went down, but based on past track records of what didn't happen with her intel, she decided to go vigilante. In her words today, she was afraid of what would happen if that group got that much clout. What they would be capable of doing."

Dom looked at his two friends. "She's never once said that she didn't do it, you know. She admits to taking the money, says she sorry that she screwed up our investigation, but she's never apologized for taking the money from the Bandits."

Brian looked over at Deke, then to Dom. "It'd go a long way if she'd tell us where the money is now. It might help with her sentencing, if we can give the money back."

"That's not going to be possible," Dom said soberly. "She doesn't have it."

"She took it, but doesn't have it? We nailed her less than forty-eight hours after the theft. Where'd it go?" Deke demanded.

"To charity."

Deke and Brian looked at each other, and then to their friend. "What do you mean, 'to charity'?" Brian wanted to know.

"She set up the siphon so that the money went from the account we put it in, through a few dummy accounts and then into the donation box of a women and children's fund anonymously. She wasn't trying to steal the money for herself, she was trying to keep the gang from getting stronger, and helping the people that group preys on. She was doing it the only way that she knew how."

"Holy cow," Deke exhaled in a rush. "Can we prove any of this?"

"Does it matter if we can?" Brian challenged. "The D.A.'s already got a guilty plea out of this. She's going to have to pay for it."

"You'd think that her lawyer would try to use this to get her a better deal, wouldn't you?"

Dom shrugged. "That's why I went to see her today, Deke. She'd been trying to tell both of them what happened, but they were only interested in her admission to taking the money."

"What can we do?" Brian asked.

"Well, about the only thing that I can think of right now is to corroborate her story. If it all checks out, I'll have to figure a way to get it to Judge Forsyth, because Daniels and Jacobs are too narrow minded."

"Not to rain on your parade, but what good's it going to do? They've already gotten the plea. They're not going to let her withdraw it. She's convicted, she'll do the time."

"Maybe. But it might also cut the sentence down. Either way, I can be her friend and be there to support her. At least she'll know that I tried.

Over the rest of the pizza and beer, they discussed what could be done to prove Bridgette's story.

"How is she doing?" Deke asked while Brian was taking a bathroom break.

Dom looked to his friend. There was sincerity in his eyes. "She seems to be holding up reasonably well. I don't think she has many friends."

"Inside or out." Both of them winced. "Sorry, that was uncalled for," Deke admitted.

"It's all right. I don't think she has many of either. I'd wondered why she hadn't made bail before the hearing. I don't think anyone was willing to stand for her."

Brian came back down the hall. "I was thinking," he said. "Jacobs asked me to take a look to see if I could figure out where the money went. If she made any of those reports via computer, there should be a record of it on hers and on the receiving one. I can try to poke around there over the next few days while I'm looking for Jacob's info. Nothing else major on the board, and I don't think I'd raise too much concern poking around."

"That's a great start," Dom said. "If you find anything, then perhaps I can try to sweet-talk Ashley into helping me dig out the file on her. I want to know why nothing was ever done."

"You know what, Dom? Let me do that. She owes me a favor, and there is no interdepartmental record denying me any access to files."

"What does that leave me to do?"

Deke smiled, "Be her friend, Dom."

ABOUT CHRISTINE CHIANTI...

Christine is the author of more than twenty titles ranging from short stories to novels. Her latest work, Virtual Reality, is the first book in the new Organized Crime Unit series, and will be available in fall 2014.

Christine is a member of Romance Writers of America and is at home in Western New York.

For more on Christine, or her work, please visit www.goldenlarkpublishing.com

CONNECTING WITH CHRISTINE CHIANTI....

www.christinechianti.com
www.twitter.com/cchianti
www.facebook.com/christinechianti

Other Titles by Christine Chianti:

Short Stories

The Shocking Truth

One Night

New Kid in Town

Sins of the Father

Witless Protection

Unbalanced Conspiracy

Now Leaving: the Comfort Zone

Doubtable Reasons

Magnetic Commodity

Deceitful Discovery

Evergreen

Novellas

Whole Once More

Novels

Dreams Series

Desert Dreams

Blue Ridge Dreams

Sleepy Hollow High Series

Fiendish Fall

Wicked Winter

Savage Spring

Organized Crime Taskforce

Missappropriated Means

www.ingramcontent.com/pod-product-compliance
Lightning Source LLC
Chambersburg PA
CBHW071151260626
47162CB00003B/996